MW01379417

Finishing Touches

LK Hunsaker

ISBN 0-7414-1647-6

Published by:

519 West Lancaster Avenue
Haverford, PA 19041-1413
Info@buybooksontheweb.com
www.buybooksontheweb.com
Toll-free (877) BUY BOOK
Local Phone (610) 520-2500
Fax (610) 519-0261

Printed in the United States of America

Printed on Recycled Paper

Published August 2003

Acknowledgements

This novel was shaped by many influences on my life; in particular, by my family. I want to begin by thanking those who were incredibly inspiring, readily giving, and always encouraging.

To my parents, grandparents, siblings, aunts, uncles, and cousins who formed the major part of my childhood existence, and to my nieces and nephews who have enhanced my adult years. I am eternally grateful.

To Marilyn Gray for the many hours spent editing and your insistence that this needed to be published.

To Jan Zalewski for the purest form of friendship, and the request not to change a word; Mary Maxwell, for keeping up with each chapter and offering great constructive criticism; Cheryl Land for impatiently asking for each "next chapter," spurring me forward; and *Writers and Friends* for technical and creative support.

To Duncan Faure, a wonderfully talented singer/-songwriter, for allowing use of your lyrics and for so much more. You are truly a beautiful soul. Rock on. Also, to Gigi Houghton and Perry Cooper for "administrative" assistance and beyond.

Finally, to my husband, for giving me a broader view of life and unlimited love and assurance. And to my children, who provide unending joy and a wider perspective of life and love.

Dedication

For Rulon – Forever.

For Elizabeth and Eric – My present and my future.

And for Mom – I am your child.

One

Jenna inhaled deeply, allowing crisp fall air to invade her body. Feeling a nip of winter creep further through her open window, she pulled the plush blanket higher around her baby's shoulders. Jenna loved the precious time spent rocking her child to sleep while he snuggled into her breast. At these moments, she felt the most connected to her only love. She also missed him the most vividly.

Lightly running her fingertips over Aaron's tiny head, Jenna studied the perfect little features, so like his father's. Daniel had never tried to conceal the pride he had felt whenever someone mentioned how much his son resembled him. He had considered the child his greatest work of art, and his most important. Jenna's husband had been many things, but humble had never been one of them. She couldn't help grinning, recalling his admission of knowing he was a very good-looking guy. And he really was, or had been. Even after he had gotten sick and had lost too much weight, his features had still been perfect and his eyes absolutely beautiful.

She snuggled her baby closer and returned her gaze to beyond the window. The view from their loft was breathtaking at this time of the year, with hundreds of maple trees along the banks of the Illinois River boasting their shades of red and yellow and green and brown. The *Spirit of Peoria*, a reproduction of the beloved old riverboats, often sailed by with passengers walking the decks or standing at the rails. Six years earlier, Jenna and Daniel had watched the *Julia Belle Swain* together whenever they caught it floating along the river. Once, covered only with a sheet pulled from their bed, they had stood before the large window and talked of taking the short cruise on the old paddle-wheel. Some day.

"*Some day*" had never come. Neither had so many other days they had planned. Their time together had centered around his painting, but then, he had told her to expect that. She hadn't argued when he had refused to go out because he was working or when she had to go to bed alone. She had been warned and had willingly accepted his terms. The naivete of youth, Jenna mused sullenly. Now, there was no later for them. The *Julia Belle* and Daniel were both gone.

His baby stirred in her arms and Jenna coerced herself to rise slowly, moving across the loft to settle Aaron in his crib. Convinced he was still slumbering, she wandered into the kitchen to pour a cup of mint tea; a habit she had developed while carrying her first child. Daniel's mother had suggested it might help settle her stomach and it seemed to work. Even well after the morning sickness was gone, Jenna had continued the routine and joked with her husband that maybe he should try it as well, to calm his nerves. He didn't like mint tea. He didn't like boats either, except at a distance. Alan had once pointed out that Daniel's work was the only interest they shared. Jenna quickly pointed out that her advanced pregnancy proved him wrong. Her best friend hadn't been amused.

Not sure what to do with herself while Aaron slept, Jenna returned to the beautifully carved oak rocking chair, a gift from her mother-in-law. Joan had been nearly as excited as her son after hearing that he and Jenna were expecting their first child, and had wasted no time making sure they had everything they needed for the baby. Jenna hadn't heard from Joan recently. She considered trying to call, but knew she would have to talk to two or three other people just to get through to Daniel's mother and then most likely have to leave a message. She wasn't up to that today. A fleeting thought of calling her own mother surfaced, then dissipated. She would just try again to invite Jenna to some social gathering. And Jenna's sister-in-law would insist on coming over and staying the day, with the kids. She wasn't up to that, either.

Alan. He would be at work, but she could talk to Cheryl for a few minutes, until her twins interrupted, and ask her to say hello. Jenna didn't want to talk to him now, anyway. She only needed to feel the connection – to know he was there.

She dialed his number without stopping to think about it. She knew it better than her own.

His voice startled her. He shouldn't be home now.

After another prompt, she gathered herself enough to answer, grimacing at the shakiness of her voice.

"Jenna, what's wrong? Are you okay?"

She hesitated again. No, she wasn't, but she wouldn't tell him that. "Yeah, I'm fine."

"You don't sound fine."

Trying to maintain composure, she fumbled for something to say to him now that he was on the phone. "I … I'm just surprised you answered. I figured you'd be at work."

"We just finished a big job. I gave everyone the day off."

"Oh? How'd it go?"

"Another Nicklaus project."

Jenna half-grinned at the term. Nicklaus had been one of her friend's first clients, never satisfied and constantly insisting on changes. When she had still been meeting Alan on Sundays for dessert and coffee, Jenna would hear about all of the complaints and revisions of the week and make jokes to put him in a better mood. It had always worked.

"Jenna?" Alan's voice called her back.

"Sorry, I thought maybe you'd heard enough complaining recently and I should just stay quiet."

"Do you want me to come over?"

Yes, she very much wanted him to come over. "Oh, no, I'm fine. I was just checking in to see how you guys are doing. Is Justin over the flu?"

"Jenna, that was two weeks ago."

She paused, holding her breath a moment and wishing she hadn't called.

"I'm coming over."

"No. Alan, it's your day off. You should spend it with your family."

"My family is fine; you're not. I'll be right there." He didn't give her time to respond before she heard the click from his end.

Oh, hell. She wasn't ready for company. She hadn't gone out in nearly a week or showered in two days, and there were dishes in the sink and baby toys and blankets on the floor. Not having time to shower and clean both, Jenna decided her own cleanliness would be more noticeable. So she checked on her sleeping son and jumped into the warm water.

The doorbell found her almost presentable while slipping into one of Daniel's shirts, and Jenna rolled the sleeves while heading to the door. A slow, deep breath prepared her for her friend's visit.

Alan glanced at her wet locks. "Hey, Jenna. You didn't have to shower for me." He gave her a small kiss on the cheek in his usual casual style and waited to be asked in further.

"You didn't have to come over." She studied her friend admiringly. All the work he did outside was so good for him. He always had a beautiful tan and his muscles were well-toned. Daniel had been very pale-skinned and burned easily.

"It sounded like you need some company. Has your sister-in-law been over recently?"

"No, her kids have been sick, too, and she didn't want to give it to us. I guess that's what I was thinking when I asked about Justin." She motioned for him to step in and closed the door softly, having learned to keep everything as quiet as possible while Aaron was asleep. He even slept as lightly as his father had.

Alan scanned the area as he strode easily to the small couch. Everything in the loft was small … except the space still reserved for Daniel's easels and canvases and large paint-stained work table.

Jenna only half-followed her friend, wishing she had cleaned up earlier. "Do you want a drink? I think all I have is juice right now, but I can make some iced tea."

"No, Jen, I'm fine. Come sit down."

Sitting alone with him was the last thing she wanted. She could hide her emotions well from everyone else but had never been able to keep anything from Alan. They had been friends since his family moved in across the street when Jenna was eleven, and she had spent more of her teenage years with him and his family than with her own parents.

As a distraction, she went to the sink and began running water into the metal basin. Alan moved to her side and took the dishes from her hands to dry, talking easily of his kids and his job. He never brought up his wife unless Jenna asked about her. She knew they got along well. They always had. Cheryl was a wonderful person, very devoted to her family and especially to her husband. And she was a neat freak. Her house was always immaculate. How she did it with three kids, Jenna couldn't begin to imagine. But Cheryl completely adored Alan and he never did anything to upset her.

A quiet fussing from the opposite end of the room drew her out of her thoughts and she went to collect her baby, gently pulling him from the crib which had claimed part of Daniel's studio space. Alan set to work putting the dishes away as she sat down to nurse Aaron. She knew it made her friend uncomfortable when she nursed in front of him, although she kept herself covered and

Cheryl had nursed all three of their babies. But there was no such thing as privacy in the loft, unless she wanted to disappear behind the curtain that hid their bed … her bed … from the living area. And she didn't want to sit back there right now. She often slept curled up on the couch instead of going to the bed alone.

Her mother had tried to convince her to move since Jenna had no further reason to live in an art studio, but she couldn't bring herself to sell it and couldn't move out and leave it empty. Maybe she would get around to redecorating some day; make it presentable for company. A useless idea, Jenna laughed to herself, since she was out of the habit of entertaining and was content letting it match her memory of the first time she had stepped inside. She still thought of that moment as the rebirth into her new life – the life of her own choosing.

Her parents had worked everything out for her from the beginning. Their only child would graduate with honors from the school close to where they had carefully chosen to live, then attend the University of Illinois, as they both had. After getting to know Alan and his family well, her mother had decided they would be the perfect match. Alan was two years older than Jenna, a very good student, responsible, hard working and well-mannered. His parents weren't in the same social class as Jenna's parents, but Alan could get there with his career plans. He would also graduate from U of I and work on building a foundation for a family the following two years that Jenna would need to finish school. Then they could marry and Jenna could start on her own career.

There had only been two major problems with the plan. Alan had been intent on getting a job after earning his associates degree in horticulture from Illinois Central College, possibly continuing school after building his bank account. And Jenna had never had any interest in marrying Alan. He was her friend – nothing more.

Illinois Central. The junior college in East Peoria hadn't entered her mind in a long while. She wondered if any of its students could possibly have memories of the school that would come even close to equaling her own. Alan had tried to talk her into going there after high school. He'd said it was the perfect place to start deciding what she wanted to do. She could take some basic classes as well as some that just sounded interesting and would eventually find something to hold her easily-distracted attention. He even took her with him during spring break of her senior year to check it out. That was where she had met Daniel.

She did like art. So Alan had asked his art professor to let her sit in on his basic drawing class. Jenna could still see it clearly.

The students intently studied an elegant round vase that sat atop an old, weathered crate. The vase held a large handful of wildflowers. Jenna loved the mixture of old and new, of smooth and rough, of splintering grayness and soft pastels. And the flowers were fresh. Their scent mingled with the dampness of the basement classroom.

She felt out of place being the only person, other than the professor, not trying to capture the objects with charcoal and newsprint. The quiet was disarming, broken only by the soft scratches made by budding artists and the occasional creak of metal stools or tapping of a nervous foot against the concrete floor.

The professor, a man who looked as if he had been teaching a good many years, crept silently around the circle of art tables, stopping occasionally to study a student's technique but not interfering in his work. Until he came to an intense-looking male sitting directly across from Jenna. She had noticed the guy immediately upon entering; first because he was the only one with the initiative to begin working before class officially started, and then, because he seemed totally unaware of anyone else in the room. He had the darkest hair she had ever seen on someone so pale, and had strong, but small, features. She thought he had occasionally looked over at her while drawing the still life but scorned herself for even thinking that he would. She just happened to be behind the object he was studying.

The professor stood over his shoulder. "Mr. Rhodes, you seem to have overshot the still life I so carefully set up this morning."

The young artist didn't bother to stop sketching. "I wasn't interested in drawing flowers, so I found something I was *interested in."*

Jenna waited for the reaction as a couple of others snickered. Surprisingly, the older man threw a crooked grin behind the artist's head and began moving on to the next student. "This must be why Einstein received poor marks in school."

There was no response. The interruption hadn't stopped his work. Jenna had a hard time keeping her eyes from him. He still seemed to be watching her.

With twenty minutes left of the hour, it was time for critiques. The students, all in turn, set their drawings up on an easel and lis-

tened to comments from the others. The defiant, but good-natured, young man found something constructive to say about each, and was the last to place his work up for review.

Jenna gasped. She sat for a moment staring at her own face, feeling the increasing warmth of her cheeks. He had taken the liberty of drawing her shoulders uncovered; luckily not getting any further than her shoulders, but the likeness was incredible. He received plenty of compliments from the class and the professor finally asked for her opinion.

"What?" She couldn't look at the artist who had made her blush.

The teacher smirked. "I think he should hear what you think of his work."

She felt Alan watching her. He would not be happy about this. But the class was waiting. Jenna focused on the drawing. "It's ... it's better than real life." Catching a glimpse of the artist's grin, she looked away quickly. He packed his things and left the room.

"Jenna? Jenna, what are you thinking so hard about?"

Alan's voice drew her from her memories, and she took a deep, quick breath, answering evasively. "College."

"Oh? Are you thinking about going?" He sat back against the couch, keeping his eyes away from the feeding baby.

"Going? Me?"

"Why not?"

"To do what?"

"Didn't you just say you were thinking about college?"

"Yeah, but..." She stopped short, not about to admit where her thoughts had been.

He slowly stood again and moved to the chair on the opposite side of the small end table. "Jen, I know the baby is still young enough that you want to stay home with him, but you should at least start thinking about what you're going to do."

"The baby has a name. His name is Aaron, after his father, Daniel Aaron. I know you never liked him, but I loved him and I still love him and I can't even think about the future. All I can handle now is day to day and sometimes I'm not sure I can handle that!" She lowered her voice as her baby objected and adjusted herself to raise him to her shoulder.

Rubbing his back softly helped her relax and she apologized to her friend. "Alan, you know I had no idea what I wanted before Daniel, and I sure as hell don't know what to do now."

"I know." He had lowered his eyes while she was refastening her nursing bra but now faced her directly. "Jenna, I never disliked Daniel."

"Then why did you stop coming over?"

"Because he didn't want me here."

"I wanted you here."

"You could have come over any time. Cheryl loves visiting with you. You didn't have to isolate yourself just because Daniel wanted to be isolated."

"He didn't want to be isolated, he just…"

"Wanted to be left alone to work. I know, but he did isolate you. You always had a bunch of friends in school that you never see anymore. Have you even talked with Karla recently?"

She shook her head. He was right. She missed running around with her cousin and chatting about anything and everything.

"I didn't dislike him; I just didn't like what he was doing to you."

"It was my choice and I loved being with him."

"But you lost yourself…."

"No. Alan, I found myself with Daniel. I was lost before him and I'm even more lost without him now."

He began to argue but decided against it. "Jen, come spend the day with us."

With the happy couple and their three kids? "No, thank you. I don't really feel like going out."

"Maybe not, but you need to get out of here. There's a new art exhibition at Lakeview. Why don't we go see it?"

Art? "No."

"Jenna."

"No. Alan, I can't…"

"Okay, what about the zoo? The kids have been bugging us to take them again…"

"Then you should do that. We're fine right here."

Her tone made it clear he wouldn't be able to change her mind and he gave in with a nod. "Well, I'm going to go. Cheryl didn't mind me coming over, but I think she was looking forward to having the day together, so…"

"So, you should go spend time with your family, like I told you over the phone."

She hadn't meant it as harshly as the look in his eyes said it had sounded. Well, she couldn't help that. She had asked him not to come.

Aaron started fussing for the rest of his meal and Alan gruffly insisted she not get up to see him out. Jenna refused to watch him leave, but the click of the door nearly changed her mind. The rest of the day would be just her and her baby, again.

Cradling Aaron in the other arm, she appreciated the grateful expression he threw her for allowing him to finish nursing.

At least she had him. And he was strong and healthy. How could Alan have expected that she would visit him and his pregnant wife after she had lost Daniel's first child? Her friend wouldn't have had to stop coming over just because Daniel didn't want to visit. She had wanted to see Alan, not his wife who just reminded her of what she had lost. Her husband hadn't isolated her. Losing his baby had isolated her. He had wanted children. He had wanted children maybe even more than he had wanted her. They were the link to the future he somehow knew he wouldn't have of his own. And she couldn't have handled walking around watching all of the families laughing and talking and making her feel like such a failure for not being able to carry her baby full-term.

But Daniel had loved her, even if she had failed him.

The time he had given her had always felt too limited, but it had been complete … and intense. Nothing distracted him from what he chose as his focus. And he had focused on her often enough to keep her from feeling neglected, except for their bad time. But she wouldn't let herself think about that. There was no point. Instead, she chose to remember how he had picked her out from the crowds of girls around the campus.

After the art class, Alan had left her sitting in the center area of the college. The main building of Illinois Central formed a nearly complete oval around a large open area paved with the same red brick. It reminded Jenna of an old amphitheater, the way the oval dropped into different levels. She could still clearly see the picnic tables scattered around the upper level, with students propped on their seats. A few were studying, but most were chatting with others who were between classes. The narrow mid level was interrupted by short, wide columns of brick holding small trees, providing additional seats for loungers who wanted slight shade. The lowest level, only several inches from the highest, was free of obstacles and Jenna watched three males use it as a Frisbee court. *She kept her eyes averted from the guy who had removed his shirt and shoes and was lying on a towel in his shorts with his head propped on his backpack. She thought it was still a little cool for tanning, but the sky was absolutely cloudless and the air was fresh following last night's spring shower.*

She had chosen to sit just below the highest step and nearly against one of the tree columns. She didn't need it for support, preferring to sit with her legs crossed in front. But she didn't want to be too much in the open. Pulling her eyes from the Frisbee game, Jenna went back to her book.

"What are you reading?"

The voice was less startling than the face she found. It was the defiant young artist. He casually planted himself next to her, lifting the book enough to see the cover.

"The Agony and the Ecstasy*? That's a good one. Have you read* Lust for Life*? Same author."*

"No, not yet. I just finished Love Is Eternal*."*

"Irving Stone fan?"

"I'm becoming one." She stole glances of his face as he studied her overtly.

"So, where's your friend?"

Friend. Was he trying to find out more than what he asked? "He's in botany."

"Botany? On purpose?"

Jenna couldn't help grinning at his expression, and she agreed with him. "He's studying to be a landscape engineer. He understands all that stuff."

He nodded, amused. "And you? What do you want to be?"

"I don't have the slightest idea."

His eyes pierced her skin as they ran down her arms, touched her fingers, and then returned to her face. "Have you ever considered being a model?"

Was he joking? He didn't look like he was. So, he was either hitting on her, or crazy. "I know you can't be serious." Jenna knew she wasn't model material. She wasn't built badly but was constantly fighting five or ten pounds she didn't want and her features were too masculine for her taste. She had always wanted her jaw line to be less square and her eyes to be less narrow. Her mother had taught her tricks with carefully applied makeup to round out her jaw and widen her eyes, and she had pulled her long hair into a loose bun today, leaving a couple of wisps to curl at the sides of her face. But she still wasn't model material.

"I'm very serious." The intense eyes continued to study her. "I thought you were just being modest earlier, but you honestly have no idea how beautiful you are."

Jenna again felt her cheeks get warm and pulled her eyes away to watch the Frisbee players.

"I'm sorry; I didn't mean to embarrass you. I have a terrible habit of saying what I think. But I always tell the truth, and I don't waste my time drawing or painting anything I don't want to see again."

Her son pulled away, letting her know his tummy was sufficiently filled for the time being.

Jenna studied his round cheeks and square jaw. Aaron had inherited some of her appearance, though he looked much more like Daniel. Five and a half months old already. Maybe it was time to give him cereal. Wasn't that what the pediatrician had suggested? She would have to go out to get it since she hadn't thought that far ahead. She supposed she could. It wasn't like she had any other plans. But she would most likely run into someone who would insist on offering condolences again. Jenna didn't want to deal with that today. Maybe she should have accepted Alan's offer. He was very good at running interference whenever the subject arose. And she missed talking to him.

With Aaron propped against her left side, she reached over to pick up the receiver, started dialing, then set it down again. She hadn't been very nice after he had gone to the trouble of coming over. He would understand, though. He always had. But the zoo? Did she really want to go there?

Jenna pushed herself off the couch and walked over to the sketches still hanging along the corkboard strip which ran the length of the studio wall. Finding the one in her mind, she sat carefully in front of it, holding Daniel's son close against her heart, studying the image she could still feel. Her mother asked every time she came over, which thankfully wasn't often, when she intended to pack Daniel's things and try to sell the sketches. Jenna didn't intend to do either. The loft was their home and it would stay their home.

But maybe Aaron could use some fresh air. Aaron Matthew, after Daniel Aaron and Alan Matthew. She took a long, deep breath, then made herself get up.

She again found the voice she wasn't looking for at the other end of the telephone. "Cheryl, hi, is Alan there?"

"Hi, Jenna! He's outside; we were just leaving. Did you want to change your mind and come with?"

He had told her she'd refused. He surely hadn't said how rude she had been.

"Did you need to talk to him personally?"

"What? Oh, no. Just … are you sure you wouldn't mind the intrusion?"

"Of course not." She sounded genuinely happy. "Should we come by and pick you up?"

"No, the baby seat's already in my car. I'll meet you there."

Two

She ambled, nearly scuffing her feet, toward the entrance and stopped in front of a large stone slab bearing the words "Glen Oak Zoo." The sign from which a security guard had tried to kick her off, until Daniel had shown him the half-done sketch. The sketch which had become the first of several Daniel had done as zoo advertisements to help pay for her engagement ring. The only one he had turned into a painting. He didn't care much about drawing animals, but he had enjoyed capturing images of children pointing excitedly or pulling back nervously and talking about bringing his own child to sketch with the goats in the petting area, when he had a child.

With a sigh, Jenna unhooked the buckle and pulled Aaron free from the small navy stroller that looked as if paint had been thrown all over it. Anyway, that was how Denise had explained her choice of patterns when she had given it to them. Jenna had remarked that the multi-colored splotches were too neat. The manufacturers should have looked at Daniel's jeans if they were trying to achieve an actual paint-splashed look. The colors needed to overlap and be different shapes, with finger-size streaks here and there. Daniel had laughed, suggesting that his wife join his mother's fashion design company to create a painter's line.

The baby gasped as the light breeze hit his mouth and Jenna turned his head into her shoulder, running a hand over his shiny dark hair. She stepped closer to the sign, touching her fingers to the coolness of the stone. The sensation triggered memories of her bare legs resting on top of the granite while Daniel carefully but quickly captured the scene with his charcoal stick. He always sketched in charcoal. He said he could get more life in a charcoal sketch than in a pencil sketch.

The leg that had laid against the stone had taken a while to get warm again. The other had been propped up so that just the bottom of her foot had been cold. Daniel had asked her to remove her sandals because it was more natural and fitting for a zoo sign. He had been the one to convince her that true art was more felt than learned. It had to come from deep within the soul.

"Are you coming in?"

Startled by a male voice, she calmed her son while recognition alighted. Jenna turned to face her friend. "Yeah, I was just...."

"There's nowhere in the city you can go without thinking of him, is there?" Alan set a hand on her shoulder. "That really is a beautiful painting – the one of you sitting here. It's always been one of my favorites."

She partly avoided Alan by stroking her baby's head. "Mom keeps saying I should sell it. But, it's kind of special to me, too."

"Jen, ignore her. She never understood."

"Did you?" Jenna looked at him.

He pulled his hand away. "Yes, I have always understood you ... more than you could know." Reflecting a slight sadness, his eyes averted to the baby. Abruptly, he changed the subject. "Come on, the kids are probably driving Cheryl crazy waiting to go in."

Jenna didn't protest when he took control of the stroller, but she kept her baby in her arms. And Alan didn't argue when someone remarked what a beautiful baby they had. When his own children ran to his side, however, he had to give up helping her to become father and professor, doing his best to answer the constant questions. She reluctantly set her son back in his seat and strolled along next to Cheryl.

Alan's wife was a very willing companion, always glad to have other adults around with whom she could share her daily events. Justin, her oldest, was barely four and his biggest thrill was doing anything with his father. He had Alan's medium brown hair and greenish brown eyes along with his grandmother's smaller build. And his metal-framed glasses were constantly slipping down his tiny nose. Jenna couldn't help her affection for the child. Tranquil and serious, Justin had a special kindness about him. Animals were his passion.

Alex and Rae, the twins, were nearly three and larger-boned, like their parents. Cheryl talked about them constantly; how they were more accomplices than siblings. There was never a time when only one was mischievous. And they couldn't sit still for a minute. Their older brother had been content, since birth, playing quietly with his own things, but the twins were constantly into something, and always in it together.

Jenna half-listened to their most recent adventures while watching Alan and Justin. They were so different. Justin was more like Jenna than like his father, but Alan seemed to also have a real affinity with his eldest. Of course, Jenna and Alan had always gotten along well, too. For a while, a little too well. But that had been before his marriage.

She could still feel his lips. His kiss had been more intense than she could have imagined, but she'd pulled away from him. Knowing how much Alan wanted to be with her during the time Daniel had barely noticed she was there, and after the huge fight about Jenna refusing to go to one of Daniel's shows after her miscarriage, Jenna had let her guard down enough to let Alan kiss her. But she didn't want Alan, not like that. She wanted to be needed, but she wanted to be needed by her husband, not by her friend. So she'd pushed Alan away, and he had proposed to Cheryl, who didn't want anyone but him. Jenna wondered if Alan had ever told his wife about their brief encounter. He most likely hadn't.

Wandering away from his dad, and from the twins, who were taking too much of Alan's attention, Justin came over to talk to the baby. Jenna watched the four-year-old touch Aaron's fingers softly and talk to him as if her son understood every word Justin was saying. Cheryl fussed about him being too dirty to play with the baby, but Jenna said he was fine and gave him a disposable cloth to wash his fingers.

Aaron grabbed it away and put it in his mouth, scrunching his face about the taste. Justin laughed.

"Honey, don't let him chew on that. It has soap on it." Cheryl coaxed the cloth out of Aaron's chubby fingers and pulled her son away to clean his hands for him.

"I can do it."

"I want all the germs off. Hold still a minute."

Jenna started to argue. She didn't want Justin to be afraid to play with Aaron, and her son fussed for his companion to come back. But it wasn't her place to interfere. She did notice Alan's glance. He agreed with Jenna but wouldn't interfere with his wife, either. He never had.

They stopped at the petting area at the end of their visit so Alan's children could feed the goats. Aaron wanted nothing to do with the noisy animals, which was fine with Jenna. She didn't either. Once, a long time ago, she had fed them and was disgusted by the slimy saliva their tongues left, along with the food pellets they couldn't pick up. Alan didn't care much for it, either. He joined her and Aaron on a nearby bench, commenting on Cheryl's habit of hauling her camera everywhere.

Alan hated having his picture taken. Jenna didn't especially like it, but didn't fuss the way her friend did. She watched Cheryl get a close shot of Justin feeding a very small goat; one arm propped around the animal's neck. It would make a nice photo. Jenna supposed she would have to think more about carrying a camera, to get a record of Aaron growing, but she never thought far enough ahead. Maybe Cheryl would give her a copy of that one; it would make a beautiful painting.

"What are you thinking about?"

She glanced at her friend. He was sitting closer than necessary – leaned back against the wood-slat bench; one leg propped over the other. Jenna always felt rigid in public, never able to let go of her mother's over-emphasized lessons on posture. Alan's constantly-relaxed attitude was one thing that attracted her to him. He made her feel at ease by being so at ease himself.

She turned back to watch his son. "You know, Justin is really good with animals. You should get him one."

"A goat?"

Jenna grinned. "Well, maybe not a goat. But he would love a puppy and it would give him his own playmate while the twins are entertaining each other."

"He does seem to get left out, doesn't he?" Alan sighed. "I'm always afraid he'll be too much of a loner."

"You worry too much. He's just fine, and he has a great role model." She met his eyes for a moment, then pulled hers away to focus on her own son. He was sitting happily in his stroller, watching Justin. What would he do for a male role model? Jenna had never even met Daniel's father; her own father wasn't the kind of example she wanted her son to follow, and she didn't intend to ever get married again.

Alan touched her arm. "Jen, I have a feeling Justin and Aaron will get along real well. Maybe they'll hang out together as they get older."

She looked up at him. He had read her mind again and was volunteering to take Daniel's son under his wing, just as Alan's parents had done for her. "I think that would be nice."

A flash of light grabbed her attention and Cheryl laughed at catching them by surprise. Alan stood, calling to his children that it was time to go. Jenna followed along, wondering if she would get a copy of that one, also. Cheryl had taken several pictures of Jenna and Alan together over the years and Jenna had most of them. Many of the snapshots Cheryl gave her were stored carelessly in a shoebox, but the ones of her and Alan were placed in her keepsake journal. And she had a beautiful picture of Alan and Justin on her refrigerator, beside the one of Cheryl with the newborn twins that she kept there only to curb suspicion. Actually, both pictures had only been put up recently. She would never have done it while Daniel was still there.

Cheryl wouldn't let her refuse when Alan invited her over for a barbecue. And Jenna had been glad for the offer.

Kicked back on a woven folding chair, eyes closed, Jenna listened to the crickets chirping in the twilight. Cheryl had taken the kids up for their baths and Aaron was sleeping soundly in her arms. Alan was quiet, as he often was when they spent time together. Jenna enjoyed the silences with her friend as much as the conversations. She had read or heard once that people who were truly comfortable with each other were never uncomfortable with the silence between them. She supposed that was true.

Shivering at a cool gust of air, she opened her eyes, checking to make sure Aaron's blanket was still pulled up around his head.

Her movement pulled her friend's attention from whatever he was thinking while studying his shrubs and plants, his constant habit.

"Should we go in?"

"No, the air is wonderful tonight." She loved the crispness of fall, even though it was beckoning winter to come in its place.

He chuckled. "I still think you should come work for me, as much as you love being outside."

"I don't know; that much togetherness might not be such a good thing for us." She grinned, then grew serious. "I'm sorry about being so rude earlier."

He didn't bother acting surprised at her apology. "It's alright; I know I was pushing. But I worry about you, Jen."

"I'm not much fun to be around anymore, am I?"

He sat motionless for a few seconds before pulling his chair close enough that she could nearly feel the warmth of his breath. "Jenna, you need to start letting yourself live. It's not good for you to be alone so much, and it's not good for Aaron. You saw how happy he was today. He needs to be around other people. And so do you, whether you want to be or not."

She stared at her best friend; the only guy in the neighborhood who had seen her for who she was. To him, she wasn't just the daughter of the revered hospital administrator who pushed her into being a socialite and the distant and discerning business editor who had made more playing the stock market than at his job at the Journal Star. Alan didn't care about that … then, or now.

"If I get testy with you, ignore me. I don't mean it against you. And I know you're right. It's just … hard."

"Start thinking about what you're going to do, Jenna. I'll help you any way I can. And I know Cheryl will baby-sit if you want to go back to school."

"And do what?"

"You like art and you're good at it. You'd be a great teacher."

"Art was Daniel's thing, not mine."

"It was yours before you met him. You have a lot of talent and a real love for it. Don't let him take that from you, too."

He didn't give her time to respond before standing and moving his chair back to its original position. "It's getting late. I'll follow you home and walk you in."

"You don't need to do that."

"Don't bother arguing. Just let me tell Cheryl."

After Jenna settled the baby in his crib, Alan gave her another quick kiss on the cheek and thanked her for spending the day with them. He closed the door quietly.

The loft was mostly dark and seemed emptier than it had before. She stood in the hot shower longer than usual, then sat with a cup of mint tea and thought about Alan's comment. "*Don't let him take that from you, too.*"

Setting her cup down, she wandered over to the art table, pulled her journal from a drawer, and flipped the pages until finding her favorite photo. With one of Daniel's unused sketchbooks and a charcoal pencil, she sat at his table and began a rough outline of two figures.

Three

"Jenna, I could give you more than this. I would give you more of myself than he gives you."

"Alan, don't. Don't do this to me. We're just having some problems right now..."

"Because he's completely ignoring your needs. He's not being fair to you. Jen..."

She felt his chest against hers, his hands on her arms, pulling her in. The words got lost. She knew what he wanted, but ... he stopped talking, feeling her giving in, accepting the closeness she so desperately needed. The warmth of his lips made her pulse quicken; the passion was so much more than she would have expected from this man she had known for years. The man who knew her better than anyone – better than her own husband knew her. Her husband...

She pulled away. "Alan...."

The intensity and longing in his face nearly drew her back. It had been so long since she had felt wanted, needed. But it was the wrong face. "I can't do this." Her voice was low, and shaky. Her lungs filled quickly and she stepped back further, turning away. "I can't do this. I'm married..."

"So leave him, Jenna. I'll wait for you."

Leave him? How could he think she would ever leave Daniel? He was what she had been waiting for all those years that her parents had been trying to shape her into a debutante. He took her away from that. He gave her the kind of life she had longed for. Well, for a while, anyway. But they would get it back again. They were both trying to adjust to his new success. He had a lot of pressure to perform for the public right now, to keep creating better and more beautiful paintings. He just didn't have the energy...

She missed him, though. And she missed being held and being the most important thing in someone's life. Well, she had never been the most important. His work had always come first. But she had been a central motivator for him ever since they'd met, until recently, until...

She felt Alan's gentle touch and didn't fight him when his arms moved around her waist from behind. He didn't think she was a failure. He was still attracted to her. But then, it wasn't his child she had lost.

He snuggled his face against her hair and planted a kiss on her head. Closing her eyes against the pain and the longing, Jenna felt a tear tickling her cheek. Alan pulled back and turned her to face him.

"Jen...." His fingertips wiped the moisture away. "I can't stand to see you so unhappy. He's not good for you. Leave him to his art. Leave him, Jen, and come to me."

The tears fell faster now and she leaned into her friend. "I can't." Involuntary lung spasms interrupted until she calmed herself enough to stutter the words she had to say. "I ... can't, Alan. I ... he's my husband ... I love him ... I can't ... I don't want to fail at this, too ... I don't want to fail at my marriage..."

She felt his arms get tighter around her back and a hand move up to hold her head in against his shoulder. The soft Celtic music she used for relaxation caught her attention and she forced herself to focus on the soothing strains. Eventually, her breathing slowed and the tears stopped and she held still in his arms.

"I'm sorry; I didn't mean to upset you more. I just...it's so hard for me to watch him ignore you when I would love to be the one you wanted; when I would love to be able to give you what you want from him. I love you, Jenna."

The tears started again and she pulled away. "I can't see you again, Alan. I can't do this. I'm having enough trouble trying to hold my marriage together and this isn't helping anything."

"Jen...."

"No, please, just go. I can't ... see you..."

He stepped closer again, trying to bridge the gap between them. "You don't mean that. You can't just push me away."

"I'm not leaving him. I love him and I'm going to make it work."

"And what about us ... all the years between us? You're going to let him take that away from you?"

"Alan, you're just my friend. I don't love you."

She immediately regretted the way that it had come out, but she couldn't take it back.

He lowered his head, then grabbed his coat and went to the door.

"Alan..." She caught up and took his arm. "I'm sorry, I meant...."

"No, Jenna; you don't have any reason to be sorry. You've been trying to tell me that for years and I just wouldn't listen. I'll leave you alone."

"Don't ... not like this."

He refused to even look at her. "Goodbye, Jenna." Pulling out of her grasp, he fled through the door without closing it.

She lay awake staring at the ceiling. The charcoal drawing still sat on Daniel's table. Maybe she would try painting it. But she could never do it justice the way Daniel could. And so what if she couldn't? No one had to see it. It could just be something to occupy her time. Eventually she would have to think about earning a living since the royalties and money from his sales wouldn't last forever. But, for now, all she needed was a distraction.

The sky was beginning to lighten and Aaron would soon force her to start the day. Maybe she could get an hour or two of sleep first. She could show Alan her work – he wouldn't be critical. And he would see that she did actually listen to him, occasionally.

λλλλ

"No, Baby, not already." She couldn't remember actually falling asleep, but she must have. What time was it? She turned her head to no avail. The alarm clock was blinking twelve-seventeen. The power must have gone off.

A loud clap of thunder made Aaron's cry more insistent and Jenna rolled out of bed to find him. The cold floor surged a chill through her veins. Pulling her old sweat shirt over the long T-shirt she wore to bed, she gathered her son quickly and took him back to cuddle in the blankets with her. He quieted immediately and began searching for her breast.

"Okay, okay." She pulled the garment out of his way. Rain pelted the large windows and a nearby tree danced fitfully. The weird yellow cast of the sky made her wonder whether she should find lower ground. But where would she go? She didn't know the people who lived below her, as Daniel had always made it very clear that he didn't want to be bothered. And she wasn't about to take the baby outside in this weather.

The lightening startled Aaron again and her thoughts turned to keeping him calm. He hated loud noises but loved music.

Searching her brain for a soothing melody, she began singing quietly … one of her favorites.

> *"Follow your heart when I'm not by your side*
> *I'll take you wherever I go…"*

His innocent, trusting eyes peered into hers as she sang. This is what it was all about. This baby they had both wanted so badly. A new life they had purposely created, knowing the likelihood that she would end up a single mother, though Jenna had never allowed herself to believe it would happen.

> *"You'll dance in my dreams and lie in my thoughts*
> *I'll sing you to sleep though we're miles apart*
> *So rock-a-bye baby, good night*
> *Rock-a-bye baby, it's alright…."*

She watched his perfect little face as his tummy filled and his eyelids began to flutter. When he finished, or became too tired to eat, she laid him carefully beside her and they both ignored the rain.

λλλλ

His fussing stirred her again. The clock was now flashing four-thirty-two and the sun was trying to peak through gray clouds. Lifting Aaron, she set a soft kiss on his head and set him in his crib. He protested loudly at being put down, and she quickly took care of her needs and splashed cool water on her face before returning to calm him.

Jenna wondered where Alan was working now, not having thought to ask him the night before. She hoped the job would be easier than the last one and wished she could be there for the initial planning stage. He was so good at seeing a tree- and shrub-filled landscape where most people saw only grass and dirt patches. It had been ages since she had wandered a parcel of land with him while he planned in his mind exactly what kind of foliage to use and just where it should be planted. Maybe it would be too wet today, though. She chuckled at herself. Even if it were still raining, Alan would be at the location, thinking and planning.

She could find out where he was. Cheryl would know. But then Jenna would have to explain why she was asking and wasn't sure she could. Maybe she should call Karla. It would be safer than letting herself get too close to Alan again. Well, maybe safe wasn't the right word. After all, he wouldn't hit on her now that he was married. And she had really enjoyed talking with him the night before.

Instead of calling either friend, Jenna picked up the sketch she had finished late the night before and studied the figures. Very amateurish. But it had been a while and she was out of practice. She could try it in paint instead. Were there any blank canvases left? She hadn't been able to go through Daniel's things, other than looking at the sketches. Well, Aaron had found his plastic mirror that she had placed on his blanket, so he would be fine for a while.

Lifting some partly done canvases out of the way, she found one that her husband had used and covered again with gesso, unhappy with the results of his work. She could do the same. Setting it on an empty easel, Jenna rifled through his oils, looking for the right shades, hoping they weren't too old. Choosing browns and yellows, with a red for some accent, Jenna set to work. She thought of her husband, not attempting to imitate his style, but listening to his voice describe his approach to art.

Jenna wandered around the studio side of the loft, studying the paintings; some in progress and some completed. She stopped in front of one she recognized as the sketch he had done of her at the zoo. But it was now in full color on a large canvas. Her fingers ran lightly over the blades of grass, feeling not the paint, but the sharpness of the edges. And the stone reflected the sun so well she could feel the warmth from it.

"Daniel, this is beautiful. How do you make the sunlight look so real?"

He crept close enough that she could feel his breath on the back of her neck. "I just paint it the way I see it."

"Do you always see things better than they really are? I mean, that's not me ... it's ..."

"I never see anything better than it is. I just look past the external to find the real beauty."

She caught her breath when his skilled fingers brushed her neck. She had again wrapped her long hair into a bun, leaving just a few wisps to fall in waves. When he didn't get any resistance,

Daniel slid an arm around her waist and his fingers found the pins holding her hair. It took him no time to release them, dropping them onto the floor, and he smoothed her auburn hair, then turned her to face him.

"You are beautiful, Jenna. Will you be my inspiration?"

She couldn't respond. She was having enough trouble breathing. And she couldn't pull back as he moved closer. His intensity was overwhelming and his kiss made her want more. But she couldn't. She was seventeen and her parents would have him locked up if they found out. His lips moved to her neck. How would they find out? She was supposed to be with Karla. Her cousin would cover for her, like she had for other dates. But this wasn't a date…this was…

He leaned down and gently took her into his arms, carrying her across the floor and to the other side of the room. She tried to ask him to stop, but the words wouldn't come, and he set her on his bed, leaning down to kiss her again. She didn't want him to stop. He wanted her, and he needed her, and she had wanted to be really needed for so long. Finally, someone was willing to give her complete attention, and he had walked away from his work to be with her.

"Daniel, I…."

"Jenna, I know. It's alright." He brushed her hair back again.

"I've never…"

"I know." He sat up enough to pull his shirt over his head.

She cautiously raised a hand to touch his bare chest. "I've wanted to be yours from the moment we met."

"I know."

At day's end, she had completed her first painting and begun a sketch for another. Her style was nothing like Daniel's. He had been a realist, with the touch of an impressionist. She was … well, kind of expressionist and kind of surreal. And not anywhere near as talented. She wasn't going to show this to Alan, but maybe she wouldn't paint over it, either. But she would need to get more canvas. She had seen a new art supply store the other day; one she and Daniel hadn't been to, so maybe she wouldn't be recognized there.

Four

She stepped back for a better perspective, then grudgingly went to answer the phone. Jenna would have ignored it, but it was most likely Alan since she hadn't talked to him in three days. He had left a message on her machine a couple of times; once when she had been at the art store and once when she was letting the hot shower try to wash away the caked-on paint. But she hadn't called him back. Thoughts of the past kept invading and she really just wanted to be left alone to work.

"Jenna, it's about time you answered. I've left several messages. Are you alright?"

Oh, hell. She should have let the machine pick up. "Hello, Mom. I'm fine."

"You sound tired. Are you sleeping?"

"Not at the moment."

"Jenna, I meant…."

"I know what you meant. What's up?" She looked over toward the crib. The phone must have bothered Aaron, too.

"Don't refuse before you hear me out. There's a social at…"

"No."

"Jenna…."

"Mom, I don't want to socialize."

"…there's a very nice young doctor who is not much older than you, a surgeon; he's specializing in…"

Jenna held the phone away from her ear. Not again. Daniel had only been gone for just over four months and this was at least her mother's fifth attempt at a blind date. Of course, they were all professional men – doctors, brokers, anyone who would pull her back into the right world. But it wasn't going to happen.

Aaron started the soft cry that warned her he was about to get upset. She put the phone back to her ear. "Mom, the baby's awake. I have to go."

"At least consider it. I don't need an answer now. He's a very nice man and I've checked out his record."

"I'm sure they're all nice, but I'm just not interested."

"Jenna…."

"I have to go. I'll call you later. Bye, Mom."

Barely giving her time to respond, Jenna severed the connection. The call would probably be returned quite a while later. But, her mom wasn't likely to be home if she did try to reach her. She never was, and she never had been.

It wasn't time for Aaron to be awake, so she found his pacifier and stroked his hair until he fell asleep again. She still sometimes had trouble believing that now she was the mom and he would look to her for whatever he needed. And she would be at his school events, whether or not it was something that actually held an interest for her. She would be there.

With a deep breath, Jenna straightened and sauntered over to put a cup of water in the microwave. She needed her mint tea. Actually, she needed a friendly voice. Why was it that every time she talked to her mother, she ended up calling Alan? Because he knew what she had to put up with maybe. Or because she had been running to him to complain since she was eleven. Well, she was getting a little too old for that.

The beeping pulled her back and Jenna retrieved the cup and dropped in a tea bag. She absently tugged the string while staring into the steaming liquid. The hot moisture warmed her fingers. A young doctor, specializing in … heart surgery, possibly? Maybe he could help her out if he would just replace hers so she could start over. Okay, she didn't really want that. She didn't want to lose what she did still have. But she sure didn't want to be set up, either. Especially by her mother. What on earth would make her parents think she would want her child to grow up that way? With neither parent ever around to take part in his life, any part of his life?

She walked back to the art table, where she had absentmindedly scribbled on a piece of newsprint. Alan's house – her escape. The perspective of the porch swing wasn't quite right, but perspective had never been her strong point, except when actually looking at the object she was drawing. Still, she could see it clearly. The two-story, Victorian-style house had slightly peeling white paint, a short railing around the front porch, and shrubs and trees of every kind. Alan's mom was nearly an expert on flowers and could grow anything. Jenna guessed that was where he had inherited his love of nature. Being the only boy, Alan had been given the duty of lawn care and helped his mom plant trees and trim the bushes and often just kept her company while she was weeding or watering.

The lilacs had begun to bloom a few days ago and their scent filled the air around the friendly home. Jenna's spirits lifted as she knocked lightly on the screen door before entering. She never bothered to wait for someone to answer if the large front door was open. The Taylors had made her feel like family since she had first started visiting.

Alan's mom greeted her with a smile and asked if she wanted a warm cookie. She was always baking; it was her third love, after her family and her flower gardens. Jenna accepted willingly and sat at the table, waiting for information on her friend. And she never had to wait long.

"He's not home yet. His finals are next week and he's staying late to study at the library. I'm not sure when he'll be here." Janice Taylor set a glass of milk in front of her, just as Jenna had seen in the old movies she enjoyed watching.

"I knew his car wasn't here. I just thought I'd wait, if it's okay."

"Of course it's okay, Dear. If you don't want to sit here with me and be bored, the girls are in their room. They're supposed to be studying, but I'm sure they're not. Go on up. I'll tell Alan you're here when he comes in."

Jenna grinned as she headed up the gold-carpeted stairs. Janice Taylor was anything but boring. But she knew when Jenna wanted to visit and when she just wanted to see her friend.

Amber and Carrie looked up from the magazine lying on top of their school books. Carrie, the soft-spoken fourteen-year-old, wore a guilty look. Amber, however, jumped up, grabbing the magazine, and rushed over to show Jenna their newest treasure. A smiling face headlined the front of her Tiger Beat.

"Isn't he just adorable? I saved my allowance and got it today! There's a big article about him. Do you think he'll ever come to Peoria? I just have to see him in real life!"

"I think he needs a haircut, but I like his voice." Jenna watched the girl's mouth drop open.

"A haircut? He's perfect just the way he is! I thought you liked Donny?"

"I do, but he needs a haircut. And aren't you supposed to be studying?"

Amber pulled her possession away gruffly. "Are you in a bad mood again? Alan isn't home yet, so wait and take it out on him.

He doesn't mind." The girl flopped back down on the ruffle-trimmed bedspread and returned to flipping through the magazine.

Jenna crossed the small room and claimed the wire-backed chair with matching cushion. "Sorry, I was just teasing." But Amber wasn't listening anymore. She was so sensitive. A year older than her sister, her name was well suited. Her hair was a straight brownish-blonde and just like the dictionary definition, she was "quickly electrified with friction."

Carrie, on the other hand, was very easy-going and had nearly the same shade as Alan's light brown hair.

Jenna decided to let Amber sulk. "Carrie, what are you studying?"

"I'm helping Amber with her French. She doesn't like it much, though."

"It's a waste of time. I don't know why we need to know a foreign language."

So Amber was talking to her already. She never stayed mad long. "What if you want to go to France some day?"

"Why would I do that?"

"To see all the beautiful things there – the Eiffel Tower, the Louvre...."

"If I get to travel, I'll go to California, and they talk English there."

"They speak English there." A male voice interrupted. "Maybe you should study your English grammar, as well."

Jenna looked toward the doorway and smiled at her friend. It wasn't as irritating when he corrected his sisters' grammar as when he corrected hers. Although, she didn't really mind. He always sounded so intelligent and graceful. It would be nice for people to feel that way about her.

"Mom said you were up here. She also said the girls are supposed to be studying. Amber..."

"Okay, okay." The girl closed the magazine and went back to sulking in her textbook.

Jenna tried not to grin as she stood. They never argued with him. She had always heard of brothers and sisters fighting constantly, but it didn't happen here. Amber and Carrie bickered with each other fairly often but never crossed their brother. Maybe because he was so much older.

Alan was almost twenty, the son of his mother's first husband. The girls were technically his half-sisters, but no one ever mentioned that. And Lee Taylor had taken him in as his own son. Alan got along with his adoptive father so well, that, as soon as he had a choice, he had stopped going for the once-a-year two week visits with his biological father.

"Do you want to walk down to the store with me? Mom needs eggs and it's beautiful today. I could use some fresh air."

"Sure." Jenna said goodbye to the girls and passed Alan into the hall. He always waited to let her go through the doorway first and always opened doors for her, though she often told him it wasn't necessary. It was just his nature. He was a true gentleman; not only taught, but inborn.

Stepping out into the sunshine, Jenna suddenly lost the urge to talk. She noticed the little things that were missed during every day distractions: iris beginning to push their purple skirts through the green shields, bright yellow dandelions overtaking spikes of deep green grass that needed mowing, clumps of violas growing around bushes (she loved violas and would have a yard-full when she had her own house), bits of gravel beside the road that sparkled. Crossing the road and climbing the three cracked steps up to the sidewalk that led to town, she looked at the grooved dirt that ran beside them. She remembered having helped create the little path by riding her bicycle down the small hill onto the road, as many of the town kids often did. She hadn't done so herself since her mom had caught and admonished her.

"So, what's up?"

Ignoring the intrusion of her thoughts, Jenna watched ants scurry to move away from her feet. As if they had anything to worry about. She would never purposely step on any living creature. The thought of unnecessarily ending their lives seemed inhumane. Not that she had any particular fondness for them, but as long as they didn't bother her, she saw no reason to bother them.

"Jenna?"

She gave in only partly, continuing to watch the ants. "I can't go on my senior trip."

"Why not?"

"Because Brian will be there."

"And?"

"And Mom doesn't think we'll be chaperoned well enough." Silence again came between them until she stopped at the little

bridge to pick up a small stick and drop it into the trickling creek below, pushing a strand of hair away from her face.

"Jenna, it's not ... that serious, is it? You and Brian?"

"Of course not. I'm seventeen. I don't have any interest in doing that." She moved to the other side, holding the rusty metal railing to watch the stick bounce along, getting caught for a short time before the movement of the clear water set it free. "It's just an excuse. She wants to keep me under her thumb forever."

"She just worries about you. You know, if you didn't rebel against everything she says, maybe she wouldn't worry so much."

Her eyes shot to his. "You're taking her side? Alan, I'm a straight A student because she insists on it and I'm on the volleyball team because she was captain of hers. I hate volleyball. And all I do is that and chorus. It's not like I sneak out to party like some of my friends do. I don't do anything exciting. What does she have to worry about?"

Alan set a hand on her arm. "Jenna, you know I'm not taking her side, but don't you think she can see that you don't want the life she wants you to have? She knows she's running out of time to change your mind."

"Why should I have to live that way just 'cause she wants me to? It's my life."

"Yes, it is, and you're nearly eighteen."

"And then I can live by my own rules and go where I want."

His eyes cast a warning. "Don't do something stupid just to get back at your parents. You'll end up hurting yourself more than you hurt them. It is *your life. You have to decide what you really want."*

"You have to decide what you really want."

Picking up a clean sheet of paper, Jenna began sketching the bridge.

Five

The water under the bridge became more a focal point than the old bridge itself. Though she could see it clearly in her mind, painting the clarity and translucence was another story. Not to mention the movement. And the movement was important. Water under the bridge, washing the old leaves and sticks away until they were out of sight. But were they less important or real because they were no longer in her vision?

Mixing gray into brown sienna, Jenna used her small putty knife to etch a rough line onto the canvas, added shadow until it became elliptical, then splashed a bit of white water over the side. Moving away to study her work, she realized the stick was the most realistic object in the painting. Well, she supposed that was appropriate. Water, like time, was fleeting, but the objects, or events, it washed away were still as real as if they were in plain view.

Satisfied enough to continue, Jenna found a stiff brush and dipped it into the barely mixed grayish-white. She wanted the sidewalk to stand out, as well. First, sketch in the basic outline, then, add the details – shadows, highlights where the sun hit, separations and cracks, and grass pushing over the edge. The two steps back to again get a more distant view turned her attention to a slight ache in her feet and a heaviness in her arm. Ignoring the present, she concentrated on the painted scene and the following day's events. It carried her back to her parents' home.

She made her way tenaciously to her mother's room. Another social event, or socialite event, as Jenna liked to call them, had come up at the last minute. So, again, her mom would miss her chorus concert. Well, Alan and his family were going, so she wouldn't be there alone.

Louise Givens was wearing something Jenna hadn't seen before. Like everything else her mom owned, it was meticulously fit and elegant and the black pearl necklace and earrings matched exactly.

She stood at the doorway, finally growing tired of waiting to be noticed. "You look nice. Is that new?"

"Oh, Jenna, you startled me. I didn't see you there."

Of course she hadn't. "I know you're busy, but Alan asked me to go to ICC with him over spring break to look around the campus. I wanted to answer him tonight at the concert."

"Concert?"

Jenna sighed. "My chorus concert. It's tonight."

Spritzing perfume on her wrists, she glanced at her daughter through the dresser mirror. "Oh, yes. Alan's going with you?"

"Yes. At least someone's interested."

Finally turning, her mom acted apologetic. "Jenna, you know I'm interested. But this is very important..."

"Of course it is. They always are." She changed her tone suddenly. Her mom wasn't about to agree if she got rude. "Is Dad going with you?"

"No, he couldn't get off, but he won't be late tonight. Why don't you order something from the little Italian restaurant?"

"The Taylors are taking me out after the concert."

"You mean Alan's taking you out?"

Jenna took a deep breath, keeping control of her voice. "No, Mom, his family is. So, can I go to ICC with him?"

Her mother sat genteelly on her silk bedspread to push four-inch heels onto her feet. "Jenna, I thought you applied to U of I."

"I did, but only because you wanted me to."

"It's an excellent college. Your father and I both went there and look how well we've done. Don't you want to be successful in life?"

"I'd rather be happy. And I don't want to move so far away."

"You can't be happy without being successful. And, I imagine if you go there, Alan will change his mind and go with you."

Jenna ignored the first comment. "He doesn't want to get his bachelor's right now. He wants to work first."

"He'll make more money with a better degree. You would be doing him a favor by talking him into going. And when he graduates in another two years, he can start a career while you're finishing. That way you'll have a solid basis to begin a family." She stood, testing the heels, then crossed back to the mirror.

"Mother, he's just my friend. You know I'm dating Brian."

"Yes, but he's only temporary. Jenna, he's a nice boy, but he'll never do any more with his life than his father did. You need a husband who will be able to keep you in the right society."

"I'm seventeen. I'm not ready to think about marriage. And it's bad enough that you won't let me go on my class trip. At least

let me do something half-way interesting over break. I'll be with Alan, and that's what you want."

Louise Givens paused only for a moment. "Alright. You can go with Alan to Illinois Central if you'll agree to check out U of I before deciding which one to choose. We'll make a run up to Chicago after graduation."

Jenna approached her painting again warily, then backed away and dropped her brush into the solvent. What was the point? All the painting she did wouldn't change anything and wasn't getting her anywhere. It wasn't even her palette knife; the brushes lying around weren't hers, and neither was the paint. Well, some of it was. She had found a few colors at the art store she couldn't resist and the canvas she was now using she had bought there. But mostly, it was Daniel's.

Warming another cup of water, she dropped in the same bag she had used the last time. Daniel had fussed about her reusing a tea bag, saying they could afford for her to use a new one each time. But it seemed wasteful. She had never stopped doing so, though she thought every time about his objection. Many of his comments stayed in her mind and presented themselves on different occasions. Jenna wondered whether that would ever change.

Wandering over to the window and the big oak chair, she set the cup on a small plant stand she'd been using as a table ever since the plant had died. A sudden chill raised goose bumps on her bare arms and she stood again to grab the old frayed sweatshirt she wore only in her apartment. It had a couple of small holes from where the seams had finally given and a touch of paint here and there, mostly from when she had dared to bother her husband while he was working. Sometimes it had been okay and he had responded warmly. Jenna had quickly learned to judge when she could interrupt and when she needed to keep her distance. Well, until he had become sick, and then his painting hadn't seemed as important anymore.

She still felt guilty for enjoying the extra time he had spent with her then; knowing the only reason was because he didn't have the strength to work so many hours after the cancer had taken control. And because he knew their time together would be severely limited.

Was it too cold in the apartment? Crossing over to the crib, she pulled the blanket up higher on her sleeping son and carefully touched his cheek. He felt warm enough. Cupping her hand over his tiny head, Jenna felt his slight movement. She was bothering him. He hated to be bothered while sleeping, but the touch warmed her and her baby decided to ignore it. He was so like his father. What would he do with his life? Would he be interested in art, as well? Maybe he would surprise her and do something completely different. Whatever he chose, it would be his decision. It wasn't her place to interfere.

Her tea was cool by the time she returned to the rocking chair and she set it down again. She didn't like cold tea. In fact, there wasn't much she liked cold. She never put ice in her water, preferring it lukewarm, and generally kept her soda in the pantry rather than in the refrigerator. Daniel always shook his head when he picked up her glass by mistake.

Jenna watched her husband approach. His chest muscles contracted and expanded in reply to the stretching of his arms, first overhead, then behind his back. He had been working for hours. She had made lunch, which he hadn't bothered to stop for, flipped through a magazine while sitting at the table alone, cleaned the dishes and counters, taken a load of laundry down to the machines in the basement, and was sitting with her most recent novel from the library while waiting for the dryer to finish.

Daniel set a hand on her shoulder while grabbing a glass from the stand beside her chair.

Her eyes traced his arm, fell to his stomach. She loved the warm days when he didn't bother with a shirt.

"Hmm ... wrong one." He returned it to the stand and grabbed the other, which was still colder than Jenna's, though the ice had melted. "How can you it drink it that way?"

Jenna shrugged. "That's how I like it."

He grinned, took a couple of swallows, and returned to his easel.

She watched him for a moment as he sank back into his own world. This painting was going well and he was in a good mood. Maybe she could risk an interruption before he was too lost.

Setting her book on the end table, she quietly moved up from behind and set a hand on his back, as if checking his progress. If he ignored her, she would back away again.

"So, what do you think so far?"

He wasn't ignoring her this time. She moved in closer, running the other arm around his stomach, still as flat and hard as ever, though his sister had teased him about gaining weight after he was married. Jenna didn't know how he could possibly gain weight when he rarely took time to eat.

"Are you afraid to answer? Is it that bad?" He finally turned, still holding his brush.

"You know it's brilliant. That's why you're in such a good mood." She grinned into his eyes and let a hand wander on his chest.

"I'm covered in paint. Be careful."

"Do I ever care?" She kissed the side of his neck; in the place hair didn't grow. He often fussed about the unevenness of the beard he always shaved anyway; just because it was an imperfection he didn't like. But she loved the soft places that didn't scratch her lips in the evenings when it had started to grow back in. When she was allowed to get that close.

"Jenna...."

"I know. You're working. But I need you." She moved her lips to his bare shoulder and felt him begin to give in.

"I guess I have been busy recently."

She took the brush from his hand and dropped it carefully into the turpentine.

Aaron's cry pierced her reverie. She took a deep, ragged breath and pushed away the tears that came to her eyes. Starting toward the crib, Jenna noticed the time. It was nearly six; Alan should be home by now.

Cuddling her baby in one arm, she watched him nurse for a few minutes, then reached for the phone. After waiting through four rings, Jenna paused at the voice. Wrong one.

The greeting came again before she responded. "Hi, Cheryl. Is Alan home yet?"

"Jenna! Are you okay? He's been trying to reach you all week. He even stopped by the apartment a couple of days ago and no one was there. Is everything alright?"

He came over? "Yeah, we're fine. I must have been at the store."

"Good, I'm so glad to hear from you! Just a minute, let me get him. He's been so worried!"

She listened to silence while waiting for her friend. The loft seemed very empty tonight.

"Jenna? Where've you been? I've left four messages."

"I know. I'm sorry. I just … I didn't feel like talking."

"Are you okay?"

"Yeah, I'm fine."

"And Aaron's okay?"

She couldn't help grinning. He hadn't said "the baby" this time. "Yes."

"I stopped by…"

"I know. Cheryl told me. I had to go to the store."

Silence again.

"Alan?"

"I'm here."

"I've been painting this week."

He didn't answer right away. "That's great, Jenna. How's it going?"

He sounded cautious. Jenna assumed Cheryl had stayed within hearing distance. "Um, I'm not sure. I…" She swallowed to try to keep the emotion from her voice. "I was thinking about…." She stopped again, unable to suppress the tears this time.

"Do you want me to come over?"

"Yes, but you shouldn't." Her baby was startled by a drop on his cheek, and she had to prop the phone between her neck and shoulder to adjust herself and lift him to the other side. She barely heard Alan say he would be right there.

Though Aaron's tummy filled before the doorbell rang, Jenna was still holding him, letting him comfort her. He fussed a bit when she interrupted his restful state but a kiss and a few soft words calmed him by the time she opened the door.

Alan had brought his son with him. Jenna wondered whether it had been his idea or Cheryl's.

"Justin wanted to see Aaron and I thought he could entertain him for a while. I hope you don't mind."

"Of course I don't. Come on in." She returned the boy's shy grin and led them to the living area, setting her baby on the floor beside his toys. Jenna refrained from wrapping Justin in a tight hug when he flopped next to Aaron. The cowlick at his nape had grown enough again to form an untamable half-moon, drawing emphasis to his perfect little-boy neck. There was something especially beautiful about the soft skin and ridges just below a child's hair line.

"Come show me what you've done."

The deeper voice above pulled her eyes up toward it. Alan stared down at her, a softness Jenna didn't see often seeping from his gaze. He *had* been worried. She imagined him wanting to hold and protect her the way she had wanted to hold Justin … to let him feel how special he was.

Standing, she pushed a fallen strand of hair behind her ear. The ponytail was loose, messy. She hadn't thought to fix it before he came. And her old T-shirt had a spot or two of baby food. But he was still gazing at her as if she were in a little black dress, perfectly made up. He always had.

"Jen?"

She pushed at the strand again, though it hadn't fallen. The last time Alan had come over to see her work … while Daniel had been in Chicago, at a show… Alan had kissed her, and she had nearly…. She had quit painting after that. She didn't want to quit again.

The boys laughed at some private joke and Jenna relented. Alan was married now and had his son with him. There was no danger.

Nodding slightly, she moved past him into the studio. She felt him immediately behind her until she stopped, allowing him to take her side.

His arm brushing against hers, Alan studied the painting on the easel. "I have always loved your style, Jen. I don't always understand your art, but I always enjoy seeing it."

She looked up at his strong chin, and at his gaze focused not on her but on her work. "You don't understand this one?"

He grinned, then turned to find her eyes. "Oh, yes. This one I get. And I love the water. It's so alive. It's so … you."

Six

"Well, hello, Jenna. How is my favorite daughter-in-law?"

"Hi, Joan. I'm fine. How's business?" Jenna lightly bounced her son in her arm to try to keep him from fussing.

"Oh, you know, the same. More to do than I have time for."

"And you wouldn't change that if you could."

Joan laughed over the phone line. "You know me too well, Dear. And how is my precious baby doing? Growing fast, I suppose? I really need to steal some time to come see you both again. When would be good for you? I may be able to get a couple of days … maybe … next Thursday … no, I have a meeting Friday morning…. How is…"

"Joan, anytime you can get here is fine."

"I wouldn't want to interrupt any plans."

"I don't have plans. Please, come any time. Aaron isn't growing real fast, but I'm sure he'd love to see you again."

"He's okay? Jenna…"

"Yes, he's fine. The doctor says he's very healthy; he's just not going to be very tall."

"Like his father."

Jenna's heart skipped a beat. No, not like his father. Daniel had been small because of his illness. Aaron just took after her side of the family. He was simply not meant to be tall.

"Jenna, Honey, I didn't mean…. Is that my baby I hear?"

"Yeah, I think he's cutting a tooth. He's been fussy since last night." She kissed his little cheek to try to calm him while listening to Joan throw out suggestions for easing the baby's irritation, all of which she had already heard from Cheryl. None of it worked very well. Her own improvisation of putting her finger in his mouth to chew on worked best, though her fingers were getting sore.

About to thank Joan for the well-meant advice, Jenna heard a soft knock. It had to be Alan. He always knocked quietly so he wouldn't disturb Aaron if he happened to be sleeping. But why was he here now? It was the middle of the workday.

"Joan, can you hold on a second?" She lay the receiver on the table and went to the door, hoping Alan would keep his voice low enough that her mother-in-law wouldn't hear him.

"Hey, Jen, throw some clothes on and come out to the site with me. It's a perfect day."

"I'm on the phone." She kept her own voice quiet as if she could lower his that way.

"Okay, I'll wait. Want me to take him?" He reached for Aaron before she answered and the distraction calmed the baby for a moment.

"Thanks. I'll just be a minute."

"Take your time."

He was in a good mood; his job was apparently going well. But Joan had surely heard him.

Jenna braced herself for the inquiry she expected from the other end of the line. "Sorry, I'm back."

"If you have company, Dear, I'll let you go."

The question in Joan's voice was unmistakable. "Umm, no, I just turned the television up instead of down. And Aaron was getting too hard to hold with one arm." She hated lying to Joan and Alan's glance would have to be answered. But it just felt too weird to admit how much time she had been spending with her friend recently.

Luckily, Joan was interrupted from her end, as well, and finished the conversation saying she would call before she came.

"Was that your mom?"

She went back to Alan to claim her baby. "You're in a good mood today. What's up?"

"Jenna?"

He wasn't going to let it go. "It was Joan."

"Why did you tell her I was the television? Your mom I could understand, but…"

"I don't know. It just seemed…." She turned away from his curious stare. "Why are you here?"

His silence said he didn't appreciate her being so evasive, but finally, he relented, settling onto her couch. "As I said, I thought you might want to go out to the site with me. It's beautiful today."

"Why aren't you taking Cheryl out?"

He paused again. "You know she's not an outdoor person; she still finds my work pretty boring. And I thought you and the baby … sorry, you and Aaron, could use some fresh air."

She pivoted back toward him. "Alan, when I fussed about that the other day, about you saying 'the baby,' I … you don't have to…."

"You just needed to fuss. I know. And I'm just being facetious; one of my worst faults, remember?"

She grinned. "Yeah, just one of your many irritating qualities. And you think I wanna spend the day with you?"

He shrugged. "Wouldn't be the first time."

"The baby's fussy."

"I'm plenty used to fussy babies. Go get dressed."

Jenna hesitated before giving in, the lure of fresh air and watching Alan plan a site too hard to resist. He must be in the planning stage if he was inviting her. Once development actually began, he would be too busy to visit; though she enjoyed that, as well. Just watching him work alongside his men – well, there were a couple of girls, too, but he didn't have the same kind of camaraderie with them – was very stimulating. She appreciated the respect they gave her, not because her best friend was the boss, but because they respected him as a person. And they were all as tanned as Alan, several as muscular and none afraid to model their build while hauling plants, earth, and stone.

She lectured herself silently as she changed into jeans and a snug-fitting blouse. Those thoughts were unnecessary and she felt traitorous to Daniel. His light brown eyes peered at her from the photo on her dresser. Lifting it closer, Jenna touched her fingers to the glass. Maybe she shouldn't go. Would her husband understand how she could need Alan's company so much so shortly after losing him? Would it look bad to anyone who saw them together? It didn't matter what people thought of her. She had never cared much about that. But, she wouldn't want to reflect badly on her husband, as if his death didn't matter enough. Anyone who knew them couldn't think that. But then, most people didn't know them well.

Abruptly changing her mind, Jenna pulled the blouse back over her head, replacing it with one of her husband's shirts and rolling the sleeves to just above her wrists. She hadn't worn this one yet. She could still smell him.

Alan didn't see her right away as she stepped out from behind the curtain. Aaron was chewing on one of his knuckles. So, that's where the idea had come from. She had forgotten.

"You know, maybe…."

He looked up, smiling. "I think this tooth is in. Feels like a tiny knife in there."

She put aside her previous thought and moved close beside them. "Really? It wasn't. I looked just before you came over." She leaned down, gently pushing a finger into her son's mouth. Her friend was right. She felt the sharp edge press into her skin. "His first tooth. I can't believe he's that old already."

"Goes fast, doesn't it? I already miss the baby stage."

"So you can help me. You're a great dad."

She felt his stare, just inches from her face, and pulled back. She shouldn't have...

"I'd love to help you with Aaron; anytime, Jen." He placed a hand on her arm.

"Thank you. I hate that he won't have a father around." Jenna took her son, pulling away from Alan, and kissed his cheek.

"I'm sure you'll eventually find someone else to be part of your family, but, until then..."

"No." She looked directly into her friend's eyes. "I'm not getting married again, ever."

"You can't know that now. Of course it's too soon..."

"Yes, I can. I promised Daniel forever. That's what I meant." She didn't give him time to respond. "Maybe we shouldn't go to-day. I'm sorry I wasted your time here, but..."

"Jen, don't do this. Don't pull away from me again."

"I don't want people to think...."

"Think what? That you have a friend? Well, Heaven forbid you should have a friend. You know, you had a lot of them before. Why shouldn't you have one now? Is that why you lied to Joan? Because you don't want her to think you might possibly be able to go on with your life without her son? Jenna, she has, and Denise has. Why shouldn't you?"

"It's not the same."

"Why isn't it?"

"He was my husband."

"Yes, your husband, not your Siamese twin. Your life didn't end because his did."

"I know that!" Aaron's cry made her lower her voice again. "Alan, I know. That's why I'm painting again. I did listen to you. I'm doing something. Maybe nothing constructive, but some-thing."

“Then why don’t you want to go today? You used to love it, or at least you acted like you did.”

“Of course I did, and I do want to. I love being out there with you; I always have, but…”

He moved closer to her, close enough to touch Aaron’s head to try to help calm him. “But what, Jenna?”

How should she tell him what she was thinking? That she was afraid of getting too close, that he would get too close? She didn’t dare insult him like that, but the way he kept moving in beside her, and touching her…

“Jen, it’s different now. I’m married and I’m not about to leave my family, so if you’re afraid of me proposing again, you can relax.”

She stared into his eyes. He had never been afraid to say whatever he was thinking. She loved that about him.

He took a deep breath. “I’m right, aren’t I? Because of what happened between us before?”

“I don’t want that to happen again.”

“Next time, just talk to me. Don’t make me guess.” He slowly ran his fingers alongside her face. “Jen, you’re right. I still love you as much as ever, and if I weren’t married, in time…. But I am, and I don’t intend to do anything to change that. I made Cheryl a promise, too, and she’s a wonderful person and a great mom, and we do well together. But, Jenna, she doesn’t share my interests the way you do. She supports my career because I love it, but she won’t go to a site with me and she doesn’t want to hear about it because it bores her. I’ve missed having someone who is interested. And I’ve really missed having a best friend.”

“So have I.” Her voice was nearly a whisper. Hearing that he still loved her came as a shock, though she supposed it shouldn’t. She could tell. That’s what scared her. But she never guessed that he would say it openly.

“So? Now what?”

Good question. Now what? And it was up to her. “Alan….” What was she going to say? He was standing there silently, waiting to see whether or not he still had his best friend. “Let me feed the baby before we go.”

λλλλ

The cool, late-September air had both rejuvenated and exhausted Jenna by the time she gently pulled her sleeping baby from the car seat. She shivered while waiting for Alan to remove the seat from his truck and return it to her car.

He, of course, walked them upstairs, and waited at the door.

"Do you want a cup of tea? Or I can make coffee."

"No, thanks. Cheryl will have supper ready. I need to get going." He kissed her cheek. "Thanks for coming."

Jenna shifted Aaron to one side and gave her friend a hug. "Thank you." She relaxed against his shoulder and enjoyed the feel of his arm around her.

Finally, he said good night and she closed the door. Aaron had stirred but remained mostly asleep, so she laid him gently in his crib and went to put a cup of water in the microwave. It was after six; she couldn't let him sleep long but needed a few minutes of quiet.

Staring into the steaming tea, she saw Alan's site. He and his crew had started putting in some of the bushes around the large brick house, which had been newly built, and Jenna and Alan had talked with the owners about different ideas for the rest of the landscaping. Well, Alan had talked about landscaping. Jenna had mostly listened and chatted with the elderly woman who was living there with her daughter and son-in-law. The woman had taken an instant liking to Jenna and Aaron and had insisted they go inside to sit with her a while. Her timing had been perfect, actually, because the baby was getting hungry by then. And the woman didn't think anything of Jenna nursing in the kitchen while they had tea.

She had asked them to return the following day to keep her company. Alan hadn't mentioned that he wanted Jenna there again.

Seven

Jenna watched Mrs. Goddard pour steaming tea into the delicate china cup.

She had been glad when Alan stopped by again this morning, even though she'd had to answer the door in a towel with her hair dripping water all over the floor. But sitting in a real kitchen accented with lush, green houseplants after walking around outside with her friend was very peaceful. She hadn't thought of it before, but that could be what her apartment needed. Plants. Though Jenna wasn't good with them. She had tried once, just after she and Daniel were married. But they had either been over-watered, or under-watered, or something. Only one remained and it looked sorely neglected. Of course she could find fake plants but it wouldn't be the same.

"Are they real?" Jenna noted Mrs. Goddard's puzzlement. "I'm sorry. I mean the plants. They're beautiful."

The woman grinned, pouring her own tea. "Everything my son and daughter-in-law have is real. They never settle for anything except the best." She returned the teapot to the stove and eased into the chair opposite Jenna. "That's why they chose your husband. Believe me, they did plenty of checking before hiring him. I would imagine your house is just living with greenery."

Husband? She meant Alan. "Oh, we're not married."

Mrs. Goddard glanced at the baby, attempting to hide a look of disappointment.

"I mean … Alan's married, and yes, his house is beautiful. But we're just friends."

"The baby…."

"Is mine. Not his." She hadn't wanted to talk about her personal life but felt compelled to explain. "I'm very recently widowed and Alan just makes me get out of the house now and then. We've been friends since we were kids." The woman nodded, not looking convinced. "He has three of his own, including twins."

Mrs. Goddard stirred a teaspoon of sugar into her tea. "I am sorry. But the two of you remind me of myself and my late husband. It's a shame. You would be a good couple. There is real love there." She paused only a moment. "Forgive my bluntness. When you get my age, time gets too short to wait for the right time to speak your mind."

Jenna lowered her eyes. Maybe there was real love between them, but shouldn't there be in friendship? Why did everyone else keep seeing something that wasn't there, or more than what was there? "I should go back outside."

"You haven't even touched your tea yet. And I don't get visitors often. Please, tell me about your husband."

Jenna hesitated. Tell her about Daniel? She didn't talk about him. Not to anyone who hadn't known him. But, she was still a little tired and her feet could use a longer rest.

Taking a cautious sip, she told Mrs. Goddard that he was an artist, a very talented artist, and that they had married young because her parents didn't approve and wouldn't let her see him. She had turned eighteen just after graduating and they were married within two weeks. Her father still barely spoke to her because of it. But it didn't matter, since he had barely spoken to her before then, anyway.

"You married to get away from home?"

"No. I got married because I was in love."

"But you were in such a hurry for a young girl. Eighteen is still a child."

Yes. Maybe that was true. But she hadn't had a choice.

The Chicago branch of the University of Illinois was a beautiful college, and Jenna could almost see herself spending a few years there, away from her family. But, she would be away from Daniel, too, unless he was willing to move. That could be the answer. His mother was close to there, anyway, and they could see each other freely without her parents knowing. And she liked his mom, and his mom seemed to like her, so maybe Joan would be an ally. If he still wanted her to move in with him, they could get a small apartment near campus and she wouldn't have to live in the dorms. Jenna didn't want to share a room with other girls and have to use the community bathrooms and showers. Of course, her mom said they would pay for a private room, but still ... she would rather be able to wake up with Daniel every morning. He could paint while she went to school, and she could get a part-time job if she needed to. They could make it work.

"Jenna, are you listening to me?"

"What?"

Her mother rolled her eyes. "I do wish you would learn to pay attention when someone is speaking to you. I said the president seemed very interested in having you attend in the fall, didn't he? He knows high quality students when he sees them."

She turned again to stare out the car window. "Of course he did. You send enough money every year."

"And you don't appreciate anything we do for you. We have been sending money every year in order to help secure your place here. Of course, your grades will help, as well. But there are a lot of kids with good grades. We wanted to give you a better opportunity."

Jenna stopped listening. She'd heard it before. Instead, she studied the city buildings, wondering how far they were from the art gallery where Daniel's work would be exhibited in the morning. She had barely managed to time her trip to Chicago so it would coincide with his opening. But how would she get there? She had Joan's phone number, where he was staying, but...

"By the way, your father and I have some business to attend to tomorrow. Will you be okay in the hotel alone? I promise we'll do some sightseeing on Sunday morning, though we do need to be home by early evening. But, if you're uncomfortable with that, you can come with us. I just think you would be bored."

"That's fine, Mom." She tried not to sound as relieved as she was. Was it really going to be this easy?

"Are you sure? We'll be all day, possibly late."

"I'll be fine."

"If you're sure. You can look over the materials Mr. Jakes gave you today. See what you might be interested in as a major."

Or she could sneak off to see Daniel. How would she do that? A bus, maybe. She could ask at the front desk, but they may report her to her parents. She would call Joan tonight, after her parents were asleep so they wouldn't hear her talking from the next room.

"Have I offended you?"

Mrs. Goddard's voice pulled her back. "No. I'm sorry; I was just thinking." She realized she was still holding on to her cup, and took another sip. It was finally the right temperature.

Aaron began fussing. He was tired.

"If you would like to lay him down a while, I would be glad to keep an eye on him. My old legs don't handle a lot of walking anymore, but maybe you would rather be out with your friend."

She stroked her baby's head. "Thank you, but I don't leave him." She did want to be outside. "If you don't mind, though, I think I will walk with him. He seems to like the fresh air."

Jenna hoped she hadn't offended the friendly woman as she thanked her for the tea and excused herself.

Stepping back into the sunlight, she squinted. The sun was directly above, spilling warmth through the light breeze. She wished she had worn a tank top so she could feel the direct heat on her shoulders. She didn't want it on Aaron's face, however, and pulled his receiving blanket into a curve around his head. He never wanted it over his face, but it was enough to block the rays. Her son had Daniel's paleness and would burn easily.

Finding her way to the back of the house, Jenna felt like she was sneaking around again. But that was crazy. There was nothing wrong with her being here with Alan. So, then, why did she feel guilty?

She stopped, coming into view of the landscapers moving small trees around the back yard. Alan was watching, checking the entire scene, then walking over to a leafy maple. He easily picked it up, though it was nearly twice his height, and moved it close to an elm. That really was better. He had a natural artistic eye, and Jenna did enjoy watching him work.

Deciding to stay out of the way, she sat gently in the grass, under shade of a small tree that had been put in the day before. The sod was still damp around the trunk, so she was careful to stay on the outer edge. Aaron had fallen asleep before they had turned the first corner and she was able to sit quietly and study the landscape, and the men working it. She loved trees. She loved the smell of grass and freshly turned dirt. She loved the light breeze playing with her hair and the warm sun penetrating her skin. She loved … Alan was calling to one of his employees. His voice filled the air. She loved being here with Alan. She loved … Alan. No. She didn't. She couldn't. She had been in love. It wasn't the same. With Daniel, she had hated every minute that she was away from him. She had needed to be closer. She hadn't had a second thought about giving herself to him. Well, maybe a second thought, but it hadn't lasted long, and it was just because of her age. He had been everything. She didn't feel that way about Alan. She just enjoyed being with him and loved that he enjoyed being with her.

He turned and spotted her. Obviously in the middle of giving instructions, he turned back, pointing at the horizon, then walked away from his work. He headed toward her.

She also loved how he always stopped what he was doing to pay attention to her, even if only for a minute or two.

Alan strode the distance easily, nearly brushing her arm as he sat, arms loosely wrapped around his knees. "Did you have a nice chat with Mrs. Goddard? I know she really enjoys you and Aaron."

"She thought we were married."

He raised his eyebrows.

"She said her son and daughter-in-law only accept the best – that's why they hired my husband."

The corners of his mouth turned up just enough to say he was flattered. "Well, that's nice to hear."

She waited for him to realize how it sounded to her.

"Jenna, I mean…I'm sorry. I guess I should have made it clearer so you didn't have to…"

"You let them think I was your wife?"

"No. I didn't tell them that. I had mentioned that I was married. I suppose they just assumed…"

"That it would be your wife you would take to work with you. You know what Mrs. Goddard is thinking now, don't you? I told her we were just friends, but I don't think she believes me."

He glanced toward his workers, then shifted to face her more directly. "Why wouldn't she?"

"Because she thinks…." Why had he glanced back just then? "Have you told Cheryl that I'm out here with you?"

"It hasn't come up. Why?"

Jenna felt a knot in her stomach and turned her face away.

"Jen … I thought our talk yesterday cleared things up. Why are you making a big deal out of this?"

"Why didn't you tell Cheryl?" Silence. "Alan, what if something gets said? Okay, I know and you know there is nothing going on, but … people talk … and if she hears something secondhand…."

"Okay, you're right. I'll tell her tonight that you came out with me. But Jenna, she won't care. She never listens when I talk about my job. That's why I don't say anything. It's a waste of time."

"She adores you."

He shifted again, farther from her this time. "I know. I guess I just expected her to be as involved in my career as you were in Daniel's. I would love her to want to come out here with me – to let the kids play in the grass where I could see them, and be with them more … but it's not going to happen. I was so jealous of what Daniel had and he didn't even appreciate it."

"You think he didn't appreciate me? How can you say that to me?" She jumped up, startling the baby. How dare he? Of course Daniel appreciated her. He was just busy.

"Jenna."

She felt his hand on her arm, trying to stop her from walking away. She jerked her arm out of his hand and kept going. But where would she go? He had picked them up. He was her only way home.

"Jenna, I'm sorry."

She stopped, whirling on him. "Are you? Are you trying to tell me he wasn't as perfect as I think he was just because you don't have exactly what you want? What is wrong with you? Cheryl is pretty, and smart, and a wonderful mother, and she takes care of everything so you have nothing but your job to think about … and you're not satisfied? Just what do you expect? So she doesn't like trees. So what? She loves you, and she is completely devoted to you."

"And we never argue. We never fight. We never even disagree. Maybe there is something wrong with me, but I need some excitement now and then. I guess that's why I'm always baiting you. I like seeing sparks occasionally."

As if she needed that now? Peace and contentment would be a good thing. How could he need more than that?

"Jen, I just miss having the real fire that you and Daniel had. Is it wrong to want that?"

She closed her eyes. She missed it too. And she couldn't imagine never having it.

Finally, she took a deep breath. "Then you need to make it, with your wife."

He nodded. "I can run you home, if you want."

λλλλ

Jenna pulled her cup from the microwave and dropped in the tea bag. Aaron would sleep well after two long days of fresh air and excitement. She hadn't let Alan take them home early. It would have been more than an hour's drive round trip, and she didn't have anything to be home for, anyway. He had stopped and picked up a sandwich for her so she wouldn't have to make supper for herself, then had gone home to Cheryl and his kids.

She tugged at the string, focusing on the swirls of brown leaking fragrant flavor into the water. How could Alan not be content with what he had? At least he had them. He had no idea ... but, then, she couldn't imagine not having the fire inside from wanting with every part of your being to be closer to the one you love. To not be willing to give everything and anything to make it happen.

Pulling out the bag and adding a touch of sugar, she moved to her rocker, holding her cup with both hands. The late afternoon air had gotten chilly as the sun descended and she was still a little too cool. Her hands were, anyway. The rest of her was plenty warm. She had felt that way when Joan had picked her up outside the hotel that Saturday morning. From nerves, she supposed. She had told the hotel doorman she was going for a walk when he had stopped her to ask. Her mother had apparently asked them to look out for her. It hadn't taken her long to find Joan's car just a block down the street.

And Daniel's mother had been in a talkative mood. But Jenna didn't mind. She loved hearing about how Joan had set up Daniel's first real show. And how much publicity she had managed, without telling anyone he was her son. She had wanted his work to stand on its own, not to be purchased for the sole means of buttering up to the influential fashion designer/art benefactor. They would just think this was another of her "finds." And after he was established, she would be able to brag that he was her son.

They pulled up in front of the gallery and Jenna wrung her hands together. They were cold. But her face felt flushed. Why was she so nervous about seeing him? Maybe because they had been apart for a couple of weeks. She had been so busy with end of the school year activities and with her final term paper and senior project that she hadn't been anywhere except school, the library, and her room. Well, and at Alan's now and then just to wind down. But he wasn't there much. He was graduating next Saturday and had finals on Monday and Tuesday.

"Are you coming in or should I send him out here?"

Jenna apologized for her hesitation and forced herself through the car door Joan was holding. Heat reflected from the sidewalk burned into her skin. Still, her hands were cold.

The gallery was small, barely noticeable, but there were a few people straggling in already. Jenna watched them, fascinated by the whole scene.

"The early birds." Joan took her arm, as if expecting Jenna to bolt. "They always come early to get the first peek at a new artist, then stand back and watch other people's reactions. Spies, I like to call them."

"Journalists or art critics?"

"Oh, no, neither. You have much to learn about the art world, Child. Journalists are very obvious – always with a notebook in hand and usually with a cameraman in tow. Critics come fashionably late. They like to make an entrance, though they always appear to be trying to hide who they are. Rubbish. The important ones know they're recognized. The others are sure to make their presence known."

Jenna let Daniel's mother pull her toward the door. Joan would make a good critic. She was well-dressed, but not extravagantly. And everyone either made a point to say hello to her by name, or glanced sideways at her, jealous of the attention she was getting. Jenna wondered if she should have dressed better. She had worn her nice pants and her favorite blouse, but it didn't compare to the women in dresses and suits and salon hairdos. She had left her own hair down, with just one small barrette holding the right side back. She looked childish compared to all of the city women. Would she embarrass Daniel? What would he be wearing?

He probably wouldn't have time for her, anyway. His mom would keep him too busy showing him off and he would have to chat with the art patrons.... Maybe she shouldn't have come. What would she do while they were busy? She hated standing by herself and looking as if she didn't belong.

Jenna tried to be friendly and sound intelligent to everyone she met. And Joan was introducing her as a friend of the artist's, which seemed to bring her some respect. She really should have dressed better.

Inside the gallery, she stopped. Daniel's art was everywhere. It was wonderful. The soft light being cast upon each painting by the fixture above brought out the highlights in his work. They seemed to be alive in this sterile, beige room. Forgetting about the people around her, she wandered off to be closer to his paintings. The first one that caught her eye was the scene below his studio, from the window. And the window was there. She felt as though she was standing inside his loft now, wrapped in the sheet with his arms around her. She hadn't seen this one before. She loved it. She loved everything he did. And she missed him.

"This is his newest piece. He said you were the inspiration, though he wouldn't explain why. Would you have any idea?"

She looked up at Joan and nodded. Then she turned back to the painting. She missed him.

"Joan, Darling! You must introduce me to the artist. These are magnificent!"

Jenna turned to see a heavy-set woman burdened with too much jewelry smiling broadly at Daniel's mother.

"They are good, aren't they?" Joan played the benefactor part well, maintaining a professional distance from her son. It was a good thing she had decided to keep her maiden name, or take it back again. Jenna wasn't sure.

"Good? My dear, you're being too modest. You have such an eye for finding quality. Where in Heaven's name did you find him?"

"In a small city I happened to be in recently. I decided he should have a wider audience."

"Oh, without a doubt! He is here, isn't he? I do so want to meet him."

Joan smiled. "Of course. We were just on our way to find him. You are welcome to come with." She turned to Jenna. "Edna, this is Jenna Givens, a friend of Daniel's. She came up to the city in order to be at his first opening. Jenna, Edna Covington."

"Ahhhhh, the girl in the paintings! I can see why he chose you. He didn't have to do any touch-ups to make you look paintable."

Paintable? Was that a word? In the paintings? She thought he had changed his mind about the student series she had posed for. Joan hadn't told her...

"Come now, let's go find him." Joan avoided her glance and took her arm again, talking with Mrs. Covington as they drifted through and among small groups of people.

She studied the paintings visible from the main path while listening to any comments she could grasp from those around. Most of the artwork she recognized; some she didn't. All were just amazing. She wished Joan would release her so she could wander on her own. She wouldn't be alone here. She was very much at home standing in front of any of Daniel's pieces.

"There he is, trying to act like he doesn't belong here."

Jenna looked in the direction Joan nodded. Her breathing stopped for a few seconds. She had missed him so.

Joan released her arm and took her other companion to introduce to her son. Jenna hung back. She didn't want to be in the way. Okay, she wanted to get herself under control so she would be able to act like just his friend. And he hadn't seen her yet.

He smiled politely at Mrs. Covington and accepted her hand and obviously some compliments. He was wearing jeans and a T-shirt, with a blazer thrown over the top, most likely at Joan's request. She watched him nod slightly and treat his mother as an acquaintance, then Joan turned her head toward Jenna, and he did the same.

He immediately walked away from the women. Jenna wondered if she should meet him part way but couldn't seem to move her feet.

In no time, he was in front of her, grasping her fingers. "I was afraid you wouldn't come. Your parents brought you?"

"Well, we came to look at the college. They don't know I'm here. But I had to come. Daniel, this is wonderful. You should hear what everyone is saying. They love your work."

"I've missed you, Jenna." He set a hand on her arm and leaned in to touch his lips to her cheek. "How long are you staying?"

"I have all day. They have business."

"And tomorrow?"

She shook her head. "They're taking me sight-seeing. They want me to get to know the city for when I start school here."

He backed away slightly. "You're going to U of I?"

"They want me to. I don't know."

"I would never get to see you."

"Unless you move here."

"You're asking me to move back to Chicago?"

"No. I just thought … your mom's here, and it's a great place to show your work…."

"Jenna, I can't live in a big city. Peoria's big enough and I like it there. I may have to visit for shows, but…"

"Then I'll go to I.C.C.; I like it better, anyway."

He studied her face. "I feel like I should argue, but ... I don't want you so far away. As soon as you're eighteen, I want us to tell your parents that we're dating so we don't have to hide it ... so I can see you more often."

"Daniel." Joan announced her presence before getting close enough to hear the conversation. She had someone else who wanted to meet him.

Tell her parents? They would never have it.

The ring of the telephone startled her and large drops of tea splashed onto her jeans. She set the cup down and grabbed the receiver before it woke Aaron.

"Jenna, I got a reprieve from the meeting. I'll be at Denise's first thing in the morning. Can I come tomorrow afternoon to see you and the baby? Actually, let me take you all to lunch. Should we pick you up or would you rather meet us?"

Joan? Tomorrow? Well, Jenna had told her any time. "Sure. I'll meet you there. When and where?"

As if she had to ask. Joan always took them to the same place. Jumers. The castle-shaped restaurant really was beautiful, but too elegant for Jenna's taste, though she had gotten used to dealing with that whenever it had been necessary.

Luckily, Joan didn't hold her long and she went to grab a towel to soak the tea from her jeans. Forget it. She was too tired. Beginning to strip them off, she headed to the shower she hoped would help her sleep. Jenna would need the extra rest in order to be with Daniel's family the following day.

Eight

Jenna pulled onto Western Avenue and searched Jumers' parking lot for an empty space. She hoped it wouldn't rain. Dark clouds were threatening and the temperature had plummeted overnight. Was that why Alan hadn't stopped to ask if she had wanted to go with him again? Or had Cheryl objected? Of course, Jenna would have had to turn him down, but she would like to know why he hadn't asked.

Finding a space fairly close to the door, she eased in and cut the Mustang's engine. It wasn't a very practical family car; the van would have to replace it as Aaron grew. But she preferred driving her sixty-six Ford – a gift from Daniel after his first big success.

She sat, not moving. She didn't want to go in. They were surely there already; Joan was always early and Jenna always tended to run a few minutes late. She was so different than her mother-in-law. She never felt together enough, or smart enough, or interesting enough around Joan and Denise. Daniel's sister was a lot like his mom. Tall and thin and always dressed perfectly, even when home tending her children. Jenna liked sweats and big T-shirts.

Her son began to fuss.

"Okay, Baby. Just a second."

She climbed out after allowing herself a sigh, being careful not to hit the Cadillac beside her, and pushed her seat forward. Gathering Aaron and his small bag into one arm, she rubbed his head, grinning about the dark hair slightly curling in front of his ears. In response, he raised a tiny hand to her face and pushed his head against her neck. He loved the affection.

"There is so much of your daddy in you. He would be so proud to take you everywhere and show you off." She kissed his cheek, then noticed a couple staring.

Jenna ignored them. It used to bother her that Daniel's notoriety for being rude kept people from speaking to her, but now she considered it a blessing to be mostly left alone. Though occasionally, she wished his public image hadn't been so negative. People had no idea how wrong they were about him.

A shiver crawled across her skin, pushing her toward the entrance.

Giving Joan's name to the maitre d', Jenna followed the man through the dining room. She studied the sparkling chandeliers that echoed crystal candle holders on each table, enjoyed the scent of exquisitely-prepared entrees and focused attention on the classical music emanating from all around her. Anything to avoid stares coming from strangers at surrounding tables. Most of the diners were in business clothes. She still didn't dress well enough for Joan's crowd.

"Jenna, Dear."

If Joan was bothered by her attire, she didn't let it show. Her mother-in-law performed the social touch of the arm and peck on the cheek. Denise gave Jenna a warm, sisterly hug and claimed the baby, who was hesitant to go to his aunt. They hadn't seen each other often enough.

"I'm sorry I'm late. He slept longer than I expected and he gets grouchy if I wake him up too soon."

"Nonsense, you're fine. Denise and I were just saying we should do this more often. We do miss seeing you both." Joan tugged Aaron's sweater from his arms. "I swear he gets more handsome every time I see him. You do look like your father, don't you, my love? Jenna, please, sit. We've ordered drinks. Get whatever you like."

The maitre d' had waited, and Jenna thanked him for pulling her chair out, then requested an iced tea, without the ice, from the young waiter who had come over immediately.

Jenna fidgeted with her silverware while watching Denise entertain her son. She would have preferred to keep hold of him, to give her hands something to do. Joan asked how they were and what the five-and-a-half month old was doing by now. Denise chatted about her own children and related how much she loved working part-time just to be out of the house.

The waiter returned with the tea but had forgotten to leave out the ice. Well, she wasn't going to send it back. She hated doing that.

"Excuse me, but she specifically asked for no ice."

"Joan, that's okay."

"Now, Jenna, Dear, I may not see you often, but I do know that you don't like anything too cold. Please bring her another glass."

The young man apologized and left quickly. Jenna wished Joan hadn't noticed.

"You know, Daniel always laughed about that. He thought it was the funniest thing to order iced tea without ice or to keep cola in the pantry so it wouldn't be cold. I'll never forget his look when he first realized.... Jenna?"

She looked up at Denise.

"I'm sorry. I wasn't laughing at you."

"No. I know you weren't."

"Are you alright, Dear?"

Joan's hand on her arm wasn't what she needed now. She breathed deeper to calm herself with her eyes turned down. She didn't want to be here, pretending everything was okay.

"Maybe we should order." Joan pulled back and picked up her menu, as if she didn't already know what she would have. Jenna's mother-in-law had a specialty in every restaurant she frequented.

Jenna perused her menu. Not especially hungry, and uncomfortable with the plush surroundings, she searched for something simple and easy to eat. Finally deciding on tortellini – no cutting or crunching – Jenna returned the menu to the waiter and tried to stay conscious of her posture. Her mother had nagged endlessly about her "lazy shoulders," convinced it was a sign of low class. Jenna had often been convinced the hospital had sent her home with the wrong parents. Except that she looked too similar to her father, which also gave her mother fits. High-class ladies were supposed to have fine, delicate features. Like Joan ... and Denise.

Aaron began to fuss and Jenna was glad to take him.

Following the conversation proved difficult, with the baby squirming and glances and whispers coming from nearby tables. She picked at her meal, accepting the offer of a box for the remainder. And she let Joan talk her into dessert. Aaron finally relented and sat in the high chair, gnawing a teething biscuit.

"So, Jenna, I saw the Russells the other day and they asked me about you. They want to know when you're coming up to Chicago to visit. They would dearly love to see you and the baby again. Aaron was just a tiny thing when they saw him at...." Joan sipped her coffee silently, avoiding talk of the funeral. "And they aren't the only ones. I'm asked about you quite often." She set her cup down carefully. "I was wondering if you were up to a visit yet. Next weekend there is an opening by a young man who has some potential. We could do some shopping and throw a little gathering for a few friends and attend the show."

"I don't do art shows anymore." Jenna hadn't meant to sound so unfriendly, but she didn't want to be around those people. She didn't want to walk into a gallery and know it should be Daniel's work there.

"Dear, it won't go away because you run from it. I know. I've tried."

"I can't do it. Not yet."

Joan touched her arm again. "Come back to Chicago with me. We don't have to go to the show, but you should get away. I'll take you shopping and spoil my grandson."

Jenna averted her eyes. Joan always had a bunch of people around her. She wasn't ready for that.

"Well, we'll talk more. You will come over to Denise's with us so we can chat?"

"It's going to storm soon. I don't want to have to take him back out in the rain."

"Of course not. It's been too long since I had a little one. We'll go back to the loft with you."

Back to the loft? Jenna hadn't counted on that. She had cleaned that morning, but … her paintings were still on the easels. And she didn't intend to share them with anyone, except Alan. She couldn't refuse, though. So she nodded. "Okay, just give me a minute when we get there. I wasn't expecting company."

Joan smiled. "Dear, we're not concerned about a dish or two in the sink. You have your hands full right now and I do wish you would let me hire someone to help you…"

"Thank you. I don't need help, I…"

"Jenna."

She turned her head. Her mother. What was she doing here?

"I tried to call to ask you to lunch. I can see I was too late." Louise Givens semi-politely forced herself to greet Joan and Denise. She didn't approve of them any more than she had approved of Daniel.

"We were just finishing." Jenna glanced at the woman and younger man beside her mother.

"Yes, well … Jenna, since you're here, I'd like to introduce you to Mrs. Douglas and her son, Robert."

Not again. She stood on command and took their hands. The woman who looked slightly older than her mother was wearing a double strand of pearls around the folds of her neck and large pearl clip-on earrings. They weighed her ears down too much, though she was a stout woman. She was studying Jenna as though she were a piece of meat in the supermarket. The son was in a light gray shirt and darker gray suit pants, most likely custom-tailored, with an exactly matching tie. He wasn't tall, but his shoulders were quite large and his chest tapered into a slim waistline. If he studied her the way his mother had, Jenna didn't bother to notice.

"It's very nice to meet you." He smiled. His handshake was weak; she didn't like that in a man. "Your mother speaks very highly of you."

Of course she had. She was trying to auction her off again. "Thank you." She pulled her hand away and turned slightly. "This is my mother-in-law, Joan and my sister, Denise."

The strangers said hello, with a curious glance at their companion. Of course her mother hadn't told them she was…

"She's no longer married. I keep trying to convince her to come home again so she won't be alone."

Jenna bristled. "I am not alone. I have Aaron." She went to pull her baby from his chair, then turned back. "And I'm not dating, so stop trying to set me up."

Her mother fumed but held her tongue for the moment.

Jenna didn't care. She'd had enough. "Joan, thank you for lunch. I'm going to take him home. Come by if you want; I'll be there."

She said goodbye to Denise and gathered her belongings, not listening to her mother explain how she wasn't herself yet.

"Jenna, I'll call you later. We can talk."

Her mother had to get the last word in. But Jenna didn't feel like answering, and she most likely wouldn't pick up the phone later.

λλλλ

She sat, nursing her baby. It had started to rain just before they had reached the apartment, and she stared out at the drenched leaves. Well, there weren't many leaves anymore. Most had fallen off and had been trampled or blown away, or washed down the river. The trees were still beautiful to her. She loved the pattern they made against the sky, even when the clouds made them hazy.

If she could paint well enough to do them justice, Jenna would never stop painting them.

Daniel had been more into people, but his painting of their window – it had been his window at the time – had been an eye-catcher at his first show. He'd had several offers on it but refused them all. She was glad he hadn't sold it. It was theirs. She didn't want it to belong to anyone else, though Mrs. Covington had offered quite a lot for it.

Jenna could see it hanging in the gallery. The likeness was so great she was convinced she would be able to feel the warmth of the glass if she'd let herself touch it.

She stood quietly by Daniel's side, trying not to let the crowd around them bother her. A group of girls about her age were watching him, hoping to catch his attention.

"I don't normally make such an outlandish offer for new artists, but there is something about this one. I would just love to have it over my fireplace. Can you see that? A window over the mantel?" The constantly happy lady turned her eyes back to the painting.

Joan glanced at her son, questioning him again.

He shook his head.

His mother gave in. "I am sorry, Edna, but the ones meant for sale are marked. This one isn't. Maybe you could take another look at some of the others?"

Jenna knew her eyes had to be larger than usual. She couldn't believe he wasn't accepting her offer. Five thousand dollars was an incredible amount for a painting by an unknown, though the lady insisted he would not stay unknown for long.

Mrs. Covington ignored Joan and faced Daniel. "Well, I may have to settle for another one for today. But if you change your mind, you will give me the first chance to buy it?"

Daniel grinned. "Of course, and thank you." He set a hand on Jenna's back and addressed his mother. "I'm taking Jenna to lunch. She was nice enough to come all this way; I guess I shouldn't let her starve."

"We have a buffet arriving shortly. I assure you, it's the best quality."

"I'm sure it is, but it's hard to talk here. And I want to hear her opinions." He didn't wait for more arguments.

She walked calmly alongside him, though they were stopped several times before escaping through the heavy front door. He led her down the busy sidewalk, helping her dodge the fast-walking business people and trudging younger people. As they moved away from the gallery, his hand found hers and he flagged down a taxi.

Daniel opened the back door, then slid in next to her, throwing an address at the driver. The lurch of the car pulled her closer against him, or was it the arm he'd wrapped around her shoulder? Either way, she wasn't going to fight it. His scent mingled with the mustiness of the old taxi. His warmth invaded her. She wanted to tell him so much – how she had missed him, how proud she was of him, how.... His fingers brushed against her face and, very gently, he lifted it to his own. He searched her eyes ... and she tilted her head just enough....

The touch of his lips burned into her memory. His fingers entwined with her hair, locking her head into his possession.

Sliding her hand down his arm, Jenna drew the courage to go further. Her fingers slipped underneath his blazer, around his waist. His skin was tight under his T-shirt, allowing her to feel his ribs move with his breathing. She drew closer. And he kissed her more deeply.

Then he backed away, just enough to again search her eyes. Jenna knew the driver was watching in the rear view mirror and she was slightly embarrassed at the thought. But it had been so long. And she wanted to be even closer.

"Daniel..." Her voice came out as a whisper.

"Shhhh, don't talk. We'll be alone soon."

His lips returned to hers and she delighted in his touch, his taste. When he again released her, Jenna leaned her head down against his neck and shoulder, still caressing his back through the soft material. Alone. They weren't going to a restaurant. She closed her eyes, waiting for the taxi to stop moving, basking in the feel of his hand running through her hair.

The movement stopped and she pulled back to let him pay the driver and slide out of the car. She followed closely and brushed against him while he held the door. They didn't talk as he grasped her hand and led her up the steps of a large red brick building. The row of townhouses was well-kept, with pink and white blooms sparsely decorating the small patches of grass between the many sets of stairs. Jenna assumed it was Joan's house. Would she care that they were here alone?

Daniel released her hand to pull keys from his pocket. He unlatched the regular lock with one and the deadbolt with another, then stepped inside.

She moved just barely past him so he could close the door, again locking it. It gave her a funny feeling. Jenna's parents never had the door locked when they were home and didn't always remember when they went out. Their back door was never locked.

"I hope you don't mind not staying for the buffet. There isn't much here, but we can find something." He removed his jacket and hung it carelessly on the cherry-wood coat stand.

"I'm not hungry." Jenna watched him. And he came back to her.

"No?"

She shook her head slightly.

"Neither am I." He studied her face, then let his eyes fall for a moment. "You look good."

"I ... was worried it wouldn't be dressy enough. Everyone else..."

"Is too pretentious. I like how you dress." His hand moved to her shoulder and slid slowly down her arm. "Do you want to see the rest of the house?"

She nodded and pretended to be interested in the furnishings and paintings and collectibles Joan had very carefully displayed. He didn't say much about them and didn't linger in any one room very long. She followed him up the carpeted stairs and into a room with more paintings, but also sketches, framed and unframed. And a bed stuck back in the corner to make room for a large art table.

"Your room?"

"Whenever I'm here. I keep telling Joan to convert it to a guest room, but she refuses. There is one spare room, though. So, if you ever need a place to stay in Chicago..."

Jenna moved in and wrapped her arms around him. She loved being here where he had grown up, with all of his beginning work.

"Or ... you could share my room." He pulled her closer. "Just one thing, though. Joan knows you're not eighteen yet. She strongly advised me to wait until you're legal. She doesn't know..."

She reached up to kiss him. She wouldn't tell Joan anything. And she would soon be old enough that no one could stop them.

Contrary to his own words, he stepped back just enough to reach the small buttons on her blouse.

The doorbell made her jump.

It pulled her back to the present. There had been no interruptions then and she wanted to stay there. But her baby objected to the distraction, as well, and started to fuss. She put herself back together and tried to calm him, and herself, as she answered the door. Luckily, Jenna had taken the time to put her own paintings out of sight before she'd begun feeding Aaron.

"I dropped Denise off at home. She thought you and I might like to be alone to talk." Joan touched the baby's cheek then pulled the suede coat off her shoulders.

"Would you like some tea? I was about to make more."

"That sounds wonderful. Let me take my grandson."

Joan wandered the studio with Aaron while Jenna put the water on to heat. She stopped in front of the zoo painting, then turned. "You know you were very important to him, though I doubt he showed it well enough, except in his work."

Jenna didn't answer. Why would Joan think she didn't know she was important to her husband?

"I suppose it was my fault. I was never much for showing affection. I do hope he was better about that with you." She paused, waiting for a response she didn't get. "I have always liked you, Jenna. I was so happy he found you. I was afraid he would spend what he had of his life alone because of his passion for painting, for creating something that would last." She looked down at Aaron. "I think knowing he was leaving a son made it easier for him. But this really hasn't been fair to you. He should have told you..."

"It wouldn't have mattered." She turned away to place the tea bags into two cups, then watched the pot. What was the saying? A watched pot never boiled? Well, it did. Eventually.

Joan came up quietly behind her. Aaron was starting to fuss. "I think he wants his mom."

"He was eating before you came." She still faced the stove. "I guess he's not done."

"Well, let me finish with the tea. I'm not much of a cook, but I can manage that."

Jenna couldn't help a slight grin. She knew better. Daniel had told her that his mom was a wonderful cook when she wanted to be. But she generally had other things to do.

Aaron grew more insistent so she accepted Joan's offer and took her son to her favorite armchair. Nursing in front of her mother-in-law didn't bother her. Joan had nursed both of her children until they were nearly a year old, unlike Jenna's mother, who had only used a bottle because researchers had said that it was better for the baby. Jenna didn't believe for a minute that her mother had thought that was true. But it had worked as an excuse.

Joan set Jenna's cup on the table and sat across from her. She didn't look at home here; it was much too casual for her style. But, to her credit, she tried to act as though she was comfortable. "Your mother is trying to set you up already?"

Jenna nodded. "I can't imagine why she would think…."

"Because she never accepted your marriage. She refuses to believe it was real."

"And now that he's gone, she thinks I'm just going to write the last six years off and suddenly start doing what she wants."

"You won't let her do that to you?"

Jenna looked up. "Of course not. He will always be a part of my life. And he taught me that it's okay to be who I am."

Joan grinned. "Have you started painting yet?"

Painting? She didn't know…

"Daniel told me. When he knew he wouldn't make it. He wanted me to support you the way I supported him all those years when he was starting out. He said you have real talent with nature."

She shook her head. "No. I'm not a painter. That was his thing. I … I just dabble now and then. It's nothing."

"You're doubting that he knew talent when he saw it?"

"No, but…"

"I'd love to see something you've done. And if you haven't yet, think about it. Unless you have other plans."

Jenna looked away. She didn't have other plans. She didn't have any plans, but painting was Daniel's thing. She wasn't going to interfere with that.

"What do you do with your time, Jenna? Other than the baby, I mean."

How could she answer that? She wasn't going to tell Joan she had been spending a lot of time with Alan, or that she was doodling, and sometimes painting. Other than that, she sat around daydreaming about the past. But she didn't suppose Joan would want to hear that, either.

"You know, depression is a sneaky thing. It attacks while you're not looking, and I know the signs." She studied Jenna's face. “I want you to come for a visit. It’s too hard to make yourself get out when you’re alone. And you know how pushy I can be.” She smiled.

Jenna felt a tear run down her cheek and reached up to brush it off. Depression? Is that what was wrong with her?

Aaron had fallen asleep. So he was just tired, not hungry. She refastened her bra, trying not to move more than necessary.

“Dear, you are a wonderful mother, but you have to take care of yourself, too. It isn’t good for your baby for you to be so unhappy. And I promised Daniel I would look after both of you.”

Her tear multiplied and Joan took the baby from her arms, managing not to wake him. “Come, Jenna. Lie down a while and I’ll make some phone calls.

Nine

Joan placed the call to Jenna's mother.

Jenna had stalled as long as possible. Her nerves were frayed. She couldn't deal with the arguing and questioning, and worse, the lecture she would have received. Her mother-in-law, on the other hand, had no qualms about telling Louise Givens she was taking her daughter to Chicago. Jenna thought Joan was a bit too happy to do so.

They had spent the day before with Denise and her kids, shopping and lunching. And they'd had supper at her house, with her husband. Jenna liked Terry. He was nothing like Daniel; very quiet and relaxed, but with a sharp wit. She supposed his calm nature was necessary for a veterinarian. He loved animals, sometimes to a fault, and would have had a house full if his wife hadn't overruled him. They did have two cats that loved to rub against Jenna's ankles. She liked cats okay but had to keep Aaron in her arms, or in someone else's, so they would stay away from him.

Exhausted by the time Joan dropped them off after the visit, Jenna had gone to bed early. She'd meant to call Alan. He had to know she would be away for a while. How long, she wasn't sure. But after stumbling through the day, Jenna had been unable to force a phone call to her best friend.

Now, she was packed, and Joan was waiting on her to finish feeding Aaron so they could leave for the city. Denise would keep on eye on the loft and Jenna had told her downstairs neighbor that they would be gone. She had to call Alan.

"Is there anything else you need me to do before we leave?" Joan hovered nearby, completely unused to waiting on anyone.

"No, I'm ready as soon as he is."

Joan nodded. "Well, don't rush him. It's a long ride for a little one. Maybe he'll sleep most of the way if his tummy is full. You do have a juice bottle, just in case?"

"Yes. It's in his bag."

Joan wandered over to the studio, again studying Daniel's artwork. How was Jenna going to call Alan? She should have made herself do it the night before, or this morning before Joan came. But, her mother-in-law had arrived early, before Jenna had even showered. That was an excuse. She just didn't want to make that call, either.

Aaron pulled away. She had to think of something.

Putting herself back together, Jenna hoped evasiveness would work. "Joan, if you want to take him down and put him in his seat, I'll be right behind you." She would have to check the car seat's latch before they left, not because Joan wasn't capable of hooking it right, but because Jenna would be uncomfortable the whole three hours they were in the car if she didn't.

Joan gathered her grandson, asking him enthusiastically if he was ready to go. He smiled widely.

When the door closed, Jenna took a deep breath and picked up the receiver. It rang four times. Five. Maybe they had gone out. Well, she could call from Chicago…

"Hello?"

He sounded hurried. "Alan? Is everything okay?

"Jenna! I was just on my way over. You didn't return my call yesterday and didn't answer again this morning and I was worried…"

"Yesterday? You didn't leave a message?" She hadn't thought about checking last night, but the light wasn't blinking now.

"Yes, I did. You didn't listen to it before you deleted it?"

"I didn't … you must have dialed the wrong number."

"Jen, I know your voice when I hear it." He paused. "What's going on? Where were you?"

"I … umm … Joan's here. We went out." And she was waiting in the car.

"She's there now and you called me?"

"Well, she's outside. Waiting for me." Did he hear the tremor in her voice?

"What's going on, Jen?"

"I'm … we're going to Chicago. I just called to let you know so you wouldn't worry. She wants to spend some time with Aaron."

"For how long? Do you need me to pick you up next weekend?"

Next weekend. No, she imagined it would be longer than that. "Thank you, but … I'm not sure how long we're staying. I just … Joan thinks I should get away for a while."

He was silent again. What was he thinking?

"Can you wait ten minutes? I'll be right there."

"No. She's already waited longer than she wanted to, and I really need to go. I just…"

"Jenna."

She waited. Why was this bothering him?

"I'm not sure this is a good idea. I want you to wait 'till I get there so I can talk to Joan. Have you told your mom yet?"

Her mom? "I saw her a couple of days ago. She tried to set me up again."

"I know. She wants me to talk to you."

"She what?"

"She came over yesterday, to ask me to encourage you to date."

Jenna felt her jaw clench. How dare she?

"I told her it was too soon for that and she needs to back off. She's pretty ticked at me now."

Bless him. Of course she would be angry, but Alan had never cared about angering her mother. She sighed. "Thank you. Alan, I have to get away from her for a while…"

"Are you sure it's her you're trying to get away from?"

She held her breath. She knew what he was asking.

"Jenna, you know…."

"Alan … don't. I have to go."

"Jen."

"I'll call when we get back."

Silence. Just for a moment. "Call me when you get there. I'll be home. And Jenna, I know where Joan lives."

λλλλ

She stared through the car window at Lake Michigan, looking past the walkers and joggers. Jenna loved this part of the drive, where she could see small boats anchored in the cove, and those a little farther out with their sails wide open. It was chilly, the last day of September, and had to be even more so on the lake. But she wouldn't have minded being out there with them.

"You do like the water, don't you, Dear?"

"Yes. I always wished that…." She stopped. She would never complain about Daniel to his mom.

"That Daniel shared that love with you?"

She glanced over at Joan. The bumper-to-bumper traffic didn't phase her. And neither did talking about her son. Maybe nothing did.

Joan swung from one lane to the other, dodging slower cars. "He was always afraid of water. I even had a hard time getting him to take baths when he was little. I'm not sure why."

Jenna turned back to the lake. "The same reason Cheryl doesn't like being outside, I guess."

"What?"

"Nothing. I guess some people just aren't into nature." She shouldn't have mentioned Cheryl, but maybe Joan wouldn't recognize the name. Anyway, she let it go.

Jenna glanced behind her to check on Aaron. He was still asleep, luckily. His little head was tilted to one side, resting against the soft material of his car seat, his mouth open just slightly. He had stayed awake for nearly an hour, which was unusual, but maybe because they were in Joan's car instead of their own. He was always more comfortable in familiar surroundings. She hoped being away from home wouldn't be too hard on him.

The scenic drive gave way to city buildings crowding each other and pedestrians darting between the slowing or stopped cars. Jenna couldn't imagine just stepping out in front of a moving vehicle. Peoria's traffic wasn't nearly as heavy, but she always waited on the traffic light to tell her it was safe to cross.

Joan pulled into a parking garage. "I do need to run into the office. You can come in and say hello."

Jenna took a deep breath. It was starting already; the socializing. Maybe she shouldn't have come.

Taking her usual space, Joan switched the engine off.

"Aaron's still asleep. I'll just keep him in the car so he doesn't get grouchy."

He started stirring.

"Well, now you don't have an excuse." Joan gave her a knowing grin and opened her door.

λλλλ

She awoke to a light tapping … someone at the door. Who was here so early? Her eyes parted against their will and took in her surroundings, forcing the realization that she wasn't home. And the knock came again.

Aaron was still asleep in the crib on the other side of the room, so she pushed herself up out of bed and shuffled to the door, peering out into the brightly lit hallway.

Her mother-in-law was adorned in a straight skirt and matching jacket, carrying her heeled shoes by their straps. "Jenna, I'm sorry to wake you, but I have to get to the office. There are eggs and bread. Help yourself to whatever you can find. I'll be back to pick you up for lunch. We'll go to The Zodiac Room. I'm not sure what time I'll be free. I'll call." Joan took a breath. "Did you sleep alright?"

Jenna nodded, more asleep than awake. She must have slept hard after the long period of tossing and turning.

"Okay. My number's by the phone if you need anything."

She waited until Joan started down the stairs and shut the door again. Aaron moved a bit but wasn't ready to get up, so she went back to the Queen Anne-style bed and slithered underneath the covers, allowing her head to sink into the deep pillow. She had decided to stay in the guest room rather than to be in Daniel's room, without him.

But she couldn't sleep.

Instead, memories of the first time she had been to Joan's apartment invaded her mind. Jenna was certain she and Daniel had conceived their first child that day – the daughter who would have been six years old now. Jenna missed her, too.

She got up again and left the room quietly. Taking the few steps down the hall to her husband's room, she brushed tears from her eyes. And she stopped at the door.

Daniel's bedroom still looked the same. His sketches adorned the walls. His art table still took up much of the space. And his bed was still pushed back against the far wall, staying out of the way.

She stood a long while, feeling him there; feeling herself with him there. But she didn't go in.

Time slipped past until Aaron began to fuss, forcing her return to the present.

λλλλ

The Zodiac Room, on the fourth floor of the Neiman-Marcus building, was one of Joan's favorite places to lunch. It reflected her personality. Just off Lake Shore Drive on Michigan Avenue, the elite restaurant boasted valet service and old-fashioned elegance. The bar held no interest for the designer, but she had a set table in the art deco room.

Jenna didn't like any of it. It was too showy; too…

"Joan, darling! I have been trying to call you for the last week! You are the hardest person to reach!"

Aaron fussed at Mrs. Covington's grating voice. Jenna attempted to disappear into the furniture, behind her mother-in-law.

"Yes, you know what they say, Edna; no rest for the wicked." Joan turned to pull Jenna up beside her. "You do remember my Daniel's Jenna?"

Was she always going to introduce her that way? She had hoped the day before at the office had been just a slip. At least Aaron was quieting.

"Why, of course! Jenna, Darling, you look wonderful! How are you?"

"Fine, thank you. How are you, Mrs. Covington?"

"Oh, I'm always wonderful. I have found a treasure, an absolute treasure! Joan has been helping to convince the gallery to show his work and we finally have a date! You simply must come with her to see this young man's work." She stopped. "Oh, Darling, I'm sorry. I shouldn't be discussing this in front of you. Joan, do call me. We'll talk later."

Mrs. Covington was attracting attention, as usual, and Jenna focused on her son, trying to ignore the looks and whispers.

The woman didn't quit, never willing to let go of conversation. "Jenna, Darling, what a beautiful little boy. I'm afraid I don't remember what you named him."

Fighting to remember her manners well enough to not embarrass her mother-in-law, Jenna forced an answer. "Aaron, after his father, and it's fine. I think it's wonderful that Joan is still supporting art. There are a lot of young artists who deserve the recognition."

"You were always the sweet one. You should come with Joan to see him, then. He is a modern artist, nothing like Daniel, but I enjoy his work. It's bright and makes me happy. Will you come?"

Jenna hesitated. After what she had just said…

Joan set a hand on her arm. "Jenna and the baby just arrived yesterday. We haven't talked yet about our schedule."

"Will this be a lengthy visit, then?"

"That depends on Jenna. She's welcome to stay as long as she likes, and you are welcome to come over this evening, if you would like. Jim and Lois will be there, and a few of my co-workers. But, if you'll excuse us now, I don't believe the child has eaten yet today."

"Oh, of course. I'm keeping you from your lunch and my male friend is most likely wondering what's become of me. I am sorry. I will see you tonight, then?"

Joan agreed politely, then signaled to the maitre d'. He nodded and led the way to the back of the room, to a private spot next to the windows, pulled a chair away from the table to make room for the stroller and beckoned to a waiter who appeared immediately.

Joan was right. Jenna hadn't bothered with breakfast and the scent wafting from a filet mignon at an adjacent table surged a hunger pang. Daniel's favorite meal. She ordered her customary tea without ice, which didn't even phase the man, then looked through the menu while holding Aaron on her lap. Until he reached for the tablecloth, and she shifted him to her shoulder and let him pull on her hair instead. He loved pulling on everything recently. Good thing she didn't have a sensitive scalp.

"We must find someone who will sit for you while you're here. A mother needs her time away."

"Oh, I don't leave him yet."

"Never? You can't be serious? He's nearly six months."

"I have no need to leave him."

Her mother-in-law would have argued if the waiter hadn't come back with their drinks. This one had remembered to leave out the ice.

She decided on the restaurant's classic tuna pecan sandwich and thanked the waiter, noticing glances from the filet mignon table. The whispers around the room made her self-conscious. Maybe they weren't talking about her, but then, why did she keep feeling their glances? Joan was pretending not to notice. She was very good at that. While her own mother would have been making a point to talk to everyone she even vaguely recognized, Joan was the opposite. Most of the patrons knew her, or at least knew who she was. But she acted as though she and Jenna were alone in the room. She had said a few years before that her unavailability made people more interested than if she were friendly to just anyone. But, if Jenna hadn't known her better, she would have thought Joan a real snob.

"I hope you don't mind that I've invited a few people to the house tonight. Only close associates and a few friends. Nothing fancy."

Jenna pried Aaron's fingers off her ear. "What should I wear?"

"Anything you like. As I said, it's nothing but a little get-together."

Maybe she would wear her old sweats. Joan did say "any-thing." But, she supposed she wouldn't. Remembering that Joan very often had people over, Jenna had brought many of her nice clothes. In fact, she only had two of what she called house outfits with her; one to wear while the other was washing. She basically lived in the same old clothes day after day, anyway, only pulling out something decent to leave the apartment. Unlike Joan, who stayed in her work clothes until after her evening shower, when she replaced the meticulous garments with a long robe. Jenna simply slipped into clean sweats until changing into a long T-shirt for bed.

Lunch conversation centered around Joan's work and troubles with her newest client. Jenna only half-listened, trying to keep Aaron happy as they ate by giving him pieces of bread from her sandwich since he preferred her food over his teething crackers. Once, they were interrupted by someone Jenna vaguely remembered meeting at one of Daniel's shows. The lady wanted to see his son, and of course, told her how much he looked like Daniel and said she was so sorry for her loss, and the loss to the art world. Jenna thanked her politely and wished she would go away. Why did she care about the loss to the art world? It would keep going just fine without him, with some new kid taking his place. Maybe Mrs. Covington's "treasure."

But, she made it through lunch and looked forward to getting back and being alone. It seemed funny to think about slipping back into her sweats while walking through the polished marble foyer and out into the main building.

"I have to put in just a little more time at the office today. You can come visit a bit while I'm finishing."

To the office? She had assumed Joan would take them back to the apartment first. Aaron would need to eat again before long.

"I'll pull the curtains closed when the baby gets hungry so you'll have privacy. It won't be more than an hour or two."

Behind Joan, who was outpacing her, Jenna grimaced. She always had trouble keeping up with her mother-in-law. Whenever Daniel had been with them, he'd walked more slowly for her and had asked Joan to do the same. Being five-eight and mostly legs, Joan didn't realize how hard it was for someone three inches shorter and not all legs to walk as fast, especially with a baby on her hip because he didn't want to be in his stroller.

Finally, Joan turned. "Oh, Jenna dear, I'm sorry. Here, let me take him. You must be getting tired."

She didn't argue. He was getting too heavy to carry around and Jenna hadn't made herself lose the extra pregnancy weight. The additional six or eight pounds were enough to make a difference in how she felt. She supposed she should start thinking about getting rid of it. But, for what reason?

Approaching the elevator, Jenna paused on the face of a man stepping out of their way. Tall and sturdy, but thin, he had a very classic look, highlighted with a speckled tan sweater and brown twill pants. He glanced over while chatting with a companion, then returned his gaze to her own and smiled. She turned her head away. He wouldn't have looked twice if she still had the baby in her arms. But still, it was nice. Maybe she didn't look all that bad.

Ten

Jenna found herself thinking of him as she prepped for Joan's second soiree in two days. The guy at Neiman-Marcus. Why was his smile still haunting her?

He was cute, in an adult way. Young, but not boyish, and appeared … well, normal. There was nothing different about him. His gold-brown hair was in medium layers, perfectly combed, and he wore wire-rimmed glasses that were barely noticeable, blending in with his natural coloring. So what made him stand out so much in her mind?

His smile. It was genuine, showing true sincerity. And he appeared comfortable with himself while leaving out conceit. How did he get that way? What was he doing with his life that made him so content? And why had she been so rude?

Jenna studied herself in the standing mirror. The Victorian frame didn't match the image the glass reflected. She hadn't bothered to change after finally getting back to the apartment and was still in her soft cotton-polyester pants and long sweater. The outfit hid her shape well. She could just as well have been wearing a sack. But, it had been good enough for the guy at Neiman-Marcus. It was good enough for Joan's … whatever they were. She didn't have to impress them.

After spritzing a touch of soft musk on her wrists, Jenna collected her son from the little crib his father had used. Aaron had been politely fussing at her while she was dressing, having pulled himself up to stand at the wooden rails. He thanked her for the rescue by pressing his mouth against her cheek.

Wiping the baby drool, Jenna returned his kiss. "And why would I want to leave you with a sitter? You're the one who gets me through the days." She stroked his soft hair and grimaced at his chubby hand yanking her not-so-soft locks. "Ouch!"

He laughed.

"That's not funny. That hurts."

He looked at her face and gave her hair another pull.

"Aaron…." Despite knowing she should discourage him, she found his laugh too uplifting and kissed his head. "Okay, let's get you changed. They'll be here soon."

He didn't want to be down but tolerated it since she was staying right there. And she didn't bother to change his clothes. He was fine the way he was.

Jenna sat and held him a while after covering the fresh diaper, enjoying their private 'talk,' until forcing a deep breath to give her courage to start the evening. The first of many long ones, she assumed.

The doorbell rang as Jenna reached the bottom of the staircase. She and Joan nearly collided in the entry.

"Oh, there you are, Dear. I set up the playpen so you wouldn't have your hands full all night. Go ahead and find yourself a drink while I get the door." She didn't wait for an answer before turning to greet her company.

The first few intrusions weren't bad; an associate from the office whom Jenna had met already and three people she faintly recognized from the gallery. And they were just talking business, mostly leaving her out of it. She hadn't put Aaron down. She wanted his company and he was happier that way. One of the women had tried to take him but he'd refused outright, as only a young child was allowed to do. Jenna apologized perfunctorily while thinking adults could learn something from babies.

Hoping she would be able to sneak away since she had made an appearance and no one was talking with her, Jenna edged toward the hall with the guise of making Aaron happy by staying on her feet.

Her escape nearly complete, she neared the stairs.

The doorbell rang. Jenna sighed. Again? How many were coming?

"I'll get it." Talking to no one, she propped Aaron on her hip and turned the antique, gold-finished knob. Mrs. Covington ... and...

"Hello again, Jenna! And how is the young Mr. Rhodes tonight?" She touched Aaron's chubby calf and he pulled away.

"Shy, as usual. How are you?" Jenna glanced at the man hanging just behind. Most likely the "treasure."

"Oh, wonderful as always!" The bubbly woman swept past Jenna into the hallway, pulling her guest along.

Jenna closed the door and started to ask them to go on in.

"I *must* introduce you to this brilliant young man. I mentioned him briefly at lunch, if you remember, and thought I'd bring him along. Jenna Rhodes, this is Trevor Dade."

He took her hand. "Jenna Rhodes? You're not *the* Jenna Rhodes?"

She raised her eyebrows at the guy. He was roughly her age and obviously trying to make a statement with the long blonde bangs hanging partly in his eyes, and long, loose black clothing accentuating his overdone thinness. "I'm sure there are several. Rhodes is a fairly common name."

"You weren't married to Daniel Rhodes – the painter?"

Her stomach tightened. She should have known anyone in Joan's circle would recognize her name.

"Well, of course!" Mrs. Covington beamed, gloating about her … protégé … showing that he had studied his predecessors. "I did tell you that you simply *had* to come tonight." She protectively held his arm. "Trevor is not much into the socializing arena. I had quite a time convincing him that he wanted to be here. Much better than going to some bar, now, isn't it?"

"You still live in Chicago?" He paid no attention to the woman clinging to him.

Jenna fidgeted with Aaron, as a distraction. He was sitting calmly in her arm, watching the conversation. She would have loved for him to interrupt.

He didn't.

"No, I'm just visiting Joan."

"Oh? Why did you move away?"

Move away? He hadn't studied them very well. "We never lived in Chicago. Daniel had moved before I met him. We just came up a lot for his shows."

He nodded, keeping a piercing stare directed mostly, though not completely, at her eyes. "There were rumors he had a kid, though most say it's just a rumor. I guess they were wrong."

A rumor? They had kept track of every detail of Daniel's life while he was still painting, and his son was just a rumor?

"Jenna, Dear, are you going to invite them in or leave them standing in the foyer?" Joan took Jenna's side, but spoke to her guests. "Edna, I'm glad you could make it. And this must be Mr. Dade."

Jenna watched the introductions, and the way Trevor Dade was using a rehearsed politeness that didn't fit him. And he refused to go along to the main room with Joan until Jenna went first.

He used the same politeness with the other women, only coming to real life while speaking of his art, and grabbing every opportunity to find his way to Jenna, though she tried to keep her distance. Of course he just wanted to get inside details of Daniel's life. She was used to that. Her only purpose in his world, as most people had seen it, had been to play the supportive wife and feed information to the curious. Although, she hadn't been just playing supportive as she'd been accused of more than once, and she never told anyone anything about their personal lives. It was none of their business. But she didn't feel like dodging questions tonight.

"You dig modern art?"

Jenna turned. How had he come up behind her without notice?

"I know your other half was a realist, but I'm kinda curious about what you like."

She paused. Had anyone asked her art opinion before? If so, she didn't remember. "I'm not really into modern art, no offense intended."

"None taken." The sly grin thrown at her didn't appear fake. "What are you into?"

Was that a come on? He was standing closer than necessary and she didn't have Aaron to serve as a buffer since Joan had insisted on taking him. She stepped back slightly. "I've always liked expressionists, and some of the surrealists."

"Oh. Van Gogh and DuChamp?"

"Well, yes, I like Van Gogh best of the expressionists, but my favorite surrealist is Marie Cerminova."

"For real? She's not much known."

"And you're surprised I know anything except Daniel's work."

"No. I think you probably know a lot. And you think I only wanted to talk to you because of your old man."

"Yes, that's what I think. And don't call him that."

He grinned. It was crooked and accented his city speech. "Well, Edna is chatting with a gallery about setting up a show for my work, which you just said you have no interest in, but you could drop by if it does happen – just for kicks."

Her reproach obviously had no effect on him. "If Joan is working on it, I'm sure it will happen." She glanced over at her mother-in-law and her son.

"And you'll be hangin' with Joan when she drops by?"

To an art gallery opening? Most likely not. "I'm not sure I'll be here that long. As I said, we're just visiting. But good luck with it." She turned away before giving him time to object.

Staying close to Joan until Aaron began fussing for his supper, Jenna managed to avoid any further conversation with him. There was really no reason for the avoidance. He was being polite enough. And he seemed honestly interested in her opinions, which was nice, although it could be an act. Either way, she didn't want to find out.

She relished her escape from the small crowd and went upstairs and into the guest room with her son, then stopped. It wasn't where she wanted to be. Grabbing a receiving blanket, she found her way back out to the hallway and to Daniel's door. She hadn't been able to make herself actually walk into the room since they'd arrived, and hesitated. The bedroom reverberated with his presence. Jenna could almost feel his fingers running through her hair and his breath on her skin. But she didn't retreat this time. She wanted more.

Slipping out of her shoes, she folded a leg in front of her on his bed, using it to help support his son while Aaron ate. The silence, broken only by occasional suckling sounds, only heightened her sense that Daniel was there with her. Would her baby be able to feel it? His innocent round eyes peered at hers, communicating the best way he knew. Did he miss his father?

Pushing the thought from her head, she concentrated on the drawings of strange faces and studies of the masters. His version of the Mona Lisa could easily rival Da Vinci's, though it was in charcoal instead of paint. He'd told her he had done it in oil, but hadn't been happy with the results, so painted over it. She wished he hadn't. More than once while they were together, she had insisted on keeping a painting or sketch he wasn't happy with. He had never understood why she'd wanted them, but now, she was obsessive about keeping everything and was glad she had argued with him.

Well, they hadn't actually argued. She'd only had to promise to keep them to herself. No one had seen them still, and she liked having a part of him that no one else had. They could study his public paintings all they wanted. His private sketches were hers.

She had teased him about how the staunchy critics would react if they had seen any of his private work. The sketches he had done only for himself. The ones she had done of him, as a joke, while he was asleep. And while relaxing in the Jacuzzi. That had to be her favorite. On their third anniversary.

"Fine way to spend your anniversary. Are you wishing you could be somewhere more secluded?"

Jenna smiled at Rosalyn Russell. "Not at all. I love seeing him enjoy his work so much. It's a wonderful turn-out."

"Well, of course it is. He is quite a name in Chicago. We all keep wondering when you'll give in and move here."

Jenna studied her husband across the room. These events were becoming so much easier for him than they had been in the beginning. Still, he was always ready to leave. "I would be very willing to do that, but Daniel says there's less to distract him in Peoria."

"He does still hate crowds, doesn't he?"

"I guess, but not so much." She caught his eye. He was radiant tonight. Maybe not the right word for a man, but he really was. His stylish suit jacket and contrasting shirt and tie over nicely-fitting blue jeans truly emphasized his personality, and his build.

She watched as he broke off the conversation with potential buyers and made his way through the crowd. Stopped briefly a few times, he didn't allow himself to be detained very long. Jenna was glad to be his destination.

Daniel slid an arm around her, speaking to Mrs. Russell out of courtesy until Marilyn excused herself to find her own husband.

"I'm sorry we had to spend the evening this way."

"I'm not. This is what you do and I'm happy just to be here to share it."

His other hand brushed her face. "We won't stay long. Joan booked us a room at the Regency ... her anniversary gift ... the wedding suite, with a Jacuzzi."

He had been true to his word.

They had left early, ordered room service with wine and candles, and drifted between the bed and Jacuzzi. Daniel had finally pulled his sketchbook from the bag he carried as religiously as his wallet and captured her relaxing in the warm bubbles with only a glass of wine. Using only one side of the page, he had asked her to finish it. With some persuasion, and maybe too much wine, Jenna had dared to mess up his drawing by sketching her husband beside her on the page.

The difference in quality and style were unmistakable, but he had loved it.

Every show since that one had ended the same – in a posh hotel room where Daniel made up for the time he had spent getting there.

Eleven

Jenna closed her book. Five days in Chicago hadn't helped her feel at all better. But five days wasn't very long; her mom would tell her she was being too impatient again. And maybe she was. Jenna supposed there could have been some truth to at least parts of her mother's lectures, though she hated accepting the admission, even in her own mind.

Aaron played contentedly with the safety mirror on his blanket, pawing at the blurred baby in its reflection, then chewing on the frame holding it. She watched him for a moment, took a deep sighing breath, then moved to a small window, brushing the lace curtain away. It wasn't dark yet, only threatening darkness. Still, there was nothing to see. Joan's living room ran the length of the apartment, with windows at each end; one facing the street, the other overlooking a bit of grass interrupted by another row of townhouses. An under-grown sapling with few yellowed leaves stood in between the buildings. Jenna imagined it didn't get much light, or attention. She missed the lush, stately trees outside her own window.

Letting the curtain fall back into place, she returned to the couch, picking up her book. She didn't bother to open it. Used to the smell of paint as a backdrop to her reading, she found it nearly impossible to concentrate on the story while sitting in Joan's potpourri-scented apartment.

Her eyes drifted to the phone. She hadn't talked to Alan since the night she had arrived, and then just briefly. She supposed she could check in to let him know everything was fine.

The receiver grew warm in her hand. What if Cheryl answered? Well, then she would talk to her instead and try to sound as though that was what she had wanted.

She dialed quickly before changing her mind. An imperceptible sigh of relief escaped when she heard his voice.

"Alan? Hi, I wasn't sure you'd be home yet."

"Jenna, I was hoping to hear from you tonight. I just walked in, and I was thinking about calling...."

"Oh, then Cheryl's probably wanting you to go eat."

"No. She's not home ... PTA meeting."

Good timing. Should she have known that?

"Are you home? I can pick you up and we can find something..."

"No. I'm still in Chicago."

The silence seemed longer to her than it must have to him.

"You know when you're coming back yet?"

"I don't know."

Another pause. "Jenna, is Joan close by? Is that why you're so quiet?"

Quiet? "Umm, no, she's out. You can't hear me?"

"I hear you fine when you talk. What's up? What have you been doing?"

"Oh. Well ... nothing much. I don't even know why I called. I just ... wanted to let you know everything's okay."

"You've been in Chicago for a week and haven't done anything? Wasn't the point of you going so you could get out of the house?"

Was it? "Well, we've had lunch a few times, and Joan had some people over the first two nights. She's helping some new abstractionist. That's where she is now ... at his opening."

"And you didn't want to go."

"I don't like abstract art."

"And if it had been surrealist? You still wouldn't have gone."

No, she still wouldn't have gone.

"Jenna, I know you don't want to be there. Just tell Joan. She'll understand."

"No, I don't want to be here. But I don't want to be home alone, either. And I have nowhere else to go." She held her breath until she could speak calmly again. "So tell me what I should be doing."

"You know I can't tell you that." His voice had softened. "If you want a path, Jenna, you have to make one. It's your life. It's up to you."

"I don't know how." She brushed a tear off of her cheek and wiped the wetness from the receiver.

"Come home, Jen. Running away isn't helping you."

Aaron scooted closer and tugged at her leg.

"I have to go. The baby's hungry."

"How's he doing there?"

"Not sleeping well. I usually have to put him in bed with me; then I don't sleep."

"Careful. He'll get used to that and you won't sleep until he's four."

She chuckled, remembering how long it took for Alan's oldest to start sleeping on his own. But Justin had colic as a newborn. Anything that had stopped his crying had been worth doing.

Aaron started to fuss about not being picked up. "Well, I'll call again … sometime. Give the kids hugs for me. They're okay, right?"

"They're fine, and I will. Take care of yourself, Jenna."

She nodded. Futile, since he couldn't see her, but it was the best she could do. "You too."

Replacing the receiver, Jenna pushed away more tears and went to find a tissue. She needed to calm herself before trying to nurse. Aaron would feel her tension otherwise.

After blowing her nose and running cold water over her face, she stood, staring at her reflection. She detested crying. She detested the weakness she felt in herself recently. And she detested feeling helpless to stop it.

The tears strengthened and Jenna grabbed more tissue. It had to stop. She had to take control again. Her emotions hadn't been so tight in years, not since the few months after her miscarriage.

At least then she had been able to blame her hormones. The doctor had said it was natural. But, Daniel pulling away hadn't helped either. Maybe it *had* been her imagination, as he'd said. Maybe it *was* purely coincidental that demand for his art had increased and he'd had to do so many shows. And maybe she should have objected to him going to Chicago without her.

It wouldn't have happened then. Alan wouldn't have moved in the way he had if she hadn't cried in front of him. If she hadn't been so sick of being left alone that she had gone to his apartment…

"Jen, you need to do something of your own. Stop being so dependent on him that it kills you when he's away."

"It's not that." She flopped onto his couch, pulling a leg in front of her.

"Then what is it? Why are you so upset?"

Jenna pushed a tear away. "He's been so distant since … he's always so busy, even when he's home. I miss him."

"Because you are too wrapped up in his life. You need more than that." Alan moved closer, towering above. "Jenna, you have a

right to live your own life instead of just following someone else's."

"I am living my life. This is what I wanted."

"No, it's not." Lowering himself until his eyes were just below hers, he set a hand on her exposed ankle. "This isn't what you wanted. You expected more from him. You expected him to always pay as much attention to you as he did before you were married."

"I was young. That's not realistic; he has so much work to do."

"That's an excuse, Jen. He could alter his schedule if he decided to. But you don't push him. You have to tell him what you want."

"I can't. I don't want to change him."

"Why the hell not? He's changed you!"

Her eyes jumped to his. Alan didn't swear, ever. He was mad, either at her or Daniel. She wasn't sure which.

"I'm sorry. I shouldn't talk to you that way. But he didn't have the right to change you." Alan's free hand drifted to her face. He touched her gently. "Jenna, you are perfect the way you are. Either insist that he leave you that way ... or leave him."

The brush of his fingers against her cheek, and her hair, and the closeness, mental as well as physical, lowered her defenses. A very slight move toward him was all it took for Alan to slide his hand behind her neck and pull her closer. And he kissed her.

He was warm, and inviting, and she clung to him while he kissed her more deeply. She had to stop him, to push him away. But Daniel hadn't even touched her in over a week, maybe two. She wanted to be wanted like this, like nothing else in the world had any meaning.

Alan pulled her down to the floor, still owning her mouth. Her knee slid between his legs ... one hand thrust against the cold wood floor, barely holding her body above his. The other cradled on his shoulder, feeling his strength.

His fingers crept under her shirt, ran slowly up her spine...

She shoved against him, breaking the kiss. "No!"

"Jenna...."

"No! Alan, I'm married, and you're dating..."

"So we'll leave them. I would be better to you. We could do everything together. You can help me set up the business ... help me run it, and still have time for your painting, and..."

She shook her head, wrenching away. "No. Alan, no. I can't. I don't want to leave him. He's what I want." Hoping her shaky legs would hold, Jenna stood, quickly gathering her things. She was to his apartment door before he caught up, grabbing her arm.

"Don't go."

Without looking at him, she jerked away and ran down the hall...

An insistent cry pierced her thoughts.

Aaron. She had left him too long.

Splashing her face again quickly, Jenna yanked several tissues from the box and went to find him, cuddling him close, letting him calm her as she calmed him. The memories were too strong now. She wasn't ready to go home yet.

λλλλ

"Good morning, Jenna." Looking up from her newspaper, Joan eyed her too long. "The coffee's fresh and it looks like you need it. Didn't you sleep well last night?"

"No, I ... how'd the opening go?" She poured herself a cup while listening to Joan's account of the gathering. It hadn't gone as well as Daniel's, of course, but then, few first openings had.

Jenna sat across from her, enjoying the morning peace before her son awoke. "I'm glad it went okay."

"Yes, he does have some talent that could become something. I'm not sure I care much for him personally, however."

"Oh? Why not?" She stirred perfunctorily. The cream was well mixed in by now, but it kept her fingers busy.

"A bit arrogant, I think. And quite the ladies' man – constantly paying more attention to the young women than to those who might actually provide his income. He will have to have some lessons in decorum if he expects to get anywhere."

Jenna didn't answer. Maybe he wouldn't get as far as Joan's son, who had been taught decorum all his life and had done well with patrons and critics. The girl who ended up with the abstractionist would most likely get more attention, though.

"Oh, the Russells stopped in. They didn't stay long since you weren't there as they'd hoped. I asked them to come by tonight and Edna overheard so she may be here, as well. I hope that's alright."

"Sure." As if she had any choice. Charlie and Marilyn Russell were quiet and unobtrusive. Mrs. Covington was exhausting. But at least Joan hadn't mentioned the abstractionist. And she would have the rest of the day...

"I thought we might go down to the Loop today and wander a bit. The fresh air will do you and Aaron some good. You are rather pale for having just come through the summer."

"Actually...."

"Don't even try to argue with me. Run get yourself together while Baby is still asleep and we'll stop for a croissant." She paused to finally look at her daughter-in-law, laying the paper on the table. "Jenna, Dear, I realize I sound a bit pushy, but I do want you to get on with your life and be happy again. Daniel would expect me to help you do that. So go get ready and we'll have some fun."

Jenna found herself enjoying the meander through the antique and art stores. She listened amusedly to the Chicago accents, some stronger than others. Daniel's had been barely detectable, though more obvious than Joan's. Trevor's was strong.

Pushing the last thought from her head, she picked up a vase. It had an unusual curve and distorted color – green, which generally didn't appeal to her, but this one she wouldn't mind having in the loft.

"Oh, Jenna, you do have an eye. A beautiful piece. You simply must have it for your home."

She turned it over to check the price tag. Incredible. "Not at this price. That's outrageous."

"Nothing is outrageous if it suits your needs well enough. That vase was made for you." Joan stopped the salesman and took the prize from Jenna's hands, handing it to the very attentive middle-aged man. "Hold this for us, if you would."

Of course he would. Joan wasn't asking.

Pleased at the sale prospect, the man didn't argue, but acted as though she were someone highly important, smiling with his nod before turning to store the vase at the counter.

"Joan, really, it's too much. I have no real need...."

"Need? Dear, sometimes it is very unclear what our needs are. You seem to box your needs into just the basics of living. It's such a shame. You have a superlative creative energy waiting impatiently to be let out. I saw it in Daniel, and I see it in you. You must learn to open the box now and then, Jenna. Come now, there is another store I want to browse before lunch."

Open the box? After the years of her parents forcing her to close it? She'd fought quietly against keeping it closed while still at home, and now … she had the freedom, but somewhere had lost the nerve.

λλλλ

"Edna, do come in. Charlie and Marilyn are entertaining Jenna and the baby. Oh, and you brought Mr. Dade."

Jenna jerked her head toward the door. She'd been heading upstairs when Joan had responded to the doorbell, hoping to make her escape to nurse Aaron without much notice. But Trevor's slight grin said that he'd seen her reaction to his name. Why was he here again?

"Yes, I do hope you don't mind. I should have telephoned…."

"Not at all, Edna. It's nice to see you again, Mr. Dade."

Jenna noticed the fakeness of Joan's greeting, but most likely, the visitor wouldn't. She was too practiced at the art.

"It's just Trevor. I don't go in for all that formal stuff. Hey, Jenna. I missed you at my opening."

She didn't speak. What did he mean – he missed her? And what was that grin about?

Joan turned to notice she was there, with a questioning look, then recovered quickly to fill in for her daughter-in-law's lack of an appropriate response. "I'm afraid Jenna no longer attends art shows, but I am hoping it is only temporary. And I must apologize. I nearly wore the girl out dragging her and the baby all over the Loop today." She motioned for her guests to enter as she spoke, and Mrs. Covington gave Jenna a too-long hug as she passed.

"And did you find any treasures in that part of town? I can not for the life of me understand what Joan sees in that section. She should have taken you uptown."

"Now, Edna, the Loop is swarming with potential from the art world and Jenna did find a wonderful piece for her loft. Come; let me show you. I believe she will be busy for a moment attending to her son. Mr. Dade, I think you may remember…."

Jenna watched as her mother-in-law pulled them into the apartment, allowing her to continue upstairs. She hated that she would have to return to socialize with the abstractionist.

She sat in Daniel's room for too long after Aaron had finished. Maybe she could stay for a while and move out of the guest room, into her husband's room. They had always stayed in Daniel's room together during business trips to the city and Joan had automatically tried to give it to her this time.

Aaron pushed against her. He was ready to move again.

"Okay, Sweetie." Making sure she was put together, Jenna forced her legs to take them back to the living room.

Trevor stood to meet her but spoke to her son.

A familiar scent caught her attention and she wondered where she had smelled the cologne before, while automatically getting ready to apologize for Aaron pulling away. Except he didn't pull away. He was smiling at the stranger. Mrs. Covington remarked how babies were great judges of character and the abstractionist grinned into Jenna's eyes.

He spoke quietly. "If Aaron isn't afraid of me, maybe you shouldn't be either." Then he pushed the bangs back from his eyes and offered her a drink.

"Thank you, but I think I should be asking you, since you're company."

"But I make a hell of a piña colada and Joan is being very hospitable about my using her bar." His eyes sparkled.

"I don't drink."

"Never?"

"Not as long as I'm still nursing. I don't think babies need alcohol."

"Ahhh, well, a virgin colada, then. I wouldn't want to contribute to the delinquency of a minor."

His sly grin and his accent on the words "virgin" and "minor" stiffened her back. Did he know…? Of course he didn't. No one knew. Joan and her parents had been very careful to conceal the fact that her first pregnancy had begun before she was eighteen. For different reasons, of course. Joan didn't want it to interfere with Daniel's integrity as a professional artist. Jenna's parents didn't want it to interfere with their own social status. She didn't care, herself. And Daniel had insisted that he didn't, although

Jenna was never sure he hadn't been trying to spare her feelings. The way he'd reacted when he'd found out...

"Jenna, Dear, come sit down. I'll take the little one." Joan didn't give her time to object.

Obediently taking her place, she pushed Daniel's reaction from her conscious thought and did her best to join the discussion. They were talking about designers, though, and she paid little attention to the fashion world. She supposed she should take more interest in her mother-in-law's work. But the thought of rich women trying to outdo each other with their selection of extravagant clothing held no appeal for her. She didn't even have a clue whose name was on the outfit she was now wearing.

"You know, Daniel told me that Jenna is quite the artist herself. She has yet to show me any of her work, however."

Her eyes widened, and she felt a warmness pushing into her cheeks. Mrs. Covington and the Russells cast curious glances and questions at her. Trevor stared intensely while handing her the drink.

"I ... no, I just dabble." Why would Joan do this?

"Don't be so modest, Dear. My Daniel would never compliment an artist who wasn't quite good. He was nearly as particular about everyone else's work as he was about his own."

Jenna thought of the comments Daniel had made about the other artwork at their first meeting. "Well, he's a diplomat. He always finds something good to say.... I mean, he always ... found ... something good to say about everyone's work, even if most of it was not very good. The first day we met...." She stopped. Every eye in the room was focused on her, and she suddenly couldn't speak. She never talked about their past.

"How did you meet?"

She looked at Trevor. He wasn't being facetious. He wanted to know. But she couldn't tell him.

"They were both attending the same art class." Joan set Aaron in the playpen, then recited the rehearsed story. "Daniel had an old art teacher he befriended, and even after he graduated, he dropped in on his classes occasionally. He met Jenna there and asked her to model for him."

"You were the model?" Trevor's thoughts were too apparent.

"No. It was a still-life. I was just in the classroom and he decided to draw me instead."

“She was quite an inspiration to him, and I still have that first drawing.” Joan suddenly disappeared into the den and came out holding an elegantly framed charcoal drawing.

Jenna’s cheeks became warmer again. Trevor was staring at her portrait, which looked as though she were uncovered.

“Darling, it’s beautiful. And just why have you been hiding this away? It should be shown with the rest of his work.”

“No. I don’t want it shown.” Jenna stood and collected her son, ignoring Mrs. Covington’s further questions. “I’m going to try to get him to sleep.” She also refused to answer Joan’s apology for embarrassing her and fled up the stairs to the guest room.

Twelve

"Can I come in?"

Jenna glanced up at the voice, nodded, then returned her stare to the bit of dark sky she could see from the bed. She assumed her mother-in-law's guests had retreated, leaving the two women to nurse their wounds privately. Joan, of course, would have brushed it off, apologizing for chasing Jenna from the room and continuing to be the perfect hostess. Jenna had changed her baby and held him until he relaxed enough to let his eyes droop. Placing him in the crib, she had settled onto the bed, crossing her legs in front, and had been sitting, staring out the window at nothing for however long it had been.

"Jenna, Honey, I am sorry if I embarrassed you. That wasn't my intention. I simply thought that if you had a slight push, you might open up a bit and let us see some of your work."

She shifted her eyes to the floor. "It's really not that good. I'm not the artist. Daniel is … was. Why do I keep doing that?"

Joan sat close, wrapping an arm around Jenna's shoulders. "You're trying not to let go. But, Honey, you having talent of your own won't change anything that Daniel did, or was. There is no reason for you to hide your own gifts."

"I don't want to try to be what he was; I could never even get close. There just isn't any point." She jumped up, with the ruse of needing to check on her sleeping son, and stood at his crib trying to escape Joan's questioning.

"How long have you been creating art? How old were you when you began?"

Jenna took a deep breath. Her mother-in-law wasn't going to let up this time. How old? She turned slowly, directing her voice away from the baby. "I don't know. I can't remember not doing it. It just…"

"It's just a part of you; a part you shouldn't bury with your husband."

Jenna blinked back tears that were trying to push their way through. "I don't know how to do this. I don't know how to let go and move on. Move on to what?"

She paused a moment before speaking. "To whatever it is that you need to do for yourself. Not for me. Not for your parents. And not for Daniel. For yourself, Jenna. What is it that you want?"

"Joan, I don't know. I really don't. I've been doing some art again … because Alan pushed me into it, but it's not good and it's not what I want to do for a living or anything. I don't want to get so wrapped up in it that I neglect my son."

"The way Daniel neglected you for his art."

"I didn't mean that."

"Yes, you did. Maybe you didn't mean to say it to me, but you did mean it. And I know he did. Jenna, I talked with him about it. He assured me he would make time, and he was so sorry … after…"

"I don't want to hear this. It was fine. He gave me everything he could. He gave me his son, even though he knew…." She wiped the wetness from her cheeks and let Joan move in to hold her.

"It wasn't fair to you, Jenna, but I'm glad you stayed with him. He was truly much happier after finding you, and never would have gone as far without you. But he would never want to hold you back."

λλλλ

She couldn't sleep. At least Aaron was.

Pushing her feet into her slippers, she grabbed the baby monitor and went into Daniel's room. She could smell him, or imagined she could. Joan was right; she would let him down by withdrawing and doing nothing. But she wasn't qualified for anything.

She sat softly on the old stool by her husband's drawing table and looked out the window into the blackness. October had descended quietly. So far, it was still fairly warm. By the time the end of the month arrived, winter would be announcing its impending onslaught. Jenna never looked forward to the winter. She could never get warm enough. But she did love the turning of the seasons; the day she would step outside and feel that Halloween was near. The sudden crispness signaling childhood trips with Alan's family to select the roundest, most perfect pumpkin to shape into a jack-o-lantern. Even after she had married, Jenna had refused to let go of the tradition, hauling Daniel out to the patch and ignoring his raised eyebrows. One of the few things she had absolutely insisted he do with her.

For the children who would come trick-or-treating, she had said. He had known the kids were only half the reason. But each year, Daniel had become more involved, talking to the little ones who ran up to the door of their building, proudly dressed as superheroes or goblins or princesses. He had even sketched a few.

The kids. Whatever Jenna decided to do with her future, she was sure it would involve children.

A flash of an old idea returned. She could go back to ICC and get a teaching certificate. Teaching art wouldn't require her to paint like a professional. She simply had to know the techniques and learn how to describe them to others. Working with children would be easy for her. And no one could say she was trying to fill her husband's shoes.

Even in the brief moment that she could see herself using her art in a productive way, with the satisfaction of having some control over her life, Jenna realized a bit of inner peace. Rising again, she went to the bed in the corner, drew back the covers, slid out of her slippers, and curled up with her husband's presence supporting her new thoughts.

λλλλ

She woke to her baby's muffled cry. It was late. He rarely woke before she did anymore.

A deep yawn as she rose accentuated her more relaxed air. Her slippers were left behind. She wanted to feel the soft carpet gently tickling her bare feet. It reminded her of fresh spring grass through which she loved to walk.

The light cry for attention quieted as she approached her son. He held his arms out, waiting for her to comfort him.

"Morning, Sweetie." Jenna kissed his head and sat to nurse him. What would they do today? Maybe tell Joan she was ready to go home this coming weekend. She wanted to be back in her loft, surrounded by her things. She wanted to tell Alan her thoughts about going back to school. He would be proud of her, and he'd said Cheryl would baby-sit. Aaron was six months now. There was no reason she couldn't leave him for just a little while now and then. She wouldn't go full time; that would be too much. But a class or two.... It would take some time, but that was okay. It would be a start.

When her baby was sufficiently full, she went to find Joan, still barefoot.

The apartment was dark. Jenna twisted the black knob of the nearest living room lamp to cast a soft glow into the room. The grayness of the sky wasn't helping. She pushed the curtain aside. Joan had already left for the day. Well, she supposed she could wait to tell her when she came home. While she stood, staring out at the apartments across the street, the mist gave way to small drops of rain. She watched a while longer, as the drops grew in size and determination, until Aaron began yanking at the lace in her hand.

"Oh, no, Honey. Grandma wouldn't like that. Let go now." She carefully pried the tiny, plump fingers from the curtain and moved away. There was no point in irritating him by continuing the struggle. He settled for his squishy bright yellow plastic book of farm animals. Jenna set him in his playpen and returned to the window. So, it was fall now, already into the school year, but she could begin with the January term when Aaron would be closer to a year old. Would she start with art classes, in which she had the most interest, or get the basic classes out of the way first? Maybe one of each. She could do her language or math homework first, then do her art as dessert.

Dessert. That sounded good. With a glance back at Aaron, she went to the kitchen, searching first the cabinets then the refrigerator. Nothing much. There was plenty of fruit and she usually settled for that, but it wasn't what she wanted today. She supposed she should have a normal breakfast instead of the chocolate cookies she generally had at home. Giving up, and deciding it wasn't quite worth taking a taxi in the rain, Jenna returned to check on her son. He was fine; still making the little book squeak from the pressure of his palm.

Flopping down on the end of the couch, she picked up the phone. He was most likely at work already.

Cheryl answered, as Jenna expected.

"Hey, Jenna! Alan said you called the other day. Is everything okay? He said you sounded a bit upset."

"Oh, you know, off and on, but I'm okay. I … just wanted to let you know that I'm going to try to be home this weekend, if Joan can get the time off."

"Wonderful! I'm sure he'll be glad to hear it. Just a sec, let me get him before he leaves."

Get him? He should have been at work by now. She waited, wishing she had held out a few more minutes. Why didn't she want to talk to him? She was ready to go home … to tell him…

"You're coming home this weekend?"

She froze, only a moment. She wasn't ready. What was wrong with her?

"Jenna?"

"Sorry. Umm, maybe, if Joan can get the time."

"Well, if she can't, let me know and I'll come get you."

No. She didn't want that. "Alan, no, that's okay. I don't want to upset Joan. I can wait until next weekend if it works better for her."

"Jenna, it's no problem."

"Please, I'd rather."

He was silent, very likely making it more than it was. Honestly, she didn't think Joan would appreciate her arranging her own ride back. It would look ungrateful.

"Okay, but let us know one way or another."

"I will, and thanks for the offer."

"Anytime." He was holding back. She could hear it.

She answered the normal questioning and asked her normal questions, then hung up and took a deep breath. Maybe she should've talked to Joan first. Well, it was done; she was committed.

The doorbell startled her. No one ever came over while Joan was away. She glanced at her son, then wandered over to peer out the peephole.

The abstractionist. Why?

After a slight hesitation, she unlocked the deadbolt and opened the door just enough.

He grinned. "It's wet out here; are you gonna let me in?"

"Joan isn't here."

"Now, you don't think I came to see Joan?"

"Then why did you come?"

"I brought lunch. You like Chinese?" He held up a brown bag spattered with rain spots on the top and a slight grease stain on the bottom.

"Lunch? It's only ten."

"Yeah, well. I don't do the breakfast thing, so I do lunch early. Are you still full from bacon and eggs?"

"No. I haven't eaten, but…"

"Great. So open the door just a couple more inches, why don't you, and we can eat together."

She hesitated still. She didn't want him there – not while Joan was away.

"I'm not gonna bite … unless you want me to." He winked.

Why did this guy think he was so funny? He was much too full of himself. But, it was raining harder and he was already wet, and he'd gone to so much trouble…. But was he safe?

"That was a joke. Don't look at me like Jack the Ripper. I'm completely harmless. Well, not completely, but close enough." He seemed to never stop grinning, but his eyes were kind and Aaron had accepted him fairly well the night before.

She stepped back, allowing him room to enter. "Take your shoes off. I'll get a towel."

"Wow, you sound like my aunt. Must be an adult thing I haven't learned yet."

Jenna didn't bother to answer. She went quickly to the linen pantry and found as close as she could find to an old towel. He thanked her when she handed it to him, again with a grin. He gave her the brown bag. It did smell good, grease and all. Trying to be a polite hostess, she waited as he dried his head and rubbed the towel up and down his arms. And they again traded packages.

He followed her to the kitchen and asked where to find plates. She pointed to the cabinet, then went to check on Aaron. Her son was standing, holding on to the edge of the playpen, and smiled as he saw her. He wouldn't be hungry yet, but she didn't want to leave him alone in the living room, so took him in her arms and returned to their visitor. The abstractionist had found the silverware and had everything set up by the time she strapped Aaron into his high chair.

"I didn't know what you liked, so I got some of this and some of that." Trevor greeted the baby by rubbing his head, then opened boxes as he chatted, acting as if he and Jenna were old friends who normally ate lunch together. She was uncomfortable – not frightened of him, but … wary of his intentions.

Aaron gave her a distraction, though, and she tended to him even when he didn't need it. He was quite content gnawing on his biscuit and intermittently picking at the rice she put on his tray. She never bothered using the plastic dish she had for him, since he always dumped it over first thing. And a spoon was just in his way. It generally ended up on the floor.

"Do you plan to have more?"

Jenna finally looked at the man across from her, waiting for clarification.

"More children. You're good with him."

Her jaw clenched. He had no right…

"Was that a bad question? You know, I don't have any manners. I just say whatever comes to mind."

Which was a bit refreshing, in a way. "No. But that's not something I can do on my own, so pretty irrelevant, I would think."

He chuckled. "Well, I didn't mean now. I meant … if you get married again. Do you want another kid?"

"I'm not getting married again."

"Never?"

"No." She turned to her food, hoping he wouldn't push her further.

He didn't. They ate in silence for longer than was comfortable.

Eventually, her manners took over. "This is very good, thank you."

The abstractionist grinned. "Well, good. I was afraid you were only eating it so you wouldn't offend me. That is what your clique does, right? Me? If I don't like something, I flat don't eat it. No offense meant, but what's the point? Not everyone likes the same things, right?"

Her clique? And just what did he mean by *her* clique?

"And I offended you again. Wow, that's easy to do, isn't it?"

"I'm not offended; just wondering what you meant by 'my clique.'" Okay, if he liked directness, he might as well get it from her.

"The uppity class, of course. Isn't that where you come from? I know it is – I can see it in your actions and your speech. Not that that's a bad thing. You don't seem quite as uppity as most of them. But still, it's there."

"If you think I'm uppity, why are you here?"

He shrugged. "If you're so bothered by me, why did you let me in?"

"It's raining. I may be uppity, but I'm not cruel."

"No. I know you're not. And I don't think you like being uppity. Thought you'd like to try something else for a change."

The glint in his eyes gave more meaning to his words than what he'd actually said. For a moment, only a split second, she was intrigued. Try something else? No, not what he had in mind. She didn't want that, not from Alan, not from the abstractionist ... not from anyone.

She pulled her eyes away. Hopefully, he hadn't read her first thought.

He made idle chatter, with her and with Aaron, as they finished, then insisted on helping with the dishes, though she tried to dissuade him. He wasn't one to be easily dissuaded, and she wasn't used to that. She had always been able to stop Daniel with a word, and she could with Alan. Maybe she shouldn't have let him in.

He worked closely to her, occasionally running his arm into hers. She didn't believe for a minute that it wasn't on purpose, either. Two or three times, she had backed off, finally giving up because he kept following. And it was slightly comforting, in a way, to know he wanted to be there.

She pulled away abruptly. "Don't you have to get back to work?"

"Work?"

"You don't have a job? Other than painting, I mean."

"I work nights so I'm free all day."

"Nights? What, security or something?"

He laughed. "Hell, do I look like a security guard?"

No, he didn't. He was too scrawny.

"I'm a bartender, at a shabby little club I'm sure you would never lower yourself to be seen in. But it suits me, and it gives me great ideas for paintings." He shoved his bangs away from his eyes. They fell immediately back in place. "Guess I just made you even less interested, didn't I?"

He wanted her approval. Why, she couldn't imagine. He seemed to have everything together and was living the way he wanted to live. What could her approval, or opinion, matter to him? Jenna took advantage of his openness, deciding to ask. "Why do you care what I think?"

The abstractionist stepped closer. "Cause I'm willing to admit I'd like to try something different." He touched her fingertips, very briefly, then turned away. Heading toward the door leading to the hallway, he paused and looked at her again. "Don't worry; I'm leaving. But I'll be back, and I hope you'll let me in again."

Thirteen

Jenna lay in Daniel's arms; her head propped against his chest and shoulder. She debated whether this was the right moment to tell him. Or, she could wait a while. It wouldn't be obvious for several weeks. And the longer she waited, the closer she would be to eighteen. Would he change his mind about wanting her to move in? He still wanted to tell her parents they were dating; to face them and admit he was seeing their daughter and let them know he was in love with her. Of course, he had agreed they maybe shouldn't tell them the full extent of their relationship. Not yet. But Jenna couldn't even agree to let Daniel meet them. They would object, strongly. And she didn't want him insulted.

"What is it, Jenna?"

She pivoted her head to meet his eyes. "What?"

He grinned. "You can't hide your thoughts from me. There's something bothering you."

"Oh, am I that transparent?"

"To me you are." He stroked her hair and kissed her forehead. "What is it?"

She cuddled closer against his bare skin. She didn't want to ruin this moment; they were too few. "I ... was just thinking of my parents. I think they're starting to get suspicious."

"We need to tell them."

"No. Daniel..."

"Jenna, this is bothering you too much. I don't like for you to have to sneak around behind their backs. If I had known before..."

She tensed, tears suddenly pushing to her eyes. If he had known ... if she hadn't deceived him ... they wouldn't be here together now. "You do regret it."

He pulled away, enough to lift her face to his. "No. That's not what I meant."

A tear refused to be held back any longer. She turned her eyes away.

"Oh, Jenna, I'm sorry. I didn't mean..."

"Yes, you did. I should've told you, and now you regret it, and I can't change it."

His fingers forced her chin up until he found her eyes. "Jenna, no. I only meant that it's too hard on you." He wiped a few more tears from her face. "Would we be here like this now if I regretted being with you? Do you think you are forcing me to make love to you?"

She couldn't answer. He didn't act like he was being forced, but ... the way he had reacted when she'd told him she was seventeen.... How would he react knowing she was carrying his child?

"I love you, Jenna. And I don't regret anything. I just don't want you to have to hide from your parents for another month. We need to tell them we're dating. I'll talk to them, make them see..."

Her tears strengthened. It was too much. They couldn't tell her parents. She wouldn't be able to see him again, not until she was eighteen. By then, he would find someone else ... someone older, and she'd have to do it alone...

He pulled her against him. "Shhhh, Honey, don't cry."

"We can't ... we can't tell them. You don't know them ... they'll..."

"Okay. Okay, Jen. If it bothers you that much, we'll stop talking about it. It's only another month. We can wait. But you will *move in with me then. You do still want to?"*

She nodded, rubbing her head against his chest.

"Okay. Calm down, now. Everything will be alright."

She clung to him, concentrating on his breathing, the rise and fall of his chest. She couldn't believe everything would be alright, but it was for the moment.

A loud clap of thunder made her jump. Coming slowly to her senses, she realized it was Daniel's pillow she was clinging to. The image of him had been so clear in her mind that awakening without him stabbed pains of longing into her heart. She silently cursed the thunder for taking him away.

The monitor on the stand next to their bed told her the storm had also bothered her son. But she didn't want to leave Daniel's bed. She waited. Maybe he would go back to sleep. Still holding the pillow, Jenna sank her head into it, attempting a return to where she had been. It didn't work.

Forcing her feet to the floor, she finally set the pillow down and pushed herself to stand. Then she stopped. Aaron was quiet; maybe he had been too tired to let the storm continue to bother him. He should have been, as long as it had taken to get him to sleep. She usually didn't mind rocking him for as long as it took, but the night before it had irritated her. Exhausted, she sat down again, listening. His sudden quietness was too eerie.

Nearly to the door, she paused when it opened. Joan had him. That explained the silence.

She hoped the darkness would hide her mood. "I'm sorry he woke you. I thought he might go back to sleep."

"I guess he doesn't take after his father in every way. Daniel always slept best during storms." Joan caressed the baby's head.

"He doesn't like noise."

"No, neither did his father, but for some reason he liked storms. He was always a bit odd." She grinned, remembering.

"I'll take him so you can go back to sleep."

"Are you okay, Jenna?"

"Yeah, just tired, but moms are supposed to be, right?"

Joan waited.

"Actually, if you're free this weekend, I think I need to be home."

Her mother-in-law nodded. "Well, I was hoping you would stay longer, but I'll take you. You'll be okay there?"

Jenna claimed her son. "Yeah, we'll be fine."

Unwilling to leave her husband's room, Jenna cuddled Aaron in next to her on the bed. She wouldn't sleep now, anyway. The dream had taken her home … too far home. Her parents had been furious. And Jenna had been furious with Alan for helping them find Daniel's loft, even if he had been worried about her.

With the threat of her father pressing charges against Daniel, Jenna had finally blown. She hadn't even told Daniel yet that she was pregnant. But in the middle of the yelling, with Alan barely preventing her father from attacking Daniel when he looked like he wanted to himself, she told them all. She had admitted that she was pregnant – almost four weeks pregnant – and that everyone would know and she didn't care. She would wait for him if he went to jail and take care of her child on her own until he was free. Or do it completely alone, if she had to.

Her parents, after beginning to breathe again, had argued between themselves about how to handle her "*situation*." She had ignored them. She had ignored Alan's stare.

Daniel moved slowly closer. Jenna waited nervously. Her parents were too busy arguing to keep them apart. Finally, he reached a hand to her face, sliding his fingers into her hair.

"You won't be alone, Jen. I'll be here."

With a sigh, Jenna gazed at her sleeping son. She wished they'd had him earlier. Daniel would have been a wonderful father, for even a few years.

λλλλ

Thinking she would be lucky enough to get away before the abstractionist honored his word about coming back, Jenna began packing while her son slept. With not much to pack and three days left, it wasn't necessary, but she was restless. She hadn't called Alan back to let him know, as he'd asked, but there was time for that. And she'd been busy.

Joan had insisted on taking her to lunch twice during the week so far, and the Russells had come over the night before. She hoped that would be the end of company. Entertaining wasn't her thing. It was exhausting.

Standing in her room, deciding which clothes could be returned to the suitcase, she was startled by the doorbell. Not wanting it to wake her son, Jenna hurried down the stairs before it rang again.

Trevor. And it wasn't raining this time.

"Told you I'd be back. Have plans today?"

Yes. She was packing, but didn't tell him that. "Why?"

"Well, thought you might keep me company. There's something I've been wanting to do, but don't know anyone else who might be interested."

"In what?"

He chuckled. "Are you going to let me in?"

"I don't know. It's not raining, so I wouldn't be cruel not to, would I?"

"It would be more cruel not to, since it's not raining. I wouldn't want to think we were only bad weather friends. Or do I need to go get more Chinese food to coax the door open?"

She grinned, unwillingly, and only for a moment. "No. I just ate."

He passed her more slowly this time when she moved back. She smelled the cologne again, still unable to place the familiarity.

Trevor walked into the living room, then turned. "So where's the little guy?"

"Asleep."

"Does he sleep long?"

"Why?"

"Well, so we can go, of course. Unless you have a sitter you call for last minute interruptions by crazy men who want to take you out."

She stared until her bearings returned. "I don't use sitters and he may be a while, so maybe you should find someone else…."

"Jenna, I don't want to do this with someone else. I want to do it with you." His face suddenly lost the momentary seriousness and regained its grin. "And I won't bite, unless you want me to."

"Shouldn't you be spending time on your painting? I know they'll be wanting to do more shows."

"They can wait. I paint because I enjoy it. I'm not about to let it rule me, not for anyone. It isn't art if you do that; it's work, and then what's the point?"

Of course. That was how she felt, too. It had been one thing she hadn't understood about Daniel, until he became sick. Then she knew why he'd been so driven; he had wanted to leave as much of himself behind as he could. But the abstractionist couldn't see that far into the future. He was probably about Daniel's age chronologically, but he was so much younger. And his exuberance was contagious.

"Do you want something to drink?"

"Sorry, that's my line. Sit down and I'll see what I can find."

"You're not at work here. I'm supposed to be the hostess."

He grinned. "That role doesn't suit you. I'm more comfortable with it." With a wink, he passed her, heading to the kitchen.

She sat, pulling a knee up in front, wrapped by her arms. What was he trying to accomplish? She wasn't encouraging him in any way, and with his looks, he could easily find someone without … complications. Why was he wasting his time?

Handing her a can of soda, the abstractionist sat a little too close. He chattered with her as comfortably as he had the day before. Luckily, he never seemed to run out of things to say, so she didn't have to answer much. Jenna used the opportunity to study him, doing her best to try to figure what he wanted. Secret information about her husband was a possibility, though he hadn't mentioned him again. And what would be the purpose? Daniel had been an artist; everything people needed to know about him, they could see in his work. Nothing she could say would matter.

"So … you've never shown your work to anyone except your husband?"

She paused. Nothing had come of Joan's remark until now. How much should she tell him?

"Okay, so I take your silence as a negative, but why is it such a big secret? Are you embarrassed to be an artist?"

"I'm not an artist; I just dabble now and then."

"So why does it matter if someone sees it? Let me guess. You're actually better than the great Daniel Rhodes and you don't want to show him up."

"Not anywhere near."

"Then why has no one seen it?"

"Someone has."

"Oh? You mean your parents and you think they just say they like it because they're your parents."

"No." Her parents had never been interested in her art. "A cousin … and a friend. Like I said, it's not good enough to show."

"Then why would your husband have told Joan that it was?"

Why? She had no idea.

"I'd like to see some of your work."

"I don't have any with me."

A soft cry broke off the response she didn't want to hear anyway. Was she paranoid, or were his eyes following her, tracking her path to the stairs? A deep breath accompanied her escape. How would she get out of going with him to … wherever he wanted to go today? Maybe she could say Aaron was not feeling well, or was too grouchy.

Turning into their room, she doubted he would believe that. The baby smiled at her sight, reaching out happily, waiting to be held. He didn't look anywhere near sick or grouchy.

He would be hungry, though. She wasn't about to nurse in front of the abstractionist, but could she just stay upstairs that long without telling him? Maybe she could get him to leave by saying she had to feed him and that he needed a bath … anything.

Gathering Aaron into her arms, she did stop and change him first. Then she braved the downstairs again, and the living room.

Trevor was perusing Joan's book collection, most of which her mother-in-law hadn't read. They were for show. But they had provided Jenna with entertainment whenever she was in town.

A small baby noise turned the artist's head, and he smiled at Aaron.

"Hey, Partner. Wanna go sight-seeing?" Casually presenting himself to them, he took Aaron's hand.

Her son smiled, grasping the strong fingers.

"See? He wants to go. I'll take him while you put something warmer on. It may be chilly."

"I don't know...."

"Don't even argue. I've been sitting here waiting for the little one and you're not turning me down now that I'm revved up for it."

"But ... he needs to eat ... and...."

"So fix a bottle and bring it along."

"He doesn't use a bottle."

"Oh. You're one of those natural people. Hey, that's cool. So it can't take long. I'll wait."

Too befuddled to argue, she nodded and went back upstairs.

She hated cabs. They always scared her, zipping in and out of traffic. Luckily, they had a fairly short ride before stepping out beside a boat dock.

Jenna looked at Trevor.

"It's an architecture cruise of Chicago's most interesting buildings. I've wanted to do this for a while, but like I said, didn't have anyone else who wanted to go, and I hate doing stuff alone. Figured you wouldn't mind, seeing as you're into art." He read the hesitation on her face. "Unless you don't like boats. Damn, I hadn't thought of that. Can you handle boats?"

"I love boats."

His relief was too obvious. "Cool. Then let's go."

"No, I..." She didn't want to go on a boat with him. She'd wanted to go with Daniel.

"What?" He was studying her.

Aaron pulled at the hair hanging beside her face. When she grimaced, Trevor took the baby's hand away gently, allowing his fingers a slight brush of her cheek.

She met his eyes. They were still waiting for her answer.

"Nothing. Okay."

His grin was more gentle, reassuring.

Jenna soon found a pride at being there with him, listening to his comments about certain aspects of the tour. He had studied architecture, and he knew art. He knew the different styles, techniques, thoughts that went into each structure. He knew pieces of art within some of the buildings, pieces he thought she should see. And she found herself wanting Trevor to show them to her.

He spent quite a bit of time helping with Aaron; talking to him, holding him, grinning at people who cooed at the baby. He acted more a father than even Alan had.

Alan. She hadn't called him yet. Maybe she'd been too hasty. There were a lot of things in Chicago she had always wanted to see but hadn't found the time. She could stay another week, now that she had someone willing to show her things she had interest in. After all the time she had spent following someone else's interests...

"Jenna?"

She let his eyes touch hers.

"Are you listening to me at all, or have I been talking too much and boring you?"

"Oh, no. I'm listening. I just got lost in my thoughts a moment. I'm sorry."

"No problem. I tend to get too wrapped up in my own voice."

"No, really. I'm enjoying this. Keep talking."

He searched her face. "Are you? I don't want you to do or say anything just to make me feel good. Be honest."

She was being honest, and somehow, she knew she could be with him. "So, are we touring the insides of the buildings tomorrow? Or do you have other plans?"

The abstractionist was taken aback, then he grinned. "No, I have no other plans tomorrow. Is the same time good for you?"

"Yes."

Fourteen

She let Joan carry the conversation during dinner while her thoughts turned over the events of the last three days. The abstractionist had surprisingly come to be a pleasant companion. He didn't remind her of the past and didn't pry. And he didn't ask anything more than just to spend time with her.

Jenna and Aaron were scheduled to go back to Peoria the day after next, but she hadn't told him. She hadn't called Alan yet, either. Thinking seriously about staying another week, Jenna struggled to find an excuse. She hadn't told her mother-in-law about Trevor. Joan knew nothing about the two days of sightseeing trips, though the way she kept studying Jenna implied that she knew *something*.

And why was Jenna hiding it? She and Trevor were just friends; there was nothing wrong with that. He had been very much a gentlemen, and other than the slight brush of her cheek, he hadn't even set a hand on her. It kept their relationship comfortable. Her thoughts of Daniel remained, of course, but they hadn't haunted her as badly since the architecture tour. Maybe she would be able to get back into the art world in this roundabout way. Ease into it by focusing on different mediums. The building styles had been fascinating. She wouldn't mind taking a sketch book and recreating the angles and shadows and lines…

"Jenna?"

She looked up at Joan. "Yes?"

"What on earth is keeping you so deep in thought?"

"Architecture." It slipped out before she could stop it.

Joan raised her eyebrows. "Architecture?"

"Well, buildings." She replayed the partial truth she had started earlier. "You know, while Aaron and I were out walking … I was looking at buildings. The differences. Thinking about how old some had to be compared to others. The line they made against the sky, and…."

"And I thought you were more into nature than architecture. Isn't that why you hang out with that friend of yours? Alan, isn't it? The one who does the gardening?"

Alan? Why had she brought him up? "He's a landscape designer." She pushed at her remaining vegetables with a fork. It had always been a struggle to make herself eat them, any of them.

"Yes. Well. I thought it was your love of nature that drew you to him. I've never heard you talk about being interested in buildings before."

Because she had never thought about it before, at least not consciously. "Well, there isn't much to see in Peoria, as far as architecture. Most of it is pretty plain. So I guess I just didn't have a reason to think about it before."

Joan waited; knowing there was more than Jenna was saying. She was fishing for information about her relationship with Alan, too. But there was nothing more to say about it. They were friends. He was a landscape designer. What more was there? Nothing she was going to admit to Joan.

"There isn't a lot around this neighborhood worth seeing, either." She threw Jenna a pointed glance. "Now, if you go into the middle of the city, or along the shoreline, you'll find buildings worth your concentration. Maybe I can take the afternoon off tomorrow, before you leave, and we can drive around to find something more interesting. I can pick you up early and we'll have lunch. What do you think?"

Trevor was supposed to be over again, but she couldn't tell Joan that, either. He knew a mostly unknown art gallery, sporting unknown artists, that he had talked her into going to with him. She most definitely couldn't admit she was going to a gallery.

"Well, actually, I was thinking I might stay a little longer, if you wouldn't mind. You're already cutting your schedule back for me, and I know you're busy right now. So, maybe next weekend would be better for you? And maybe sometime before then we could sight-see?"

"That would be wonderful, Honey, if you want to stay. But don't feel like you're putting me out. If you need to get back..."

"No. I don't. I guess I was just having a bad day when I said that."

"And you're feeling better?"

"I guess so."

Joan perused her face. "I'm glad. I was hoping a different atmosphere would help. For a time, I was afraid it was making it worse."

"Maybe it did, at first. But I've always liked being here."

Daniel's mother smiled. "I was always sure you did. I kept trying to talk Daniel into moving, for his sake and yours."

"I tried, too – once. He wasn't interested."

"No, I know. He never liked it here." She leaned back a bit from the table. "Now that you are free to do as you choose, Jenna, you might think about it. I can help you find a place."

Move? Permanently? No, she didn't think she could. The loft was her home; their home. She didn't want to leave it.

"Thank you, Joan, but … I can't. Not now."

λλλλ

The "gallery" was well-disguised. Smoke burned into her nostrils upon passing Trevor through the entrance, a heavy burnt-wood door with cross beams separating from it. She hoped the abstractionist wouldn't end up with slivers in his fingers.

He motioned for her to proceed, but she waited. Jenna had no interest in leading the way. She could barely see after the brightness of the noon sun. Covering Aaron's head with his thin blanket, protecting him from the nicotine-laden air and from anything else floating around, she stayed close behind her companion. She didn't notice any artwork. She saw bookshelves, dusty and untouched, small grimy tables with somewhat matching chairs, a few slovenly dressed patrons slumping over a counter that separated them from dusty glass bottles on warped wooden shelving, and a girl with piercings in places that made Jenna cringe. This couldn't be called a gallery in any sense of the word.

Trevor greeted a couple of guys who acknowledged his presence. They stared at her the way they would a leper. He didn't seem to notice. "This is a friend of mine. She's into art."

One nodded, the other continued to stare.

The abstractionist pulled her past them, around a corner. The slight strains of acoustic guitar playing a blues number – Jenna had no idea which one – became louder, pulling her eyes to one of the slightly larger tables. She turned away when a broad-shouldered black man with a gray-sprinkled beard noticed them. He was sitting alone, a cigar burning on the table within his reach.

"Hey, D-Day, what ya got there wi' tcha?"

Trevor grinned. "Only the prettiest thing you'll ever set eyes on."

The man laughed, halting his plucking of the strings. "Yeah, yeah, you been feedin' those lines again, ain't ya? Don't listen to a word he says, Darlin'. Run while you got the chance."

Jenna glanced at the abstractionist. He was still grinning.

With a slight pressure of his fingers against her back, he indicated for her to sit, pulling out a chair. She hesitated.

"I don't bite, Darlin', not hard anyways, with these pretend teeth."

She looked back at him. That was Trevor's line; well, a variation of it. Which one had taken it from the other?

Aaron woke when she sat down. Not happy having his face covered, he yanked at the blanket.

Trevor reached over to snuff out the cigar. "Sorry, you'll have to let it burn away after we're gone. Don't think his mom wants him to pick up that habit yet."

"You got a babe with a babe? D-day, don't 'cha tell me you're handling another brother's woman. I'll kick your white ass right on out o' here."

"Now, how long have you known me?" He rubbed a hand over the baby's head. "This is Daniel Rhodes' kid, and his widow, Jenna."

"Well, I'll be. You're pullin' my old leg. No one like that would be hangin' round wi' chyou."

She looked from one to the other. So, she'd been right. His only interest for her was her husband. Did he think she could help his career by people knowing they were…?

"Tell me the truth, now, Darlin'. You ain't the painter's ole lady. He's just settin' me up for a laugh."

Jenna considered lying, telling the man that she wasn't who Trevor claimed, just as a way to get even. But she could never deny her husband. "Yes. I'm Jenna Rhodes."

"The painter's lady?"

The painter's lady. That pretty much described her. Daniel's wife. His son's mother.

She took a deep breath, raising her chin just a bit. "Yes, Daniel was my husband."

"Well, I'll be." He squinted at her. "There's a lot of sadness in your eyes. He was a good man, was he?"

Her steadiness faltered. Trevor was watching her. So, he wanted to know what she thought of Daniel? Fine. He should know.

"Yes. He was a very good man. Caring, kind … obsessed with whatever he was doing." She stroked her baby's hair. "He very much wanted to be a father, and he loved holding him…" Emotions got in the way, and she stopped.

Trevor lay a hand on her shoulder. She enjoyed the touch – the warmth.

"So what do you think of the gallery?"

He was changing the subject, and she was grateful.

"Well…"

"You haven't even looked at the paintings yet. C'mon." He stood abruptly and pulled the chair out for her.

Following, she finally realized he was referring to the framed … artwork, if it could be called that, encircling the room. It was abstract and made no sense to her. One, she could tell, was supposed to be a nude … male or female, she wasn't sure. Picasso-style, but not as sharp. The rest, well … they looked like Daniel's palettes, where he mixed the paint he used on his work. Except for the ones with sharp lines. She just didn't get it. What was the point?

"You're not impressed."

"Well, I just … I guess I'm not as trained in art as I should be. I don't see what you're seeing."

"You're not supposed to see what I see. That's the idea. It should be personal. You can take away whatever you want from it."

He moved closer, pointing out a particular piece with blue and green shades and tints. "What about that one? How does it make you feel?"

Jenna studied the painting, following the lines and changes of hue and trying to find a pattern, something that would give her a clue as to what it was supposed to be about. And trying to ignore his scent. Finally, she sighed. "I don't know. It doesn't make me feel any way that I can tell."

"Because you're keeping your mind too closed. You're thinking inside the lines."

"I'm sorry – I can't help that. It's the way I was raised." Her tone was too sarcastic and she turned from him, embarrassed.

The silence was soon overtaken by soft guitar wails.

"Can we go? This isn't the place for a baby." Her eyes burned, from the smoke, she told herself.

λλλλ

Jenna bathed Aaron, and then showered quickly after the abstractionist left them at the apartment. Everything they'd been wearing was thrown into the washer. Joan would notice the smell on their clothes otherwise.

With the baby in one arm, she ran water into a cup and pushed it into the microwave. While it warmed, she set Aaron in his high chair and handed him a hard biscuit. He munched it gratefully. Hopefully, he hadn't inhaled enough smoke to do him any harm. Jenna had tried to cover his face again as they left, but he wouldn't have it. He kept pulling it off and smiling at her. But they hadn't been there long.

The beeping drew her attention from him and she went to drop a tea bag into the cup, carrying it back to the table. She tugged the string, watching the steaming water slowly darken. It reminded her of the watercolors she had worked with for a while.

She'd enjoyed trying it and had turned out some relatively decent work, but her hand was too tight, so Daniel said. He had told her to loosen her grip slightly and let her feelings about her subject take over. When she tried, the results were even worse. He'd said her feelings must have been too intense; she was too uptight. His "messing around with it" had turned out wonderfully, absolutely beautiful. She gave up on watercolors.

But she did love them. The variations in intensity and clarity that could be achieved were unlike oil. There was a softness to it.... It didn't matter. She didn't have the skill it needed.

After mixing just a touch of sugar into her cup, Jenna picked up the pencil and pad of graph paper Joan had left on the table. Joan had notepads or graph paper everywhere so her ideas could be immediately saved no matter where she was. And there were always drawing pencils nearby. Maybe that had helped prompt Daniel into his art – watching his mother constantly doodling dress designs. Denise, however, had no artistic interest, other than in following, and actively supporting, her brother's career.

A figure of a lady began to emerge from the page; a Victorian lady. Jenna worked on the details of her robust gown. Delicate lacework, pearls and flowers, a plunging neckline with not much to support it. Gathers on the front, at the bottom, pulling the hem up to reveal sleek, toned shins. More flowers to tie the gathering. Then shoes ... no, no shoes. She was barefoot ... barefoot ...

walking on a cobbled path. The stones were smooth, but round, with crevices that would catch a spiked heel. On either side was grass, wiry and bent. The girl's only choices were to stay on the hard, stone path or swerve off into the prickly half-dead grass.

Jenna set the pencil down, studying her work. It reminded her of the drawings she had done in high school, the ones she had given to Alan. She wondered if he still had them. He should have thrown them out years ago, after she had finally let him know there would never be anything more between them than friendship. He had to have claimed to like them only to spare her feelings. He had said they were her. Her thoughts and emotions. They were just quick sketches; nothing more. But she had given the whole stack to him when he'd asked – to save them from the garbage.

Aaron coughed, choking.

She bolted out of the chair, grabbing him. He coughed a couple more times, then stopped, breathing normally, and chewing the rest of the crumbs in his mouth. She had to force herself to breathe again.

"Don't do that to me!"

He chuckled and grabbed the finger she pointed at his tummy. He wasn't even bothered. Of course not; he had no idea yet about the fragility of life. How quickly you could lose someone. How it could shatter your world.

She held him close, ignoring the soggy bread slobber he was rubbing on her shirt.

A click from the hallway told her Joan was home. Jenna stepped out to meet her.

"Jenna, what's wrong?"

"Oh, nothing. He was choking on his biscuit. It scared me."

Joan set her briefcase beside the coat rack, then shrugged off her suede jacket, hanging it above. "It gets less scary after a while, when you start to realize it's a common baby thing to do." She rubbed Aaron's head. "You're getting your mommy all messy."

He smiled at her, reaching for her face.

She backed away, instead taking his chubby arm in her hand. "Oh, no, I've been through that enough already. I'll take you when you're cleaned up."

Jenna followed her into the living room. She must have driven her kids crazy with her obsessive cleanliness. Or maybe she hadn't always been that way. How could you be? With constant baby drool and diaper changes and toys around and food spilling over the high chair…

"So did you do anything interesting today?" Joan slipped out of her shoes and picked through the mail on her side table.

Interesting? "No, not really."

"Are you getting bored being in the house alone?"

"I'm not alone. I'm happy with Aaron as company." Again, she wasn't lying; just circling the truth.

"Well, I have half of tomorrow free. We can take a drive up through the older part of the city. I'm not sure you've been there before. There are some very pretty old houses on certain streets. At times, I've longed to buy one, but I have no need for such extravagance. And I certainly wouldn't want to intrude in the wrong circle." She said all of this without so much as looking up. Her sarcasm wasn't well hidden. Although Joan was very successful and had more money than she could ever want to spend, she was new money and was unmarried after three unsuccessful attempts. The women in the "wrong circle" preferred suffering silently in horrible marriages than facing the humiliation of failure. Jenna thought they were crazy. Why would being stupid enough to stay miserable be less a failure than daring to find something to make themselves happy?

Her stomach twitched. What right did she have to judge? She enjoyed Trevor's company but was shielding herself from him. It was different, though. She was merely protecting herself from more pain.

"Jenna?"

She looked up, erasing her thoughts from her face.

"Does that sound alright?"

"Oh. Sure. I don't have plans."

No lie, not even circling. Trevor had asked again, about her running somewhere with him the next day. She'd refused, still not telling him she would be around an extra week. He would stop coming by, thinking she was gone. And she still hadn't called Alan.

Fifteen

"This is nice. Did you do it today?"

Jenna glanced toward the kitchen door, where Joan was holding her sketch. "Oh. Yeah, I was just doodling. I forgot I left it there."

"I'm glad you did. So my Daniel was right; you do have some real talent."

"No. It's..."

"You?"

She paused, letting Aaron slip down to the floor. He immediately began creeping back to the bookshelf with trinkets decorating it.

"I don't know. I wasn't thinking about it. I just tend to pick up a pencil when there's one beside me."

"I'd love to see this in paint, on canvas."

Jenna rose to grab her baby. "Aaron, no, Honey. They're not toys." He fussed a bit. "I think he's getting hungry. I'll be back." She didn't wait for Joan's answer before leaving the room. Her mother-in-law had suggested once that she could stay downstairs instead of hiding; a receiving blanket would work fine. And she had, in her own loft. For some reason, she just couldn't do it in Joan's living room. People did tend to drop in at Joan's, unlike at home, and that would be too uncomfortable.

Of course, she had nursed in front of Daniel. It was a bittersweet memory, how he would gingerly touch his son's fingers as she sat on the bed beside him. On the days he'd had more energy, he had let his own fingers roam, teasing her.

She stirred inside, then took a quick, deep breath to calm herself. She missed his touch, the way his eyes took her in, caressing her even when he wasn't able to do more than that.... Forcing her thoughts elsewhere, Jenna replayed Joan's comment about her drawing. "*So my Daniel was right; you do have some real talent.*" The Victorian girl had emerged subconsciously. Had Jenna actually been drawing herself? She could, at times, picture herself long ago, dressed as a lady, mingling in a large ballroom. Except she didn't much like to wear dresses. She hated wearing hose and heels. There was nothing practical in that. In jeans or sweats, she could sit in the soft, cool grass when she pleased, or on old dusty park benches, or … on a granite zoo sign. Off which side of the stone should she step? The Victorian girl would have a rough time with either path – continuing on over the hard cobblestones or veering off into the sharp browned grass. Was there a better choice? Was there any choice?

Aaron pulled away, needing a pause from his hearty imbibing. Jenna rubbed his back, letting her eyes drift around Daniel's room. This was an artist's room – careful decorating cast aside to make space for things more important. She had always had to keep her room the way her mother wanted it – perfectly matched and spotless, and much too pink. She didn't care for pink, either. How would she do Aaron's room, if he had one? That was another thought. He would eventually have to have a room, not just a space in the corner. Maybe she could do a partition. It would cut down too much on the studio space, though, and there would be no soundproofing. They would have to move when he got older.

He released the air in his tummy, then hinted that he was ready to finish his meal. He had eaten his carrots well earlier. She was surprised he was still as hungry as usual. But he was growing, already wearing size nine month clothes though he hadn't reached seven months in age. He grinned from one side of his mouth when she stroked his cheek. He especially looked like his father when he grinned.

Jenna lingered after Aaron had finished, walking with him around the bedroom, touching … caressing … Daniel's sculpture in the corner. It was an abstract, done as a class requirement. He had never said what it was supposed to represent, and she couldn't begin to tell, but she did like the lines. They were smooth and flowing, unhurried and uninterrupted – the way he'd always worked. Of course. It represented his personality. Funny she had never thought about it before.

Abstract. A genre he had said he'd never understood. The sculpture in his room was the only one he had kept. The rest had been garbage. She had a hard time believing it was possible for Daniel to have created garbage.

The half day of touring old houses with Joan turned into a day-long marathon, including lunch with two of her work friends and the rest of the afternoon in the office. They tried to include Jenna in some of the design discussions, then tried to hide their surprise about how little fashion knowledge she had. Not to mention her disinterest, which she had trouble hiding.

It didn't seem to bother Joan. She smiled patiently and showed her some of what they were describing in fashion terminology. The buildings had been more interesting.

Aaron was restless by the time they returned to the townhouse. He was tired, and tired of being contained all day. Jenna had a hard time keeping up with his exploring and fussing, and finally took him upstairs to see if he would settle in early. Lying beside him in the guest room, she refused to make herself get up again after he fell asleep. Joan would just have to understand.

λλλλ

On Monday morning, she called Alan.

Luckily, she reached Cheryl instead; explaining that next weekend would be better for Joan to drive them home. Alan had been trying to call; first the loft, then Joan's house. Her mother-in-law hadn't said anything. Jenna apologized for worrying them and promised to call just as soon as she returned home. She supposed her friend would get over being mad that she hadn't called earlier.

Flipping through the television channels in an attempt to occupy her restless mind, Jenna paused at a man leaning over his garden. She listened to his advice on weed prevention, emphasizing organic methods as he pulled perfect red tomatoes from the lush greenery. Maybe she should try gardening. Alan would help her, she was sure. But she had nowhere to put a garden. Besides, she had trouble keeping indoor plants alive. She switched the channel.

By the time Joan arrived home, Jenna had finished the novel she'd started the week before, had spent considerable time playing with Aaron, and had watched an old-ish romantic comedy. She was ready for her mother-in-law's company.

The following days were mostly the same and she found herself wondering whether she should let Trevor know she was still in town. No, she'd ended that and had no use in getting it started again.

Thursday morning, she found a sketch pad and drawing pencils lying on the kitchen table. A hint from Joan, obviously. She wasn't going to give into that, either. Until Aaron was napping later in the day and she went into the kitchen to make herself a cup of mint tea. The pull of the art supplies was too hard to resist, possibly because she was bored. With no conscious idea about what to make of the blank page, she let her hand guide her. An old table emerged, with smoke rings rising from it, and the briefest hints of artwork in the space behind. The old musician holding his guitar intercepted the emptiness between. It wasn't a very good likeness, but the idea was there. She could nearly smell his cigar.

Dropping the pencil, she grabbed her cup and went back to the living room. Trying to sit, her thoughts bothered her and she went to the window. Sunny, with no breeze that she could see. All was still except for the cars moving in both directions below and a few people strolling the sidewalks, some in shorts, others in light jackets. A nice day for sight-seeing.

The lace fell back between her and the outside world. Shouldn't Aaron be waking soon?

She jumped at the ring of the phone. Hesitating, Jenna moved over to it, let it ring once more, then raised it to her ear, warily greeting the caller.

"So you are still here."

Trevor. How did he know?

"If you didn't want to see me again, you could've just said so. Remember? I like directness."

"I wasn't lying. I had planned to leave last weekend. I just … we changed our plans."

"And you didn't keep my number?" He sounded hurt.

"I have it." And why hadn't she used it?

"Oh."

She needed to say something. There was no reason to leave him with bad feelings. Nothing came out.

"Well. I'm sorry I bothered you. If you're ever in town again and feel like looking me up … but I guess you've made it clear that you won't. Safe trip, Jenna."

The click at the other end stopped her protest. She held the receiver still for a moment. Her bridge painting came to mind. She was sure burning hers.

Setting the receiver down, she took a deep breath. It was most likely for the best. She would be leaving Chicago soon to go back home. He wouldn't follow. Unlike Daniel, Trevor was a city boy and would stay that way.

λλλλ

Joan carried Aaron into the loft, leaving Jenna free to set her bags down and return for his car seat. Denise had taken care of the one plant Jenna had been told couldn't be killed, an ivy with broad leaves. It looked better than when she had left. And the windows had been opened occasionally so it didn't smell like old air. But it was different. Her home felt emptier than it had when they'd left three weeks before.

She closed the door and made her way to the kitchen while Joan settled Aaron into his playpen. "Do you want some tea?"

"Thank you, Dear, but I think I'll run over and see Denise and the kids while you're settling in. Is there anything you need from the market?"

Jenna turned after setting the microwave to warm her water. "Oh, I'll have to go pick some things up, but I think I'm okay for today. Tell Denise hello for me, and thanks. I'll give her a call later."

"I'll do that."

Her mother-in-law turned toward the door, and Jenna wandered into the studio. She barely heard the door click open, then shut, before reaching out to touch one of Daniel's paintings that had been left upon an easel. The zoo sign. She could still see him standing before it, putting the finishing touches on the canvas before turning to take her in his arms for the first time. Their first time, only a few weeks after they had met. Closing her eyes, she could feel him again, caressing her hair, loosening the pins that held it in a bun and helping it fall to her shoulders. Moving closer against her…

"Jenna?"

She jumped, turning to find her mother-in-law.

"I'm sorry. Are you alright?"

"Yeah, I … I thought you left." She tried to push the image from a moment ago out of her head.

"You were quiet on the way back, and seem … are you going to be okay here alone?"

"I'm not alone. He's still here."

Joan's eyes widened. "Jenna, I don't think I should leave you. Why don't you pack up a few more things and we'll all go back to Chicago tomorrow."

She was tempted for a moment. She could handle living in Chicago; but she couldn't leave. "No. This is my home. I think.... I'm thinking about going back to I.C.C. to go into teaching."

"Teaching art?"

Jenna nodded.

A slight smile replaced Joan's look of concern. "I can see you as an art teacher. Let me know if you need anything. Of course, you can do that in Chicago, too, or transfer there if you decide."

"Maybe ... eventually."

"Well, you will call me at Denise's if you decide you need anything tonight? The baby is tired from the trip; you should keep him in and let him get readjusted."

"Okay." She accepted a rare hug from Joan, then watched her leave.

"Well, Sweetie, just you and me again." Answering Aaron's call to be picked up, she held him tightly. "Guess we should check the machine."

The light blinked too many times in a row for Jenna to bother counting how many there were, so she hit play to begin wading through. Several from her mother and a few from Alan. He did sound worried. Her mother was annoyed. Jenna would deal with her later.

There was a message from Karla. Jenna hadn't heard from her in quite a while; since the funeral. She and her husband had moved to the East and Jenna missed her. The message was short, with a telephone number attached. Starting to dial, she paused and decided to see if anything else on the machine was pressing.

Just Alan. The newest message was strained. Maybe he was mad, but there was something else. It was too disturbing to ignore.

With determination not to let his anger provoke her, Jenna picked up the receiver and dialed his number. He had several messages waiting for him, too. When the beeping stopped, she briefly let him know she was home safe, then hesitated, and told him to stop by when he had time.

Something was definitely not right. They never left the machine unchecked for so long. She could try going over, but there wouldn't be any point if they weren't home. She would have to wait until he called back.

No. His mom. She would know if ... and Jenna hadn't talked to her in a very long time, either.

Again, she dialed. This time it was answered quickly.

"Mrs. Taylor?"

"Yes?" A slight pause. "Jenna?"

"Yes, how are you?"

"Sweetie, how are you? I've been asking Alan about you and he never says much. You know how he is. He did say you went to Chicago. Are you still there?"

"No, we just got back. I tried to call Alan and got the machine. Is everything okay? His last message…"

"Oh, you haven't heard, then. They're in St. Louis. Cheryl's mother is not doing well and you know how close they are. I tend to think she's making more of it than it is, just to have Cheryl home with her, but I could be wrong."

"What happened?"

"She hasn't taken care of her diabetes – you know she never did. But I'm sure she'll come out of it, as usual. I would imagine she's still trying to convince them to move down there."

"Alan won't move."

"No, I don't think so, though it might be better for him if he did. Not that I want him farther away, you understand, but it does tend to strain their marriage. Oh, I'm not supposed to know that, so you won't say anything?"

"Of course not." Strain their marriage? She couldn't imagine. Alan and Cheryl were so close.

"Enough of that. How was your trip?"

"Oh. It was … interesting."

"Yes, I'm sure it was. Joan is such a fascinating person. And how is the baby?"

"Wonderful; still easy."

"And growing fast, I'm sure. You'll have to bring him over sometime and we'll sit and chat."

Jenna grinned. "I'd like that."

They agreed to meet on Sunday afternoon, both excited about the prospect.

Leaning back into her rocking chair, teacup in hand, Jenna felt a bit of peace. An afternoon with the Taylors was long overdue. It would only be missing Alan. "*Strain their marriage…*" Had her friend been hiding this from her on purpose? Or maybe she had been too caught up in herself to notice his troubles. That couldn't go on. He was still her best friend.

Sixteen

Glancing at her parents' house, Jenna pushed it out of her thoughts and turned her car into the driveway across the street. She pulled in behind their silver Ford, leaving the space to the side for Alan's car. Silly, she supposed, since he wouldn't be there. But it had been his spot for so long, she didn't feel the need to intrude.

The wind chilled her as she opened the car door. Fighting the gusts, she pushed hair back out of her face and took a moment to again admire the old house. She had always loved it, not only because of its occupants, but because it was … charming. The spaces were well-proportioned and looked as though they had been planned for both friendliness and privacy, whichever was needed. The girls had fussed about it looking too old and being too drafty. To Jenna, it simply looked like a real home.

A stir at the window caught her attention. Not more than two seconds later, Carrie bounded from the front door.

Holding her hair out of her eyes with one hand, she pushed the seat forward to retrieve her son. She didn't have time to pull him out before being descended upon.

"Jenna! Mom said you were coming, but I didn't quite dare believe it! It's been so long! Oh, let me take him!"

Handing Aaron to the little girl who had grown enough to tower over her, Jenna grabbed the diaper bag and pushed the door closed. "Yes, it really has been too long. How's school going?"

"Oh, college is SO much better than high school! Jenna, he's just precious. You have to let me baby-sit for you sometimes."

"Careful, I might take you up on that." She grinned and followed Alan's sister to the door.

The sudden converging of people frightened her son and Jenna reclaimed him before they had even reached the small entranceway. Aaron refused to go to anyone else, clinging to her neck, but Jenna enjoyed the warmth of their welcomes and hugs. She could see them as her family.

The aroma of baked chicken forced the realization that she hadn't bothered with breakfast or lunch. Suddenly, she was famished. Possibly, it was mental; the thought of Janice Taylor's cooking would give anyone hunger pangs.

Settling into the living room, Jenna studied the group. The girls had switched roles from when they were children. Carrie talked incessantly, interrupted occasionally by her parents. Amber had grown into a very mature young woman. The light freckles she'd hated had all but disappeared, and her straight hair fell most of the way down her back. The man she introduced as her fiancé was also quiet, though friendly. A banker. Jenna never would have guessed that Amber would find her match in a banker.

They had met in a theatre class two years before. He wrote plays. Interesting combination. Amber had graduated, not exactly with honors, but with determination. She had no interest in acting, though her fiancé credited her as having the talent for it. She wanted to start with backstage production and move up to directing and producing. Jenna decided she wouldn't be at all surprised to see Amber's name on a film sometime in the future.

Time flew, dinner was wonderful, and the descending dusk caught her unaware. Aaron had finally relaxed and spent quite a bit of time with Carrie holding or chasing him. Amber didn't have as much luck.

Eventually, Jenna stole away to find the restroom.

Coming out, she stopped at Alan's old room, which had been turned into a den. She stepped inside cautiously. His aura was still present, with a few pictures and a couple of small trophies he had left behind that had never been taken down not quite matching the room's generally soft feel. There was also a large box on one of the shelves marked with his name. Apparently, more keepsakes he had left.

She checked back to see if she was missed yet, then wandered deeper into where she shouldn't have been. The lid of the box was loose, not taped down. She wondered what he'd thought okay to leave behind that his mom couldn't part with. Brushing off a slight trepidation, Jenna pulled the box onto the desk and quietly lifted the lid. She had to know, right or not.

Most was school stuff, certificates, special papers and projects, some memorabilia from baseball games and vacations ... and a large manila folder. It was familiar. Pulling it up out of the jumble, she looked inside.

Her drawings.

He hadn't thrown them out, but he also hadn't taken them.

Jenna perused each one, still not understanding why he would have wanted them in the first place. Realizing too much time had passed, she slipped them back into the box and returned it to the shelf. Somehow, it satisfied her that he couldn't throw them away.

λλλλ

Shivering, she hurried to the door of her building, cuddling Aaron into her for warmth. It felt like snow, though it was only October. The Taylors had invited her to join them for Thanksgiving, if she didn't have other plans. She didn't have, though Denise would most likely invite her, as she had every year. It would be hard to go there without her husband.

Watching the steps around her wrapped-up baby was difficult in the dimly lit stairwell. She wasn't out after dark often; it was too quiet.

Nearly to the top, she stopped suddenly at the sound of feet and a presence above her.

"Jenna?"

Her wide eyes found her friend.

"I got your message. I didn't figure you'd be out so late."

"Alan. You scared me." Breathing again, she continued up the stairs and went past him to her door, digging for her keys.

"How was Chicago?"

What was wrong with her? He had obviously just come from his in-laws and she hadn't even asked.... "Oh." She turned the key, then faced him. "How's Cheryl's mom? Is she okay?"

"Nothing serious. How did you know?"

"Your mom. When I got your message then called and didn't find you.... Is everything okay?"

He took a deep breath, studying her eyes. "Maybe we should go in. It's too cold out here for Aaron."

Jenna nodded and led him into her house. Attempting to avoid the conversation she didn't want to have, she went to set her son in his playpen and pulled his coat off. "Do you want something to drink? I can make coffee."

"That sounds good. I'll help you make it."

"No. I'm fine. Have a seat; I'll be right there."

Alan ignored her, coming to her side soon enough to reach the coffee she would have had to stand on her toes to grasp. She didn't drink it very often, but Alan did. And he looked like he could use it.

After silently working together, they stood in the kitchen waiting for the brewing coffee. Jenna did like the smell of it, more than the taste.

"So her mom's okay, then? And Cheryl isn't too worried?"

"As okay as ever. And no, I don't think she is. But she stayed in St. Louis ... with the kids."

"She what?" Jenna thought of Janice Taylor's comment, about the strain...

"That's where she wants to be and this was just an excuse to get there. I'm in the middle of a very large contract at the moment and she kept complaining about me being gone so often ... and suddenly her mom was very sick."

"She lied? That doesn't sound like her."

"No. I think her mom just gave her an excuse. She does tend to choose convenient times to not feel well." He leaned back into the counter, pushing his palms against the edge, his elbows bent behind him. "I told her I had to get back, that we'd return soon and stay longer when I could afford the time away."

"And she refused to leave?"

He shook his head. "No. She would've come back if I'd pushed it. But I didn't want that kind of tension."

"But Alan ... you couldn't have stayed? Just a couple more days? If she's been missing you, you don't want to be away from her now."

"Jenna...." He caught himself, then looked away. "So how was Chicago? You haven't told me much."

He was done talking about himself; it was more than he had in a long time.

She turned to check on the coffee. Not done yet. The machine was much too slow.

"Did you go to any shows?"

She raised her eyebrows. He had to know better. "No. I'm not interested in shows anymore."

"Jen, I meant theatre. Doesn't Joan usually take you to one?"

"Oh. No, we didn't.... She didn't even bring it up. Because I said I wouldn't leave Aaron with a sitter, I suppose."

"So what did you do?"

Filling her lungs to help her relax, Jenna avoided his eyes. "Nothing much, really. I stayed in a lot, had lunch with Joan a few times and sat through some of her office work, did some reading, wandered the Loop. Nothing much."

"Why did you stay the extra week?"

He knew there was more, but she wasn't about to admit it. "This weekend was better for Joan to take off from work. I told Cheryl that over the phone."

"Yeah, she told me what you said. I want to know the real reason."

"What do you mean?"

"Jen, I talked to you, remember? You were ready to leave. What changed your mind?"

She turned again. It was close enough to ready. Grabbing two cups from the cabinet above, she scooped sugar and cream into one, leaving the other empty. Dark liquid was still dripping slowly into the decanter. She grasped the handle and waited. The heat felt good next to her cold fingers.

Aaron fussed at her. He was likely ready to eat and get to bed. It had been a long weekend.

Alan set a hand over hers. "I'll get the coffee."

She nodded, pulling away from him to go to her son. He was hungry. Well, a receiving blanket would have to work; she couldn't make him wait. And she didn't expect Alan would leave anytime soon.

Settling into the sofa, she thanked her friend for moving the little side table to where she could reach her cup. Aaron didn't care if she had company. He ate just fine, and a little too noisily.

"Did he ever start sleeping there?"

Maybe he was dropping the earlier subject. She hoped. "Yeah, fairly well. But I think he's glad to be home."

"Are you?"

Finally meeting his eyes, she grinned softly. "Yeah. I missed you, even with your questions."

He chuckled. "Guess I am doing the third degree thing again. I just want to make sure you're okay."

"Well, can I tell you something?"

"Anything."

"I did something I shouldn't have."

"You? I can't imagine." His eyes sparkled.

"Funny." She helped her son readjust. "I had dinner with your family today. That's where I was."

"Did you? I'm sure they enjoyed that. But why shouldn't you have?"

"Oh, it's something I did while I was there. I … snooped."

Alan laughed. "Snooped? Like there's anything there you haven't already seen?"

"Well … no, but … you kept the drawings. Why?"

His face softened, thoughtful, but not upset. "You went through my box. Why?"

How could she answer? She really had no idea why. "I … I don't know. I've just … been thinking … about the past … about … how you wouldn't let me get rid of them. I've never really known why it mattered so much. I guess I just wanted to know what was important enough to you to be worth keeping, but not important enough to take with you."

His head lowered, dropping toward the half empty cup he held in both hands between his knees. "It's not that they weren't important enough to take with me, Jenna. That box is full of things I had in my apartment that I didn't want to get rid of but didn't want to have to share when I got married. So I took them back home for safe-keeping." He looked at her again. "The drawings especially. They remind me of how we used to be when you did them. Best friends, with my hopes still intact about us eventually being more than that. No, they aren't your best work, but they are you."

"I should have fallen in love with you, Alan. It would've made things so much easier."

"You can't help that you didn't."

She leaned up just enough to grasp her cup. It should be tepid by now. Jenna took a sip. Not sweet enough, but it didn't matter. She didn't really want it.

"I should go."

She nodded, but he didn't move. Aaron did. Jenna covered herself and lifted him to rub his back. And Alan stayed where he was, watching her.

"Do you mind if I don't go?"

"I was hoping you wouldn't. This place is so quiet after he goes to bed." She hadn't meant to be suggestive and knew she should ask him to leave. This was too dangerous, with Cheryl out of town and Alan disappointed in how things were between them. And she wanted company. She wanted him to stay and talk to her.

They chatted more easily – about old times – while Aaron finished eating. He fell asleep as soon as he was full; at least Jenna hoped he was full so he wouldn't wake during the night to finish.

She got up to change him and laid him in his crib. As she turned, Alan was behind her.

Very softly, he touched her hair, her shoulder. Her eyes followed, but she didn't object. She did miss…

"I have to go now." He suddenly stepped back, moving quickly to reclaim his coat and head to the door.

"Alan?"

He turned, the doorknob twisting in his fingers. "I have to go out to a site tomorrow. I know it's cold, but…"

"I'd love to go."

She went to her rocking chair. Few stars penetrated the blackness, clouds she couldn't see blocking all but the brightest from her sight. Alan. What was she going to do about him? From the time she had realized he was interested, she'd done her best to discourage it, despite her mother constantly trying to push him at her. It had seemed to work, mostly. Until Daniel. Until Alan could see she was serious about someone else. He had not given up easily, trying to convince her she was too young, that he wasn't right for her. It had only made her start keeping more distance from her friend. Jenna didn't want Alan to object. Her parents had made enough trouble about it. Alan was supposed to stand beside her, support her, against her parents. She never would have expected him to take their side.

Especially when she had found she was pregnant. At seventeen.

The shock had worn off, not quickly, replaced by uncertainty, fear. The news was easier on Daniel than it had been on her. He had very bravely stood up to her parents and insisted they were getting married. He didn't ask Jenna. Her parents hadn't pressed charges because they didn't want the publicity, but also wouldn't give permission for marriage before eighteen. So they had waited only until she was eighteen and she had lived with the Taylors until then.

Now and then it had bothered her that Daniel assumed she would marry him. But what other options did she have? Her parents would never let her stay there, unmarried with a child. And she didn't want to be a single parent. Besides, she loved Daniel. She wanted to be with him. He had to have known that she would want him to marry her, to help her take care of their child.

Living in Alan's home during that time had been extremely uncomfortable. He had tried to talk her out of the marriage.

"Jenna, you don't have to do this."

"Alan...."

"Before you say anything more, I have to tell you.... I kept hoping you would see...." He moved closer, taking her hand. They were in his room, sitting on his bed. The door was open, but just barely.

"Jen, do you honestly not know how I feel about you? I haven't pushed because I know your mom drives you crazy with the idea of us being together, but, that is what I want. This ... artist ... you don't owe him anything just because.... I hate that you've been with him, Jen. I'm not going to lie. But I can get over it. You don't have to marry him. I have job offers already. I'll take the best-paying one and we can get a small apartment until I can do better."

"No. Alan, don't."

"Marry me, Jen. Not because you have to – because you want to. I've always loved you. We're best friends. We understand each other..."

"No." She bolted.

He caught up, taking her arm.

"Alan, I'm sorry. I know how you feel – I have for a while. But I don't.... I can't.... I'm sorry. I love Daniel. We were already planning to move in together..."

"You can't." Alan touched her hair, her shoulder. "You can't love him; you hardly know him."

"That's not true. All the times I've said I was with Karla recently ... I've..."

He backed up suddenly, like she was a disease.

"I'm sorry. I didn't want to lie to you, but ... Alan, it was the only way. They wouldn't have let me see him..."

"And they would've been right. Look what he's done to you. He's just completely messed up your life. This isn't you, Jen. You don't sneak around. You don't lie. You don't..."

"Sleep with someone I love?"

He shook his head. "You only think you love him because he wants you; he gives you attention you need. That's not enough. You're not old enough..."

"Stop it! You're only doing this because you're jealous! I AM going to marry him because I DO love him. And I don't need

you acting like my parents!" She hurried from his room, not stopping to answer his mom. He could tell her if he wanted to. She could think whatever she wanted to think. It wouldn't change anything. Nothing would change anything now. Her path was set.

Seventeen

"Joan called while you were in the shower."

"You didn't answer it?" Jenna picked up her son and turned at her friend's silence. "Alan?"

"Does it matter?"

Yes, it mattered. He knew it did. "What did you tell her?"

"Why does it matter, Jen?"

She stared. Was he purposely annoying her?

"You know, we've spent the last three days together and you still haven't told me anything about Chicago." Alan followed her with his eyes while she moved closer to settle in her chair. With a leg propped over the other, lolling on the couch, he looked entirely too comfortable in her home. "What's going on?"

Three days. Of casual friendship, as it should be. Why was he bringing this up again? "There's nothing going on. I don't know what you want to hear." She gently fought her son off of trying to eat. It was time for him to start weaning off of her.

"Trevor stopped by her place asking for your phone number. She wanted to know if she should give it to him. So, you made a new friend? Or is he an old acquaintance?"

Suddenly, she resented his attitude. What the hell business did he have giving her the third degree about … Trevor. He wanted her phone number? She hid her face by going to the kitchen for a bottle. Her son wasn't taking it well yet, but this was a good time to try again.

Alan followed. "He's why you stayed an extra week. Is that what the silence has been about?"

"It's not like that." Jenna fumbled with trying to mix the formula, still holding the active six-and-a-half-month-old.

Alan took him without asking. "What is it like? Why didn't you say anything?"

"There's nothing to say." She shook the bottle well and set it in the microwave. The stove took too long.

"Then why does he want your number? And why didn't you give it to him while you were there?"

"I don't know. And he didn't ask for it."

"Jen?"

"Alan, I really don't want to do this with you, okay? Can you leave it alone?" The beeping gave her an excuse to avoid the hurt look, and she replaced the top, shaking the bottle gently and testing it on her wrist. Her son reached for it.

She took him from her friend and returned to her chair.

Alan stayed still a moment before heading to the door. "I told Joan you were in the shower and would call her back. See you later, Jen."

She didn't try to stop him. Let him pout if he wanted; it wasn't her concern. She had the right to see anyone she wanted to see. She was free now, it wasn't wrong to…

Free. Was she honestly starting to feel free?

Obviously not, or she wouldn't be trying to hide Trevor from Alan, and Alan from Joan. Why did she care? Her parents hadn't stopped her. Why should anyone else?

He wanted her number. Why? Hadn't she ticked him off enough to discourage him? A flicker of a thought said she didn't want him discouraged; she wanted Joan to give him her number. Maybe he would see her again the next time she was in Chicago.

λλλλ

Alan didn't stop by the following day. And Trevor didn't call. She had yet to find the nerve to return Joan's call and have to explain why he wanted it. How much had he told her?

She spent her free time doodling, and painting. Damn. She had left her sketches in the book at Joan's, including the one of Trevor's art gallery, as he called it, and some quick drawings of the buildings they had seen together. If her mother-in-law had found it, she would have a lot of questions. Well, it didn't matter. Jenna could think of something when the time came.

She started sketching the gallery onto a large canvas. The knotted table. The old musician with smoke curling up around him. The artwork in the background. Her fingers took over, remembering the scene vividly. Jenna refused to let herself think. Thinking messed her up. Her mind's eye led her, searching for details. Then she stopped.

Dropping her brush into the turpentine, Jenna walked over to the window. She didn't see the empty tree branches. She saw water … and buildings. Beautiful structures, with her tour guide's voice emphasizing lines and styles. With seagulls calling out and fingers brushing her cheek. She should have called him that last week. They could have seen more, done more … talked about … anything. He hadn't done more than touch her lightly, casually. Somehow, it was more intriguing to her than if he had attempted a kiss. That was why she hadn't called. He scared her.

λλλλ

Searching the pantry, Jenna decided she would have to go out. The only candy left over from Halloween was baby lollypops, with the hooped handles. She needed cookies … or chocolate … something. Maybe some real food to go with it.

Aaron had loved the excitement of the children running up to ask for candy. Jenna had set up in front of their apartment building again this year, which she and Daniel had always done to keep the kids from having to walk up the stairs. Rain threatened but luckily had given all of the trick-or-treaters a break and held off until later in the night. Jenna had even chatted with one of the downstairs neighbors who sat outside with them for a while. An elderly man, he said he appreciated how quiet she kept her apartment. They never heard anything from their ceiling. He was a retired factory worker; had no idea who her husband was or why they had kept to themselves. He had offered her assistance if she ever needed it before escaping the chill of the wet breeze.

Mid-November already. She hadn't talked to her neighbor again since, but hadn't been out much. No visits from Alan, though he had called a couple of times just to check in. Cheryl and the children were home from St. Louis. Jenna hoped they were all doing well. Alan didn't say.

She rubbed a hand back through her hair. It would have to be washed before she could go out. Pushing the playpen close to the bathroom door, she gave Aaron his favorite toys and asked him to give her five minutes for a shower. He smiled. She never would have imagined a baby being so easy.

With the door partly open, she could hear him babbling to himself. It would be harder to find five minutes for a shower as he got older, without someone to keep him out of trouble. The playpen wouldn't hold him forever.

Drying herself, she was surprised by a knock on the door. Jenna slipped into her robe and rubbed her son's head, in no rush. It was most likely a salesman and she could ignore him.

The peephole disfigured Alan's face. She supposed he had finally forgiven her. Pulling the garment tighter, she opened the door.

"Hey, Jenna. I just wanted to let you know I'm on my way out of town."

"Going back to St. Louis?"

"Yeah. We're staying through Thanksgiving. Mom says you're welcome to spend the day with them, or any other day."

"Denise wants us there again."

He nodded. "I figured, but she asked me to remind you that you're invited."

"Thanks."

They stood, both waiting, until Alan began to leave.

"Alan, he's a painter." She continued quietly when he turned back. "We spent a couple of days sight-seeing. I started enjoying the art world again and it was uncomfortable. I just didn't want to talk about it."

He studied her face. "Has he called?"

Jenna shook her head. "I never gave Joan the okay. I couldn't even call her."

"You know, one day, Jen, you'll have to stop running. If you like him, you'll have to face that, regardless of what the rest of us think. It's your life." He leaned in to kiss her cheek. "Have a nice Thanksgiving, Jenna. I'll call when I get back."

She returned the sentiment, told him to drive carefully, and closed the door.

Aaron wanted out.

"Okay, Baby." Crossing the room, she was increasingly confused by Alan's remarks. *"If you like him, you'll have to face that...."* Have to face it? The rest of us? He had mentioned his mom. Had he been talking to her about it? About what? He really didn't know anything. So she'd met a painter. What was new about that? There were always artists in Joan's circle. Is that why he'd been so hesitant about her going to Chicago in the first place?

She took her son out of his crib. He wanted down. That was fine. He could explore while she made some mint tea.

"You'll have to face that." Why was he making it such a big deal? It wasn't a big deal. She and Trevor were only friends – not even friends, just acquaintances ... fellow art lovers ... nothing.... She pulled the cup from the microwave, dropped in the tea bag, and wandered over to her painting. It wasn't quite finished. The

artwork in the background had just a hint of shape. They needed to be brought to life, to be completed.

Picking up a tube of paint, she rolled it between her fingers and set it back down. Not today. She couldn't finish it today.

Going back to pull the bag from the cup and stir in just a touch of sugar, she stood watching her son while sipping carefully. Trevor had been great with him. Alan rarely acknowledged his presence. She supposed he reminded him of Daniel, and no matter what he said, her friend had not liked her husband. He wouldn't like Trevor, either. He was even more … the artist type – living on his own schedule, making his own rules, obligated to no one. And he sure looked more the part, with his baggy shirts and long hair.… She pulled herself quickly away from her thoughts.

The radio distracted her for a moment, taking her to a faraway beach where young people were running around playing volleyball and walking through the waves. She still loved the Beach Boys. Her mom had called it too simple. Maybe it was. But it was fun and light-hearted. She needed that. She always had.

Aaron looked up at her and smiled when she sang along. He liked the fun music, too.

Going back into the studio, Jenna sat at the desk and looked through her recent scribbles. The ship caught her eye. It wasn't the Spirit of Peoria. It was the architecture tour boat, still docked. She wondered if she could put it in paint well enough to be worth using a canvas. If not, she could always gesso over it.

Moving "The Gallery" from her easel, she chose her starting colors and began to wash in the blue background of the sky, a light airy color in the middle of the canvas that deepened as the brush rose higher. She wasn't sure whether or not there had been clouds that day but wanted a few wisps for variation. With a technique she had seen Daniel use, Jenna daubed the white and brushed it in. Yes, they looked like clouds. Cumulous.

She didn't stop until her son interrupted.

Her tea was cold, mostly untouched, and her feet ached slightly when she sat to cuddle Aaron and hold his bottle. He had entertained himself for a long time; she had a good outline and quite a bit of detail on the ship. It was blurry detail, a bit surreal. But so far, she didn't think she would have to gesso over it.

The next several days brought more paintings into being; buildings she had seen and some she created in her head, shoreline images with white sails of all sizes, and a view of her studio with the large window in the background. None were finished. She wasn't sure why she kept stopping before they were done. But other ideas kept floating around in her head and taking over before the previous thoughts could take full shape. Most likely, that was why she had never really gotten anywhere. She'd never been able to keep her concentration still long enough.

Joan called to check on them and Jenna did admit to filling her time with some painting, but downplayed how much. It worked though. Her mother-in-law sounded relieved, and maybe … well, Jenna wasn't going to become one of her artists to be put on display. It was just a hobby, not for show.

She did need to go to I.C.C. and check on classes that would be starting in January. The thought of teaching was becoming more appealing. Hopefully, she would be able to make herself stick with it long enough to get her degree.

λλλλ

Denise not only invited them for Thanksgiving, she insisted. Jenna delayed getting ready as long as she could, working on one of the paintings as an excuse. She didn't want to go. Joan would be there, and Terry's parents; the same crowd as the last several years, except without Daniel. She didn't want to do Thanksgiving without her husband. But she couldn't refuse Denise.

A few minutes after eleven, and the last to arrive, Jenna apologized.

"Oh, no, it's fine. We're just sitting around chatting. Here, let me take him." Denise took Aaron, though he tried to refuse. "Take your coat off and make yourself at home. It's cold today, isn't it?"

"Yeah, it feels like it might snow."

"Feels like. You're so funny. Oh, Aaron, stop your fussing at me. You know who I am." Assuming Jenna would follow, Denise led the way into her living room, announcing their arrival.

Aaron willingly went to Joan, refusing to look at the strangers, allowing Jenna to accept the traditional welcoming glass of egg nog from her brother-in-law. She assured him she was doing fine and purposely sat next to Joan.

Conversation was forced – the omission of a family member too vivid. Jenna was mostly quiet, answering when spoken to and avoiding talk of her art, though Joan tried to approach the subject.

She was glad to get up and help Denise finish dinner, leaving Aaron with his cousins and uncle.

Gathered around the large table with her in-laws, Jenna's thoughts of escape heightened. It was too much too soon. Joan noticed and set a hand on her back. Jenna fled from the table into the nearest bathroom.

"Jenna? Can I come in?"

She wiped at her eyes, trying to compose herself before turning the knob. "Sorry, I'm fine."

"It's alright, Dear. The holidays are the hardest. Come back and sit down. No one blames you for being upset."

"I don't want to mess dinner up for everyone. Maybe I should just go. I almost didn't come."

"Of course you're not leaving." Joan wrapped an arm around her. "You can't be alone today, and you're not messing anything up. We all miss him, but he seems closer when you and Aaron are here with us."

She wiped at her eyes again, then nodded. "Okay, but I do have to leave early. I promised Mom I would stop by. She hasn't seen Aaron recently."

"Are you going to be okay to drive out there alone?"

"Yeah."

The struggle to get through the rest of dinner and a reasonable time afterwards exhausted her. But she had promised her mom. Aaron had been an excuse, of course. Jenna knew her mother didn't have much interest in her grandson. Why would she? She had never had much interest in her daughter, either, especially since Jenna had married "out of her class." A promise, though, was still a promise.

Pulling into the drive, she noted the difference between the one extra car beside her and the overflowing driveway across the street. Alan's aunts, uncles, and cousins were there, laughing and hugging, truly enjoying each others' company.

Jenna sat a moment, drawing up the courage to enter her parents' house.

She couldn't stay. The extra car had held yet another single, wealthy young man, along with his parents. It proved impossible to avoid him, as her mother kept pushing them together. Aaron didn't even deter him. The guy with the obviously fake snob accent had grown up in private schools, away from home, and believed it was the best way to raise children.

Jenna asked what the point of having children was, if you were just going to give them away, then lied and said she had accepted the Taylors' invitation.

Her mother fussed, as usual. Her father didn't bother to acknowledge that she was leaving. He hadn't even looked at his grandchild. He had barely spoken to her.

It didn't matter anymore.

She scurried across the street, cuddling Aaron close; the warmth of the Taylor house flowing through her even before Jenna alighted the stairs and became sheltered within.

She settled in easily. Aaron, tired from the day's constant commotion, drooped against her until Mrs. Taylor set a thick blanket in the library where Jenna could see him through the glass doors. He stirred when she laid him down but didn't waste energy objecting.

Gratefully accepting a slice of re-warmed pumpkin pie and a cup of hot tea, Jenna claimed a space at the casually-set table. Wooden bowls filled with mixed nuts still in their shells and whole ripe fruits were scattered amongst the pie pans. Dessert time had passed already. The remaining pans were at best half-empty, cherries and filling spilling out from under the crust, cheesecake beginning to sag from the room's heat. The pumpkin pie, only now half-empty with her piece taken from it, was always the least popular. Mrs. Taylor made it for sake of tradition only, since she and Jenna were the only ones who would eat it. Jenna wondered who the third person was this Thanksgiving. Possibly Amber's fiancé.

With most of the men absorbed in a loud football game at the far end of the room and the youngsters upstairs with their books and toys, the few women relaxing at the table reveled in semi-private conversation. Amber's beau remained beside her, alternately grasping her hand and rubbing her back. A comment he threw out, breaching the no-politics-in-socializing rule, incensed Carrie and her mother had to jump in to save a quarrel.

Mr. Taylor, passing by, stopped and took a seat as his wife asked Jenna how her day had been.

Jenna hesitated. She would rather have listened to a political argument than to relive her day, but surrendered. Telling them how Daniel's family had avoided talking about him and how she had left the table, embarrassing herself, how she had been hit on for the ten minutes she was at her parents' house, she felt her neck muscles loosen.

Her hand shook slightly when she sipped her tea.

Mr. Taylor left the table again. His wife muttered a few words meant to be comforting. Carrie, for a change, was quiet. The noise of the football game took over.

Returning, Lee Taylor set a glass of wine beside her only-nibbled-at pie. Jenna started to object. She hadn't had so much as a sip of alcohol since finding that Aaron was on his way.

"It's just enough to help you relax, then you can go back to your tea." He gave her a wink and set another glass in front of his wife.

She relented. Aaron could have a bottle tonight.

Carrie, coaxing her dad to let her have a small amount of wine also, took over the conversation and began bantering with her sister. Jenna chuckled, glad some things never changed. With the alcohol's numbing effect, she loosened enough to admit she had been painting. Talking of her trip to Chicago, omitting Trevor, she began missing the whole adventure.

A noise at the doorway caught her attention.

Carrie bounded to the hall, seeing her brother, and nearly knocked him over with a hug. "What are you doing here!? Where are Cheryl and the kids?"

Jenna watched Alan's avoidance while pulling out of his coat. He used the snow as an excuse, the forecast predicting five to seven inches overnight and more in the following days. He said, glancing occasionally toward Jenna, that he had an important meeting on Saturday that he couldn't afford to miss. Cheryl had decided to stay with her family.

He excused himself to use the phone in the kitchen to let her know he made it okay. Returning in no more than two minutes, Alan again looked at Jenna.

His mom interrupted, offering pie and coffee. The group watching the game used a commercial to chat with him. Finally, he sank into the chair that Carrie had temporarily abandoned beside Jenna, forcing his sister to move down a space when she followed him.

"I thought you would be at Denise's." He thanked his mom for the dessert she set in front of him.

"I was." Jenna nervously took another swallow of her wine, now two-thirds empty. She noticed him glance over his coffee cup. "I also went over to Mom's for a few minutes. That was all I could handle. She tried to fix me up again, so since I was out here...."

"You're planning to stay a while?" He glanced again at her wine glass.

"I really shouldn't if it's going to snow."

"Where's Aaron?"

She nodded toward the library. Alan's eyes followed.

Mention of the baby started Carrie off again and Jenna fell silent. Listening to the surrounding chatter, her brain blurred. She had barely eaten and the wine added a heavy, unseen weight to her limbs. Alan watched her intently in between talking with his family. She could feel his stare but didn't let it bother her. She was letting nothing bother her tonight.

Lee Taylor refilled her drink. Jenna objected but took a couple more sips. The relaxation it gave her was addicting. Alan's eyes pierced her skin, and he took the glass from her hand. She looked at him, closely, finding a resoluteness in his face, and she didn't argue.

"Why don't you two stay here tonight? You're both tired and it's getting late. Jenna, we'll pull out the bed in the library for you and Alan can take the couch..."

"I need to get home." Jenna heard herself arguing with Alan's mom, but wasn't sure why she felt so insistent about leaving. She continued to refuse against the Taylors' objections.

"I'll take her." Alan's voice buzzed beside her ear. "Give me your keys and I'll grab the car seat. We'll come back for your car tomorrow." He took a sip from the wine glass he had taken from her.

Jenna stared at him ... too long. She couldn't refuse; she was in no shape to drive. But...

"Jen? Where are your keys?"

Snapping out of a haze, she rose, unsteadily, to find the diaper bag. The keys.... She grasped the chair for balance. Maybe staying would be better. But she didn't want to stay. She wanted to be home, in her own bed ... in.... Forcing the thought from her mind, Jenna plodded carefully to the front hall, retrieved the keys and took them back to Alan, glad most of his relatives had left earlier.

He held her hand longer than was necessary. "Are you okay?"

"I'm fine. Tired." Maybe she was holding his too long.

"Jenna, come wrap up whatever you'll eat. We'll never finish this ourselves. Alan, go warm the truck for the baby."

Jenna followed Mrs. Taylor into the kitchen, waiting for some kind of question about Alan's touch, or about the way he had been looking at her all night. It didn't come. His mom had never questioned Jenna … about anything.

Alan met them at the front door, taking the dish and waiting while Jenna bundled herself and Aaron.

Carrie hugged her. "Bring your paintings when you come tomorrow. I want to see."

"Paintings?" Alan raised his eyebrows.

"She said she's been painting again. Make her bring something so we can see."

Jenna ignored his look and didn't answer Carrie. She hoped they would all forget.

Eighteen

Jenna watched the illuminated snowflakes fly toward the windshield then dash out of the way. Some made it; others were swept off the glass by ruthless wipers. They were beautiful, as long as they weren't threatening her. She was glad Alan had offered to take her home. He had even gone over to her parents' house to let them know Jenna would be back for the Mustang so they wouldn't worry about it still being parked in the drive. Jenna could hear her mother's brain twirling until she blocked it out.

The roads became persistently more snow-packed and neither she nor Alan attempted conversation. Jenna wondered if the driving conditions were keeping him silent, though it wasn't likely. Maybe he was afraid she would mention Cheryl. Maybe he hadn't appreciated her being at his family's home, catching him in the act of leaving his wife and kids. Or maybe he didn't like that she had been drinking. But she wasn't drunk; Jenna had never in her life been drunk. She had always remained in control, unable to imagine not doing so.

Alan finally parked in front of her two-story building. Jenna hoped the tension she could feel draining wasn't obvious when she nearly leaped from the front seat to pull her son from the back. If her friend noticed, he didn't mention it. Grabbing the food from behind his own seat, he came around and closed the door.

They would have looked like a family to any casual observer, walking side-by-side to the apartment, Aaron drowsing against his mom and Alan holding the door for her. She wasn't too proud to accept his help; it made him feel better whenever he could – whenever she would let him. Leading the way through the dark stairwell, she supposed sometimes she was too proud for her own good. Why else would she keep insisting on living alone, taking care of things mostly by herself, when so many were standing by waiting to help?

At the top of the stairs, Alan took her keys from his pocket and opened her door. She had forgotten he still had them.

Jenna brushed past him into her loft. "Do you want to come in? Or do you want to get home before the roads get any worse?"

"I want to see your paintings."

She hesitated, staring at him as he stood just outside her door. Her Chicago paintings were inside, not hidden. The gallery was propped against the wall. He would want the story behind it. "Okay." Jenna serenely welcomed the intrusion of her personal space. "Come in. Just let me get Aaron in bed."

"I'm in no hurry. Think I'll call Mom and let her know we got here, though."

She nodded while stepping out of her shoes. Her frozen toes and the cold wood beneath her feet sent her quickly to the sitting area, where she had suggested adding a large rug as soon as she'd moved in. Daniel had brought one home the next day. The few paint splotches now decorating it only added to its warmth.

Pulling Aaron out of his coat, she calmed his slight fussing. "It's okay, Baby. We're home." Laying the garment over the couch to take care of later, Jenna took him to the dressing table and quickly slipped out of her own jacket, hooking it onto one corner. Her son fussed again when she laid him down. "I know, Sweetie, just give me a minute. I'll hurry."

The baby remained fairly calm while Jenna changed him and fixed a bottle, then returned to the couch, watching Alan pick up both jackets and take them over to the coat rack. No wonder he married a neat freak.

"Can I go look?" He glanced toward the studio.

Alan seemed nearly as tired as the baby, and she couldn't refuse him. "If you have to."

The corners of his mouth raised, just barely, and he wandered into the studio, switching on another light.

Jenna watched him. He first checked the easel – a view from Joan's window, the sapling pulling the eye. It was barely started and he didn't linger there. Walking slowly along the stream of canvases propped along the wall, he didn't speak and didn't stop at any one … until reaching the gallery. He bent to see it closer and stood, grasping each side. With a large rise and fall of his shoulders, Alan turned.

"This was in Chicago."

"Yes."

His eyes fell back to the canvas, then he returned it and left the studio, lowering into the chair across from her. "So you were collecting inspiration while you were there."

Collecting inspiration? Well, not intentionally. But it had seemed to work that way. She shrugged. "I've always loved the lake and the boats."

"The buildings are a new thing for you."

"Yeah. We went on an architecture cruise. It was…"

"You and Joan?"

She caught herself. But she wanted to talk to him, to have one person who wouldn't cause her to hide anything. "No. Trevor took me."

Her friend listened silently, no judgement apparent in his face.

"He knew Daniel's work and just wanted to hang around with his wife, I would guess. The guy in the painting … one of his friends he introduced me to … the painter's wife, he called me. It's supposed to be a gallery, with his work hanging in the background. Trevor's work."

"A gallery? It looks like a bar."

"Yeah, it is, but they call it the gallery."

"Is he any good?" He continued, to answer her bewilderment. "Trevor. Is his artwork any good?"

"Oh. Well, it's abstract. I don't really get it. Maybe that's why I'm having trouble finishing the painting. It's hard to imitate something you don't understand."

Alan glanced back into the studio before continuing the questions. "And the others? Why are none of them done?"

She paused, looking herself at her canvases. "I don't really know." Her son released the bottle. He'd fallen asleep.

Instead of trying to wake him to finish, Jenna rose slowly and took him to his crib, pulling the blanket to his shoulders. She shivered and detoured to push the thermostat up a touch. Saving a few dollars wasn't worth the risk of Aaron being cold.

Alan had gone back into the studio and was bent before the gallery painting.

Jenna moved up beside him. "You don't like it."

He stood. "Well, it's dark … very different than the rest. But it's good, Jen. Very quality work." He noticed her doubt. "Honestly. It's … more mature. There's a new level there I haven't seen before."

His opinion mattered more than she wanted to admit. And she thought about telling him to leave … before the roads were blocked. "Should I make coffee?"

"Do you want me to stay that long? Or are you just changing the subject?"

He was teasing, but Jenna didn't want to answer either question. She looked away.

"Jen, this … you and I … have nothing to do with Cheryl staying in St. Louis."

"Doesn't it?"

"No more than your trip to Chicago had anything to do with us."

Her eyes touched his. "Do you think it didn't?"

Alan watched her, waiting.

Jenna didn't pull away and didn't back down. She felt him getting closer, lowering his face, brushing a hand into her hair. She stayed still, wondering how long it would take before he stopped himself, realizing he didn't want this. He pushed in closer; her heart beat faster. Jenna knew she should pull back but needed *him* to stop it this time. He had to…

His lips met hers, gently, probing to see how far she was willing to let him go. Her eyes closed involuntarily. His warmth invaded. With the wine affecting her judgement, she returned the kiss. He would stop, remember his vows and … he moved away, barely. She couldn't look at him.

"Jen?" His voice was a whisper. She could feel it on her cheek. "Why are you not pushing me away?"

"Because you have to. This time, you're the one who's married. I knew you wouldn't … you would never…"

"Don't be too sure." He pressed back into her.

She let him. She gave in to the kiss, accepting his affection, his attention, enjoying the soft caress of his strong arms holding her.

No, she couldn't. He was married. If he were free, maybe…

She broke the connection. "Go."

He held still, not moving away.

"Alan, go home."

Taking advantage of his loosening grip, Jenna pushed her hands against his chest and backed toward the door. "You have to go now. Go back to St. Louis and get your family. Or stay there with them. But you can't be here."

"Jen…."

"Don't. Please. I … I have looked up to you for so long. The thing before, while Daniel was in Chicago … I thought that was just … because I was so upset and you … you would've actually taken me away from him?"

"Yes. If I could have." There was no tone of regret or guilt in his voice. "I love you, Jen. You know that."

"Then why don't you want what's best for me? Why are you constantly pushing me? You keep urging me to paint, and I do, but … I can't finish anything with you, Alan. I told you that years ago and it's not going to change."

He inched toward her, slowly, as if she wouldn't notice. "Then why do you keep letting me get so close?"

"Because I need you. You are the only friend I still have. I let everyone else go because I had you. Even Karla stopped hanging around because she warned me … and I wouldn't believe her. Daniel's the only one you couldn't chase away, though you sure tried hard enough."

"You think I don't want what's best for you? Jen, you're a painter, but you won't let yourself be one. You should be free to stay home and paint, or wander … or travel … whatever you want to do. Daniel wasn't going to give that to you. Even after he could afford to, he was too involved with his work. I could give you that. My job is flexible, since I make the rules…."

"Then why is Cheryl in St. Louis alone?"

She had him. His cover was blown, leaving him unable to answer.

Jenna had to get him out, before he could see how much it hurt her to uncover what she had never wanted to know. This wasn't her best friend. She couldn't accept it. It was just…

"I wanted to marry *you*."

"You wanted to own me, the way you own Cheryl. But that's not me, Alan. You have what you need. Why can't you see that?"

He shook his head, moving to within arm's reach. "What I need … maybe I do. But not what I want."

"Get out."

He didn't stir.

"Please. I need you to leave now."

With a slight hesitation, Alan swerved around her to grab his coat.

She held still, facing away from him.

The latch turned.

"Goodnight, Jen."

She didn't answer. Her voice would have broken.

"You should finish the paintings."

In a movie, she could see the heroine throwing a wine glass at the door as it closed. Maybe she would have, if she'd had a wine glass handy. But it would wake the baby.

Instead, she stood where she was, not wanting to acknowledge what had just happened. Not wanting to feel like her last supporting leg had just been yanked from underneath. Minutes passed, enough for the coldness in her feet to rise and consume her body. A shiver stirred her from the self-induced hypnosis and unblocked the dam holding her tears. With a slight trembling slowing her path, Jenna found her bed and collapsed on top.

λλλλ

She awoke to Aaron's crying.

Fighting the urge to ignore the child and stay in bed, still atop her blankets, her conscience took over. He must have been awake for several minutes, as he generally called to her softly before getting so insistent.

Tense muscles pulled when she moved. She was cold. Fussing at herself for being too stupid to even crawl underneath the covers, Jenna ran a hand through her hair to push it from her face and rubbed at her eyes. There were most likely bags underneath. So, she wouldn't go out today. What did it matter?

While feeding Aaron, the couch afghan wrapped around her shoulders, Jenna sat looking at her paintings. Chicago. It *had* been an inspiration. Maybe Joan was right about Jenna needing to move there, but leaving Daniel's loft was still out of the question.

Wiping away occasional tears, she thought more about the architecture tour and Trevor's voice sharing his love and knowledge freely. His fingers brushing her cheek. She wanted to see him again, just to chat and walk together. He could be a good friend, if he would settle for that. Maybe he could even help her understand abstract art. But he would push for more, too. She needed a female friend; no more males.

Carrie would come over, she assumed. Alan's sister? No. Jenna wouldn't be able to talk candidly to her. Karla was too far away. Who did that leave? No one, as she had told Alan; there was no one else.

Aaron occupied most of her day, patient enough to let her cling to him too often, smiling as if knowing she needed to feel better. The radio helped entertain them both. During his nap, she searched for a book she hadn't read. It didn't take long with very little storage room in the loft. She generally picked novels up from the library instead of buying them. This one she'd had for years and hadn't bothered reading yet. A romance; not something she chose often. Vaguely remembering that she had saved it just in case the mood struck, Jenna took it over to the oak rocking chair with a cup of tea.

Night descended quietly. She set Aaron in his crib, stood watching him for several minutes, then wandered into the studio. Standing before her most current canvas, Jenna shook her head. She couldn't pick up the brush. Alan's voice echoed in her head. *"You should finish the paintings."* The hell with him.

Quickly gathering the canvases along the wall, she pushed them into the supply closet, in the back corner. She wanted no more to do with art. Too tired to pack everything else away, Jenna ignored it and went back to her book.

λλλλ

The next morning, while waiting on her coffee, Jenna threw all of the art supplies into a box, stuck it onto one of the shelves, pushed the drawing table against the wall and contemplated how to best use the open space. Possibly a tall divider that would create a temporary nursery, or two or three together. She could buy colorful patterned sheets to tack to the inside, giving Aaron a more cheerful atmosphere, or just paint a colorful scene on them. No, the sheets would work better and be easier to remove to use elsewhere at a later time.

Since there was no real line separating the space, only the backs of the chairs and the rug marking the living area, she could extend it, pushing it closer to the large windows.

Finding the perfect sheets on one of their rare days out, Jenna stopped to look at curtains. The loft would look more like a home with some kind of a window treatment. Lace, to soften it without cutting out the light. A salesman was happy to point out that the set she was considering had a tablecloth to match, completely washable sturdy lace that could cover a plain-colored cloth or stand alone to show the beauty of the wood.

"Thanks, but I don't have a dining table."

He raised his eyebrows. “You’re just starting out then, I take it.”

She contemplated his question. He was looking at Aaron, judging her. “No. Just starting again.”

He nodded. She didn’t care what he was thinking. It was odd not to have a dining table, she supposed. And she did like the pattern of the lace.

“I need six valances and two panels.”

“Six and two?”

She thought quickly in her head, double-checking. Six valances would cover the top of the three large windows with plenty of folds, then meet one panel at each end to frame the sides. “Yes.”

“And the tablecloth?”

“Yes. I suppose I’ll be able to find a table to go with it.”

“Very well. Can I show you anything else?”

Jenna chuckled. “No, I’m taking baby steps for now.”

Nineteen

"You know, he's interested in being more than your friend."

Jenna raised her eyes to Daniel's.

"The landscape engineer. He wants more from you than friendship."

Risking another slight rebuff about moving, she turned her head to see him better. Maybe getting the two men together hadn't been such a good idea. Jenna had convinced Alan to go with her to the art show at Illinois Central two days earlier. Daniel was showing his work there and had invited her, but she hadn't told Alan that. Her friend had no idea they had seen each other more than the one time in his art class.

She was glad Daniel hadn't mentioned the invitation, or that she had modeled for him several times, always in public places, or that she'd had lunch with him more than once. Alan had caught the way the other man smiled at her when they had bumped into each other at the show. He was suspicious of Daniel's intents, but so far knew nothing of Jenna's. She wondered how long she would be able to hide it. She didn't want to deal with the fussing that would come with her refusal to stop seeing him. The modeling didn't matter. Being with Daniel mattered.

Perched atop a weathered picnic table in the city's park, arms around her knees, Jenna watched him set his charcoal and newsprint pad down and walk up to her.

He focused intensely on her eyes. "You already know he wants more than friendship?"

"Yes."

His eyes lowered a moment. A breath brought them back to hers. "Are you involved with him?"

During all of their time together, Jenna had watched carefully for a sign, anything that might tell her that Daniel could be interested in her as more than a model. She had hoped. She had even stayed up at night wondering, but so far, was never sure.

She shook her head. "He's my friend. I don't want it to be more than that."

"He does."

"I know. I haven't.... I just avoid that subject. He has to know that I don't...."

"You're sure you don't?"

"Yes. I never have."

A slight grin highlighted the sparkle in his eyes. "Good. I don't get involved with anyone even partly attached."

Involved?

Jenna had to force her breathing when he slid up onto the table, his leg brushing hers, facing the opposite direction so he was staring into her eyes. The breeze played with a few wisps of his hair. She wished it were her fingers instead of the breeze. Involved. How involved did he intend to get?

"And what about me?" Daniel studied her face as though still caught up in the sketch, trying to capture every detail. "Do I have a chance of being more than your friend?"

"You want more?"

"Yes, Jenna. I want more." Eyes burning into her skin, Daniel raised a hand to her face, studying it now with his fingers. Finally brushing them back through her hair, he cupped her head into his warm palm and pulled her closer.

His kiss sent a shiver down through her body to her toes. Still, she didn't move. She felt frozen, with a flame running through the middle, melting her from within. Parting her lips, Jenna accepted him.

Young voices were in the distance – children swinging or sliding ... something. Their parents would likely object to the couple making out on the park's picnic table. Jenna didn't care. He wanted more. How much more wasn't a concern at the moment.

Losing the touch of his lips, Jenna opened her eyes, wanting to see his. They were still closed. Daniel's chest expanded, then relaxed.

Finally, his eyelids parted, revealing the soul her world now wrapped around. His fingers returned to her face, touching her skin like a blind man trying to see her in a light most people never would. They rested on her lips for just a moment before sliding underneath her chin. "You are what I've been waiting for." The words were breathy, full. They clutched her heart.

Breaking out of the sketch pose, Jenna threw both arms around his shoulders, clinging, afraid to fall. She pushed her mouth back against his, hoping her aggression wouldn't turn him away, startling herself. Never had she been so openly affectionate in public. To be honest, she had never been so openly affectionate … anywhere, with anyone. He had shattered her natural defenses, allowing her to connect more with herself than she ever had before.

Judging from his gaze when their eyes met again, Jenna couldn't see that Daniel was at all bothered by her response. He stroked her skin as skillfully as he did his paintings, making her long to be alone with him, if only for a few minutes.

"I suppose we should finish the sketch so you can get home."

Squeezing her eyelids to block out the memory, Jenna pulled back from the window. The grayness blanketing the sky had sunk into her spirit, thwarting the work of the last week. It was nearly December now and the loft was beginning to look like a home; more hers, less Daniel's. Aaron had spent much of his energy trying to push the screens over while pawing at the red and blue sailboats and yellow ducks, until Jenna had tied them together and angled them so they couldn't move. She was pleased with the windows now highlighted with lace, though a few words she didn't want her son to learn had escaped while she'd been hammering the brackets to the wall. But overall, she felt good about the whole thing.

The wood floor needed refinishing desperately. That, she wouldn't attempt alone. Though maybe a coat of paint would work as well … off-white, to create a more open feel. And a deep purple throw rug under her living room furniture, moving the paint-spattered light brown one into the studio area. Their dark green couch would fit in well and patterned slip covers over the chairs would add some interest. A pansy print maybe – purple and green on an off-white background. She had always loved pansies.

Jenna jumped at the phone's ring.

Irritated at the intrusion, she didn't rush to answer. The machine took over. She waited. Maybe she wouldn't bother.

Cheryl's voice made Jenna pause. Alan had apparently gone to get his family. His wife wanted her to come for dinner.

Setting a hand on the receiver, she changed her mind. She didn't want to talk to Cheryl now. And she most definitely didn't want to have dinner with them. Jenna walked away and returned to stare out the window at the over-flowing river banks. Most of the snow had melted, leaving only traces of ice. Bare trees cast an intricate design, breaking the open space. The darkness of the wet branches amidst the gray sky and muddy brown water created a wonderful color scheme. She wondered how well she could imitate it. Or maybe abstract it. Use the colors more than the actual objects....

Capture the emotions the colors and lines conveyed. That's what Trevor did. He painted emotions. Daniel had provoked emotions, bending them with his brush. Trevor captured them.

λλλλ

She pulled the gallery painting out of the closet. Aaron had gone to sleep more than three hours before and Jenna needed to do the same, but Trevor's voice kept haunting her, telling her to think outside the box. She had been so rude and he was right. Her parents had no further control and neither did Alan. It was her choice; they couldn't keep standing in her way if she refused to allow it.

Trevor would be ... at work, in the bar. And she had the phone number.

Setting the painting on the table, Jenna wandered to the phone, picked up the receiver and sat, contemplating. He wouldn't want to talk to her after she had refused to let Joan give him her number. Most likely, he was flirting with some girl who was more his type. But she could at least apologize.

The telephone rang five ... six times. Maybe it was too late. How long did bars stay open?

"Hullo, you've got the Rocky Oyster."

It wasn't Trevor. Did she dare ask for him?

"Don't let the name scare you off. We're all friendly here."

"Oh, I'm sorry. I was just looking for...."

"Lady, I can barely hear you over all this racket."

Jenna paused, nearly hanging up. The bar obviously wasn't closed; she could hear laughing and music in the background, the hum of voices and occasional clink of a glass.

"Hullo?"

"Is Trevor working tonight?" She held her breath, ignoring a slight throb in her skull.

"Trevor? Oh, you mean D-day?"

"Um, yeah, I'm sorry. Is he there tonight?"

"Honey, he's always here. Hold on."

She heard the deep voice laughingly call the artist over to the phone, teasing about the caller being too lady-like to ask for him. She nearly hung up again.

"Yeah?"

Her stomach knotted. Stupid idea, calling him at work.

"What? Was this a joke?" His voice had moved away from the receiver.

"Nah, she don't talk loud enough. Tell her to yell."

A pause. "Hello?"

"Trevor, I'm sorry. I really shouldn't have called you at work."

"Jenna?"

"Yes. Do you want me to call back tomorrow, at home?"

"No! Hold on. Don't go anywhere."

She heard more laughing and Trevor's voice telling them to shut up, then the noise lightened.

"Okay, maybe I can hear you now. What's up? It's after midnight; is everything okay?"

"Well, I was just … I called … to apologize." She wrapped the cord around her fingers, entwining it into a knot.

"For what?"

Was he kidding? "I wasn't … I didn't mean to be so rude … at the gallery when … well, in general. It wasn't meant to be directed at you…."

"I know. Forget it. Are you back in Chicago yet? I tried to get your number from Joan, but she wouldn't give it to me. I guess she didn't know we'd … been sightseeing together."

"She told me. I asked her not to give it to you."

Silence.

"And I'm sorry. I just needed some time, to think. I'm still at home, but only part of me is. I keep thinking … the next time I'm in Chicago … maybe we could…."

"Do more sightseeing?"

"Yeah, or something."

Another pause. "Something … less touristy and more intimate?"

Intimate. Her stomach fluttered. The idea wasn't completely … out of the question … or undesirable.

"Guess that's not what you meant." His voice was softer, searching.

"I don't know." Her grip on the phone cord tightened. "Maybe." She would never be able to fix it. "I'd like to see more of your work. I didn't really … give you a fair chance. Maybe…."

"Come back to Chicago. I'll pick up some Chinese food and we can take it to my apartment. I have a bunch of stuff lying around there."

"I won't be back for a while. The weather is too risky to have Aaron on the roads and maybe get stuck…."

"And that would be bad? Being stuck here?"

"No, I just mean … I'm in the middle of fixing up the loft. When I get into something, I have a hard time pulling myself away."

"Okay. You need more time. I got it."

She couldn't answer, unsure she appreciated how well he understood her.

"Can I have your number? Or is that still off-limits?"

Jenna couldn't very well not give it to him, since she had been bold enough to call him at the bar. Trevor asked what time Aaron usually slept so he wouldn't wake him, then said he had to get back to work. A friendly, casual good-bye left her wanting to talk longer. There was something soothing about speaking to him.

λλλλ

Waking to a tightness in her neck, Jenna rose slowly and stretched the aching muscles. She would have to stop sleeping on the couch. It really made no sense.

Light was just beginning to filter into the room. It was too early, as late as she'd been awake, but there was no going back to sleep. Bad habit. Once she was up, rarely could she drift off again. She yawned, forcing herself up from the couch to heat her cup of water. Setting it on the microwave tray, she changed her mind. Coffee sounded better.

A strong richness soon drifted from the carafe. Biding her time, Jenna wandered into the studio, stopping at her gallery painting which she had left lying on the table. Her fingers brushed the beginning outlines of the artwork. It needed to be finished.

She backed away again.

Returning to the couch, she grabbed the remote and flipped through the channels, stopping at a home decorating show. It looked so easy. With unlimited money and trained designers, it would be. She glanced around her own home. A great candidate for a room makeover, even without professionals. Maybe this was one project she could complete.

The rumble of the old coffee pot ending its brewing cycle pulled her back to the kitchen. Dumping the water from her cup, she poured in sugar and creamer and stood waiting for the slow dripping to cease. The green vase Joan had sent home with her sat unceremoniously on the counter. While redecorating, she would have to force it to work with the pale lavender curtains and find a setting more suitable for its elegance.

Jenna let the pouring motion do the stirring and went back to the couch. Much too hot, the mug was set on the end table, nearly forgotten as soon as she pulled her legs up onto the cushions, covering them with the afghan, and let her head recline against the pillow-soft back. Dozing to the light hum of the television, she grimaced at the unwelcome ring of the phone.

Jenna sipped from her cup, waiting to hear the message. Aaron started to stir.

"Jenna? Pick up the phone."

She sat, ignoring him.

"I know you're up by now and I'll keep calling until you answer." He paused. "Jenna. This is crazy. Answer the phone."

"Damn!" She bolted, splashing the now-lukewarm coffee while banging it down on the table, and yanked the receiver to her ear. "WHAT?"

"Hello."

She seethed at his calmness. "You woke Aaron up. *What* do you want?"

"Isn't he usually awake by now?"

"No!"

"Well, I'm sorry, but you don't return my calls if I just leave a message."

She heard no actual regret in Alan's voice. "Because I *don't* want to talk to you." A surge of power swelled. Aaron began fussing for her.

"Okay, you're still mad. That's fine, but at least answer the phone so I know you're okay."

That's fine? As if she needed his permission to be mad? "Alan, I can take care of myself. Stop treating me like a child."

"Jenna, what is wrong with you? Did you just talk to your mom and decide to take it out on me again?"

She saw herself throwing another glass of wine at him, or on him. "I have to go. Aaron's fussing now that he's awake."

"Jen...."

"I don't want to talk to you right now. I'll call you … when I feel like I can. Go take care of your wife and leave me alone. Please."

A pause on the other end nearly made her reconsider. Alan was her friend….

"Jen, I'm coming over. We need to talk about this."

"No."

"I can't leave it this way. You know that."

"I won't let you in. Please, just give me some space." Another pause. "Goodbye, Alan." She quickly set the receiver down before she could hear his answer.

Aaron's fuss was a nice distraction. She didn't care that he was awake, only that Alan hadn't cared and hadn't thought about it before calling so early. They would have to go out. She couldn't handle sitting in the loft wondering if he would actually come by, or call back. Maybe she would go buy paint for the floor; Denise would watch Aaron so she could get it done without him painting his hands and knees.

λλλλ

Elbow-deep in off-white semi-gloss, Jenna stood. She hadn't realized quite how tiring it would be to paint a floor. Of course, she hadn't been satisfied to do it the easiest way, all one color with a sprayer. She had found a dark green she was sure would match the vase and had decided to accent the indentations with it before rolling over the top with the lighter color. Stroking in the green all along each crease with a fairly small brush was extremely tedious, but nearly one third of the loft was done by the time she had to stop. Denise insisted that she and Aaron stay at her house until the floor was done. Jenna couldn't argue; it would make the job easier and she wouldn't have to worry about moving furniture back to keep it safe for the baby.

The loft was beginning to remind her of an old country home. She hadn't been aiming for that. Actually, she didn't have any real direction in mind. Deciding on one thing at a time most likely wasn't the best decorating approach, but it was working so far. Something would have to be done with the walls, as well. It would come to her eventually.

She pushed the lid back onto the paint can and tapped the edges with the hammer. Heading to the kitchen to wash out the roller, she paused at the phone's interruption. Most likely Alan again. He had called twice while she'd been painting and had been ignored both times.

With a deep breath, she picked it up.

"Jenna, I was hoping you would be home. Could you come out for dinner tonight?"

Worse than Alan. "Hi, Mom. No, I really can't."

"Oh, Honey, we've barely seen you. I have your favorites in the oven so it will save you from having to cook…."

"I have plans."

"Oh? Someone we know?"

"It's not a date so don't get excited. I'm going over to Denise's."

"Oh. Well, can't you do that another night? I'm sure she will understand."

"No, I can't. She's babysitting for me while I'm painting and we're staying with her until it's done."

"Painting? I thought you had given up on that frivolity by now. You should be thinking of your future, Jenna. Come over tonight."

"I can't. My brush is drying and Denise will be holding supper if I don't hurry and shower. But thank you, maybe another night."

A quick goodbye wasn't too soon. "*That frivolity*." Her mom would have felt better if Jenna had told her what she was painting, but she had no need to try to make her feel better.

The next ring was Alan. She picked it up, briskly telling him she was busy and to stop calling her, hanging up on him for emphasis.

With the roller left to air dry over the sink, she headed into the shower, barely getting undressed before the phone rang again. Cursing, Jenna wrapped herself in a towel and stomped into the living room, grabbing the phone before the answering machine had time to start.

"STOP CALLING ME! I don't WANT to talk to you!" Starting to slam it down again, she decided to emphasize how angry she was becoming and lifted it back to her ear. A voice was there, but not Alan's.

"Jenna? Are you there?"

Trevor. Damn.

"Jenna?"

"Hi. I'm sorry. I thought it was…."

"Who? Someone's bothering you? Have you called the police?"

"No, it's … nothing, really."

"It can't be nothing if you're that upset. What's going on?"

She attempted to normalize her voice with a deep breath. It did the opposite, allowing frustrations to surface, restricting her throat.

His voice called out to her, asking simply for her to respond. But it was more. It was a beacon, pulling her mind back to Chicago, to the architecture tour, the easy conversations … the gallery….

"Jenna? Talk to me. About something else if you'd rather, but talk to me."

She wanted to be with him … walking along the pier or the city streets … anywhere….

"Jenna?"

She swallowed, forcing an answer. "Sorry. I'm here. How is work?"

He paused, then began telling her how he'd been teased about her phone call.

"I'm sorry. I won't call there again."

"No, Jenna. Call whenever you want. They have to have something to laugh about, right? Isn't that why they go to a bar?"

She didn't respond, hoping he would just keep talking, about anything. Clenching the towel tighter in her hand, Jenna settled carefully onto the edge of the chair. Her legs felt weak.

"I didn't wake Aaron, did I?"

"No. He's at Denise's. I was just getting ready to go over." Her voice was approaching normal.

"You're leaving him with a sitter now?"

"Second time. I'm painting the floor and didn't want him crawling over it."

He chuckled. "Painting the floor? Did you run out of canvas?"

Jenna felt her tension drain while telling him of her decorating. He listened patiently, whether or not he was actually interested, adding that her eclectic style would make for an interesting home. She invited him to come see if she had been successful with it when she was finished, casually, not expecting he would have any reason to come to Peoria. He didn't scoff at the idea.

They talked long enough for Jenna to start shivering. A mutual pause gave her the chance to tell him she needed to get off the phone, to shower and dress, but she didn't. Instead, she sat, holding the towel and listening to the silence on the other end.

"Well, I should let you go. I really didn't mean to hold you so long. Are you going to be late now?"

"Oh, that's okay. I'll call Denise."

"You could've kicked me off, you know."

"I guess, but…."

"You were being polite. Jenna, just tell me if I call at the wrong time."

"No. Really. I was … I'm glad you called."

"Are you okay? Can you tell me now what that was about?"

She hesitated. A part of her wanted to tell him. But she felt like too much of an idiot to be able to admit. "I just … had an argument with someone. Nothing worth talking about."

"You're okay there alone?"

"Yeah, it's nothing like that. And I'll be at Denise's overnight."

"You'll be home tomorrow?"

"I'll be here painting."

Jenna was reluctant to let him go. She held the phone a while after their good-byes, her thumb holding the connection closed before setting the receiver down and rising slowly to continue her evening.

Twenty

A light sprinkling of snow sparkling in the darkness beyond the loft's windows perfected the ambience of the evening. With her favorite holiday music in the background, Jenna added black olives to a small dish in the center of the cold cuts and cheese platter and took it over to her table. The buffet-style platters, flaunting an array of breads and cut vegetables and chips, weren't as elaborate as her sister-in-law's dinner would be the following day, but Jenna didn't have much hosting experience, or interest. She did have soft sugar cookies decorated and two cinnamon sticks simmering on the stove to scent the air. Her guests should feel the holiday spirit, whether or not she could.

She looked around her home. The floor had turned out well. Her overstuffed chair had its pansy cover – not as hard to find as she'd been afraid. And she had purchased a coordinating runner for her old coffee table, which still needed to be stripped and given new varnish. But that could be overlooked, she supposed.

After considering the matter of a dining table, she had found one unfinished at a price she could afford and had painted it the same dark green as the floor accent. The lavender lace tablecloth added a softness, pulling the eye from the curtains. Deep red silk poinsettias and bits of real mistletoe propped inside the green vase served as a centerpiece, the vase and leaves accenting the color peeking through the lavender. She hadn't bothered with a tree, not wanting to fight Aaron to keep it standing, but had found him a stocking and a baby's first Christmas ornament. The ornament, with the few others she had, hung from the curtain rods, floating just under the lace. His stocking was hooked onto the front door-knob. The gifts were stacked on the drawing table, intentionally to keep them out of reach of the nine-month-old, unintentionally adding to the décor.

Jenna checked the clock, looked around to be sure she was ready for her guests, visited with Aaron to pass time and calm her nerves, and finally set him back in his playpen to light three gold-colored taper candles standing beside the vase. She was ready when the doorbell rang.

She wasn't ready to find Trevor with Joan.

Her mother-in-law gave her a quick hug and a bottle of wine. "Something smells wonderful! I do hope you don't mind that I brought an extra guest. He had no plans and I couldn't see him spending the holiday alone. Oh, Jenna, is this the same apartment?" Joan dropped her coat onto the stand and wandered in further.

Jenna didn't mean to ignore the question but caught herself staring at the man in the doorway. How did Joan know he didn't have plans? How much had they talked? He looked nice.

"Is it okay that I'm here?" Trevor's bright green eyes sparkled.

Collecting herself, not quickly enough, she managed to answer. "Of course. Come in." She waited while he scuffed the snow off of his shoes and removed his coat, then stepped closer to take it from him. The warmth emanating from the lining penetrated her fingers.

"You didn't do all of this yourself?"

Joan's voice pulled Jenna away; she'd drifted closer to him than necessary. "Yes. It filled a lot of hours. And Denise kept Aaron now and then, so it wouldn't be impossible."

Her mother-in-law stood next to the playpen, stroking her grandson's head while studying the loft. "It's very nice, Dear. Much more comfortable for you, I'm sure."

"Daniel wouldn't like it much."

"Oh, Honey, I don't think he'd even really notice. It was just a work space to him. I kept thinking you would do something to make it livable."

"He liked it the way it was." She led Trevor into the apartment. Why had she brought Daniel up in front of him? "I have coffee made, and tea, and there's cider in the fridge. Can I get you something?"

Joan agreed to coffee while picking up the baby. Trevor insisted on helping with drinks.

He was just as at home in her kitchen as he had been in Joan's. They worked well together, only slightly brushing arms once. Again, she didn't believe it was an accident. It was nice having him there, though Daniel would probably not like that, either.

They had talked several times over the last two weeks, about decorating and his job, his art and how sometimes he wanted to paint and sometimes he didn't. How he never forced it, to the chagrin of Mrs. Covington who wanted him to produce faster. How she was nearly ready to stop backing him blaming what she thought was lack of drive. Jenna had refused to give her opinion, saying it didn't matter what she thought; he had to do what was best for him.

She poured Joan's coffee while he poured cider for her and for himself. He wasn't a coffee drinker any more than she was. Unable to think of anything to say, Jenna turned to leave the kitchen area and stopped when he touched her hand.

"You look great." Trevor's voice was barely audible, keeping the conversation discreet.

"Oh. Thank you." She pulled back, taking the coffee over to Joan. It had struck her while she had been getting ready that there wasn't much point in worrying about her appearance just for her … for Daniel's family. They had seen her at her worst. But it was Christmas Eve and her first hosted party. Her hair was in a bun, as it had been when she'd met her husband, a few loose strands slightly curling around her face. The shiny navy and green vest over her navy pants and turtleneck made her look thinner than she actually was; a trick she had learned from her mother to hide her flaws. Dark plain colors are more flattering on round figures. Not that hers was bad, just not perfect.

"You can put him down. I'm sure he's ready to wander again." Jenna pulled the steaming cup away from Aaron's reaching fingers and waited until he was off looking for trouble before handing the coffee to her mother-in-law. She gestured for her company to have a seat.

Trevor handed Jenna her glass, set his on the end table, and went to join Aaron on the floor, patiently accepting the offering of one toy after another. He was great with the baby. And Aaron enjoyed his company.

The doorbell drew her attention just as Trevor looked up to see her watching. She grinned slightly and went to welcome Denise and her family.

Opening the door, her stomach knotted. Alan. No, not now.

"Hey, Jenna. I just came by to drop off a peace offering. I know I was very out of line the other night and I've been worried…."

"I have company." She cut him off, hoping his voice hadn't carried into the room.

"Oh?" He glanced into the loft. "You fixed up the place."

"Working on it. Can we maybe do this later?"

"Alan, isn't it?" Joan had come up behind her, apparently expecting Denise and family. "I didn't realize you had invited more company, Jenna. Maybe I shouldn't have."

Alan glanced from one to the other. "No, I just barged in. I'm sorry to interrupt."

"No apology necessary. Jenna has gone all out to decorate. I'm sure she won't mind showing the place off more. Or maybe you've already seen it."

They both knew she was fishing, but Alan acted completely innocent. "No, I really haven't. It's been … a month, I think. I was just dropping something off for her."

"Well, do come see what the child has done, and totally by herself." Joan took Alan's arm, pulling him inside.

Wishing she could crawl behind her bed curtain and stay there until everyone left again, Jenna remained close to the door, allowing Joan to brag about her decorating skill, watching her introduce the two men. Trevor had stood when he saw Alan. He was holding the baby, possessively unless she was imagining things. Jenna still hung back, studying the glances. She wanted nothing to do with this exchange. They were civil, one more than the other, the differences in each glaringly obvious.

Alan finally excused himself, saying he had to get back to his family, stopping in front of Jenna to hand her a small package.

She didn't want it, whatever it was. "You really shouldn't have."

"It's nothing, Jen. Just something that looked like you."

Only because the others were staring, she took it from him, beginning to pull at the bright paper.

"No, wait 'till tomorrow. Have a nice Christmas." Alan touched a hand to her arm, gave her a quick peck on the cheek, then left with a rushed good-bye to the others.

She withdrew, taking it to the drawing table to get it out of her hands, lingering there.

"Peace offering?"

His voice had carried. Jenna turned to face Joan. "We had an argument. Guess he figures I'm still mad since I haven't answered his calls."

"Are you?"

She thought a moment. "Mad? No. I'm just … not interested in getting gifts from him."

"It must have been serious, to separate good friends for a month or so."

"Yeah, it was kind of big. And I'd rather not go into it."

Joan set a hand aside Jenna's head. "I guess this isn't the time, but if you ever need to talk.... You will always be my daughter, Jenna. And I have a lot of experience with men." She winked and went to answer the doorbell.

The smudge Alan rubbed into the evening dissipated as Jenna became immersed in her guests and playing hostess. Aaron, content to be entertained by his older cousins, and by Trevor, allowed Jenna to talk with her in-laws. Joan again suggested a move to Chicago. Terry jokingly told his mother-in-law to quit harassing his sister. Denise raved about the change in the loft and chatted freely with Trevor whenever she could pull his attention away from the children.

Trevor.

Jenna mostly avoided him, though the rest of the family treated him like ... family. She wondered if he had become a substitute, though it was hard for her to see him that way. Yes, he was an artist, like Daniel, but the similarity ended there. Their conversations had become more intimate and revealing each time. She thoroughly enjoyed talking with him.

But having him there, in Daniel's home ... in her home ... felt awkward. He kept his distance physically, sometimes simply catching her eye in a brief acknowledgement that he knew she was in the room. At times, Jenna caught herself wishing he would pull away from Aaron to visit with her. She also caught herself purposely avoiding him when he did start to approach.

He left with Joan to stay at Denise's, on her couch. Jenna half-considered offering her couch, so they would have a chance to talk, but she couldn't be quite that daring. He and Joan were only staying in town until the day after Christmas. Not long enough.

After putting Aaron in bed and cleaning up, she wandered into the studio and picked up the little box Alan had brought. With only a slight hesitation, she tore the wrapper and pulled the lid open. A gold pin, shaped like an artist's palette, with different-colored gems sparkling here and there. It was beautiful, but she didn't wear pins. Shouldn't he know that? She was twenty-four; he had know her for thirteen years. He should have noticed that she didn't bother much with jewelry, generally leaving the same pair of stud earrings in day after day instead of taking the time to change them. Another way of pushing her to be more, she assumed.

λλλλ

Fighting against the heaviness of her eyelids, Jenna realized it was early. Her walls reflected a light cast of the sun's rays, painting them a beautiful translucent, deep navy. She lay still, allowing her mind to awaken, wondering how hard it would be to imitate the effect. It was the perfect color for her loft, though maybe with a purple cast instead of navy, to go with her lavender. Her mind now fully active, Jenna rolled out from underneath her heavy blankets, pulled her robe over her shoulders to protect them from the loft's morning chill, and scuffed into the kitchen to make her tea. Warm cup in hand, she went to claim her rocker, eyes fixed on the awakening sky.

Aaron would rise soon to his first Christmas morning; not a thrilling one for him with only her as company, but there were a few toys from Santa sitting in front of the gift table. The year before had been both better and worse; the excitement of being pregnant, waiting for her son, tempered with knowing Daniel would only have a short time with him, if any. But at least Daniel had been there.

Denise's household would be roused by now, her kids clamoring about wanting to open their packages. Jenna hoped they would like what she had found for them.

Aaron stirred. She could barely see him from the oak rocking chair; his divider needed to be moved back further. Approaching nine months now, he wasn't nursing any longer. She missed it already and wondered whether she should have stopped so soon, though it did make it easier for her to leave him with a sitter when necessary. So far, she had only done that twice, but if she was going back to school.... How would she now? She couldn't possibly leave him with Cheryl, not after....

His stirring turned into a slight fuss and Jenna went to get his bottle. Well, she wasn't sure she wanted to go back to school. There had to be something else she could do. As Aaron greeted her with a huge hug and sloppy kiss, Jenna decided it didn't matter. Her current plans were already set and the future she could deal with as it came. Taking care of her baby, rocking him and seeing his satisfaction with her was enough for now.

When his tummy was full, Aaron pushed the bottle away and laid still, a chubby hand pulling softly at her hair and grabbing her mouth. He loved playing with her teeth and getting his palm tickled by her tongue. His hearty laugh always made her smile.

He bolted to sitting when the doorbell rang.

"Are you expecting company?" She chuckled at his questioning look. "Okay, let's see who it is. But if it's Alan again, I'm not opening the door."

"Ah dah."

"Door? Yeah, I heard the door. But thank you." She kissed his head and propped him against her left side. He was starting to get a bit heavy to carry around.

Jenna checked the peep hole. Trevor? Why was he here so early? Had Joan sent him so she wouldn't have to spend the morning alone?

"Ah dah." Aaron reached out and banged on the door.

There was an echoing bang in return.

The baby laughed, hitting the door again, and again came the echo.

"Okay, okay, you two will wake the neighbors." She stopped her son from banging again, then opened the door, barely.

"Good morning and Merry Christmas. Hey, Buddy."

Aaron smiled, reaching out.

"Can I come in?" Trevor's hand took Aaron's.

"I'm not dressed yet. Is Joan here?"

"Nah, it's amazing. There are actually cabs in this little city. I brought food, if that'll work again. And I can wait here if you want."

"Um ... come on in. Just don't look at me; I'm horrendous in the morning." She moved back.

Completely ignoring her request, Trevor allowed his eyes to roam her frame. He grinned.

"I told you not to look at me."

"I know, but you're wrong. You're ravishing."

She chuckled. "Okay, I already let you in; you don't have to lie."

"I don't, ever."

Jenna finally looked into his eyes. She believed him completely. "Thank you, really. But I need to change."

"No thanks needed, really." Switching a bag from one hand to the other, he slipped out of his coat and dropped it onto the rack, in the same mannerism as Joan. "Come here, Buddy, let's warm up these rolls while your mom…." He approached to take her son, then stopped, studying Jenna's face. "You don't have to change on my account, you know."

He was closer than he would have needed to be. And her uncombed hair, no makeup, and old robe didn't bother him in the slightest. Daniel would have been teasing her about looking like an old housewife. Or maybe he hadn't been teasing.

Jenna pushed hair away from her face. "I'm glad I'm not bothering you, but I'll be more comfortable dressed." She hoped her breath was okay.

His grin changed, holding something in.

"I'll be right back." She edged away, knowing he was watching her cross the room.

λλλλ

Jenna stared out the van window at the darkness. Touches of gray snow still lingered on the grass alongside the road from the light showers they'd had two days earlier. Denise's children had spent much of the day checking for new snowfall and singing "Let it Snow" in hopes of encouraging it to come. It hadn't. But Jenna had accepted Trevor's offer to drive her and Aaron home.

She had also spent more time with him at Denise's than she had the night before in the loft. He hadn't pushed it; she had. He was a great antidote to her fear of spending Christmas without Daniel. Jenna constantly found herself drawn to him. And now, in the silence of the van, even that was comforting.

She felt a kind of déjà vu when Trevor parked her van in front of the apartment building and walked in with her. Except that he insisted on carrying the baby. And that Jenna felt no hesitation in inviting him out of the biting cold and into her home.

While she busied herself pulling Aaron from his coat and changing him into pajamas, Jenna half-watched Trevor walk around the studio, studying Daniel's sketches. He had looked at them briefly the night before but hadn't remarked on them. In fact, he had only mentioned art when Joan or Denise had pushed the issue, appearing more interested in his bartending job than in his painting. Curious man.

"So, I really expected to see some of your work displayed."

Jenna set Aaron down to find his toys and wandered closer to her guest. "Why?"

"Why are you not proud of your artwork?" He turned, his eyes penetrated hers.

"It isn't anything. It's just a hobby."

"I don't believe that's true, Jenna. I saw the drawings you left at Joan's."

She averted her face. If he saw them.... The gallery sketch was there; along with a few of the buildings he had shown her.

"I was tempted to take the one of old George in to the gallery. I know he'd get a real kick out of you thinking he was worth drawing."

Her cheeks grew warm.

"Joan showed me. After that phone call when you were so upset, I went over to talk to her. Maybe I shouldn't have, but it worried me and I thought maybe she could ... have Denise...."

Jenna looked up at him. She knew he had been talking to Joan, or he wouldn't be here now. But she had never expected him to admit it. "How much did you say?"

"I told her I enjoyed your company. She figured out that we'd been seeing each other, casually. It doesn't seem to bother her."

"She wants me to move to Chicago. Did she ask you to help her convince me?"

"Yes."

Jenna turned. So that's why he was there; just one more person trying to tell her what she should be doing with her life.

"But I told her I couldn't do that. I wouldn't be much of a friend if I tried to talk you into something you weren't sure you wanted. And since you're spending so much time redecorating, it must not be what you want."

"I don't want to leave him."

"Leave who? The friend you were yelling at?"

"No. Daniel. If I leave his home ... it would be like leaving him. And I can't do that."

"No? Then why did you redo the loft into something you don't think he'd like?"

She whirled back to argue ... and stopped. She couldn't argue. She had almost completely changed Daniel's studio until it wasn't his anymore, painting him farther out of her life.

Trevor moved in. He touched her cheek, lightly caressing it with his thumb. "You know, it doesn't matter what Joan wants, or what the friend you were yelling at wants. And it sure as hell doesn't matter what I want. As you told me about my art, do what's best for you. Stay here, move to Chicago, run back and forth. Hell, move to Alaska if it strikes you. Don't let them push you. Mourn your husband as long as you need to, Jenna. But you have my number if you want to talk."

She stared. He could act very mature when he decided.

"I should go. It's been a long day and I know you have to be tired. But you did great today, trying to act like you were in the Christmas spirit." He grinned and moved away.

She called a taxi while he picked up Aaron to say good-bye, hung back while Trevor talked to her son, then walked him to the door and took the baby.

Trevor slipped into his coat and pulled a round tube from the pocket. "Oh, I guess I should give this to you while it's still Christmas."

Jenna hesitated. She felt funny accepting a gift when she didn't have one to return.

"It's not wrapped; I never seem to get that done. But I want you to have this." He pulled the cap off one end and shook the tube to dump out the contents. Propping the empty container under his arm, he carefully unrolled the slightly yellowed paper.

Her heart nearly stopped. It was Daniel's. A drawing of her he had done before their marriage, again with the suggestion that she was unclothed.

Finally, she collected her thoughts enough to speak. "Where did you get that?"

"At an estate sale, several months ago. Apparently, they had no idea what its real value was because I picked it up for next to nothing. A shame for them, but nice for me since I couldn't afford its real value." He paused, studying her. "I was surprised he would sell something that looks so … personal."

She shook her head slowly. "He didn't. A folder of his work was stolen … just after he started becoming a name. He was devastated because there were several … nothing more than that, but … yes, personal. Not meant for the public." Jenna set Aaron down to take the drawing in her hands.

Trevor nearly whispered. "It caught my eye and I couldn't walk away. This is what made me start studying his work. Of course, I'd heard the name, but.... Jenna, I have wanted to meet you ever since finding this."

She raised her eyes to his. "Me? Or Daniel?"

"You. I became interested in his work because of you, because I expected the only way I'd ever get to know you would be by studying the man you married. I never expected to get closer than that."

"So you recognized me the first time at Joan's. That was an act."

"No. I didn't, at first. You've changed. And when I heard your name, I was trying very hard to act normal so I wouldn't scare you off."

She returned her gaze to the drawing. "You're giving this back to me?"

"Yes. Though I debated it for quite a while. It's not easy to give up."

"You didn't have to. I never would have known you had it."

He touched her arm. "Knowing you means more than having some drawing. And I thought it might mean more to you."

Jenna allowed the paper to roll itself up again. Holding it carefully in one hand, she leaned against him, the other arm wrapping around his back. "Thank you. It does."

His head pressed in closer and both arms surrounded her. It wasn't threatening, or uncomfortable. She didn't pull back. He wasn't as scrawny as she had originally thought, but sturdy, muscular. She felt protected.

Minutes passed. They were both content to simply stand together, feeling the mutual need of companionship. Aaron grabbed onto her leg, pulling to his knees.

A blowing horn in front of the building pulled them apart. The taxi. Jenna picked up her baby and asked Trevor to call when he got into Chicago. More snow was expected during the night.

"I will. Merry Christmas, Jenna. Take care, Buddy." He shook Aaron's hand and started to leave.

"Trevor?" She gathered her nerve, while he turned toward her again. Stepping closer, Jenna slid her free arm around his back, inside his coat, and leaned in to kiss him.

Twenty-one

Trevor was abrupt, slightly distant, when he called to let her know that he and Joan had arrived safely in Chicago. Nothing had been said after the kiss. He had simply searched her eyes then fled to the taxi's impatient horn.

The phone conversation left Jenna with mixed feelings. Maybe she was assuming too much. He didn't necessarily want to be kissed just because he wanted to be her friend. Was she doing to Trevor what Alan was doing to her? Jenna cringed. She wouldn't make that mistake again. And she wouldn't call and bother him. He had her number.

Wandering around her home, Jenna finally sat in her rocker. What next? The apartment was clean. Aaron was napping. She supposed she could get ready and they could go out for paint, but she hadn't decided what color to use on her walls yet. Besides, Jenna had lost interest in decorating.

After staring out at the melting ice dripping from her trees, she stood again, wandered over to check on Aaron, walked along Daniel's mural of drawings and into the supply closet. She picked up the gallery. It had to be finished, one way or another, no matter how it turned out. In a half-trance, Jenna pulled out her art supplies – easel, paints, brushes, turpentine. Returning to the gallery in her mind, she tried to recall Trevors' paintings. The small versions wouldn't have to be detailed; she only had to remember well enough to get the main idea … and the right colors.

Aaron woke before she finished and Jenna grudgingly set the brush aside. She took care of his needs and was thankful he settled down with his Christmas toys and plastic books so she could return to her work. Glancing over what she had done so far, Jenna noticed that it seemed a bit distorted. Trevor's paintings hadn't stood out so much in reality. It was appropriate, though, that they took over as the main theme of her painting. The musician, sitting at the table, letting his cigarette burn away, hadn't been their reason for being at the gallery. He had only added to the atmosphere.

By evening it was done. This one felt like much more than a hobby.

Over the next three days, she finished another and started a third. The therapeutic effect of the Chicago paintings calmed her enough to pick up the phone when she heard Alan's voice. She agreed to have lunch with him two days before the New Year.

λλλλ

Alan stood to pull out the high chair and waited until the baby was strapped in, then held Jenna's chair.

She had insisted on meeting at the mall, in the food court, so if they were recognized it wouldn't look like they were trying to hide anything. The middle of the weekday wasn't a busy time and the tables beside them were empty. Still, Jenna glanced around while getting settled.

"Have you been here long?" She pulled a snack from the diaper bag to keep her son occupied, avoiding her friend's eyes.

"Only a few minutes. What do you want? I'll get it."

She tried handing him money for her order but he refused, as she expected. Aaron talked to passers-by as they waited, showing more friendliness than could have rubbed off from either of his parents.

Alan finally spoke to the baby when he returned. Aaron didn't hold grudges. He offered part of his teething biscuit.

"So, what inspired you to decorate?"

Jenna pushed the plastic fork through the wrapper and picked at her rice. The mall's stir-fry wasn't as good as Trevor's Chinese take-out. "Boredom, I guess. Didn't have anything better to do."

"Not painting again yet?"

She looked up. "Why does it matter so much to you?"

"Because it matters to you." He set his fork down. "Jenna, I know I've been overbearing, but I hate that you've been so stifled. I miss the fire I used to see in you. Believe it or not, I do have your interests in mind."

"I know you used to."

His chest rose and fell. "I've been … going through some things recently. Cheryl and I…." He stopped to let people pass. "I don't know, Jen. She wants to move back home, and I think she should feel like she is home, with me. She complains that I'm always gone and I know I work a lot, but that is how we can afford what we have. It's not like I'm spending it gambling or whatever. I want to make sure my family is comfortable. I don't understand how she expects to have it both ways."

"Alan, don't you see what you're doing?"

He raised his eyebrows, waiting.

"The same thing you criticized Daniel for. For putting his work ahead of me. You don't have to work so many hours. Your guys are very capable. I know; I've watched them. But you're so obsessed with it that you won't let go, even a little. That's what's bothering her, just like it bothered me. And that's why I don't paint. Not much, anyway. Because I won't do that to my son. And you shouldn't do it to your wife."

He stared at her, not speaking. Nothing more needed to be said. In lecturing her friend, Jenna realized Alan had been right. Daniel's obsession had stifled her. She couldn't allow herself the freedom of giving in to her own interests because she was too occupied with trying to compensate for his. She'd always had to be available for those few moments that he had been willing and able to give her his attention. She had geared herself to be the constant full-time parent because he wouldn't have been. She had pushed herself aside to make up for his overpowering presence, and then, for his overpowering absence.

Aaron banged a tiny fist against the table.

Jenna looked over at him. She would have to give him space as he grew. She would have to have something of her own so he could do the same. So he wouldn't be completely wrapped up in, and stifled by, her need of his attention.

"The artist … Trevor … he does mean something to you."

Jenna turned back to Alan. She nodded.

"He seems awfully close to Aaron."

"He likes kids."

"He's young."

"So am I. I just haven't felt like it recently."

Alan picked up his fork, held it, set it back down. "You're going back to Chicago, aren't you?"

Jenna held his gaze, wondering if her friend's marriage would be easier if she weren't so available – how much better it would be for her and Aaron if they weren't so isolated. How much more palatable Trevor's take-out had been. How much easier it was to be in Trevor's company.

She allowed herself a slow, cleansing breath, holding back tears, feeling a door begin to close. Back to Chicago. "Most likely."

λλλλ

Pulling out her suitcase, Jenna packed it with her warmest clothes and threw in most of what Aaron had. She didn't buy him much at a time since he grew out of it so quickly. It didn't take long to pack. The two canvases she wanted to take were already beside the door.

Finally, she called Denise to tell her she wouldn't make her New Year's party. The idea of driving to Chicago alone made her nervous, but it was late morning; there was plenty of daylight left so she wouldn't have to hurry. And the warmth of the sun had dried the roads.

Trevor hadn't called and she didn't blame him. Maybe he wouldn't welcome her visit. If not, she would stay with Joan for a few days and come back home. Her mother-in-law had gladly accepted her self-invitation and agreed to watch Aaron for the evening. Joan was having a few people over, as usual, but never went out on New Year's Eve.

Settling into the van, Jenna took a deep breath. Aaron was happy, always ready to go anywhere. She was terrified. But she wasn't backing out, not this time.

Her stomach settled while driving down the interstate singing along with her music. She loved the cassette player Daniel had put in the van for her. Approaching Chicago, however, the energetic strains of Sawyer Brown had to soften. She needed more concentration to get through the city traffic. Nerves flaring again by the time she reached Joan's apartment, Jenna was extremely relieved that she didn't have to try to parallel park. She could have managed it in the Mustang, with the van it would have been impossible.

Joan met her outside with a hug. "Jenna, Honey, I was so surprised by your call." She took Aaron. "I wasn't sure whether to actually expect you."

"I hope it's okay. I know it's last minute, but...."

"You know you're always welcome, whether or not you call first. Just use your key."

Mrs. Covington rushed up to welcome her the minute she stepped inside. Jenna resisted the woman's attempt to pull her in farther. She wanted to take a few things out of the van before slipping out of her coat and shoes, a much easier task than loading it had been, since she didn't have to cart Aaron along with her on each trip.

Finally settling on the couch, Jenna felt fatigue setting in with the warmth.

"So Joan says you have plans tonight. I didn't realize you had friends here."

"Oh, just one."

Joan rescued her from an explanation. "What time is he coming to pick you up?"

"I'm taking a cab. I'm not sure enough of the directions to try to drive it."

"Alone? Wouldn't it be better to have him come get you?"

She understood Joan's concern, and appreciated it, but it had to be done this way. "No. He doesn't know I'm coming and I may not stay long. But he told me which taxi to call if I ever need to. It'll be fine."

"He? It's a male friend?"

Jenna looked over at the nosy lady. She kicked herself mentally; it would spread quickly that she was dating again, whether or not it was an actual date.

"Oh, Edna, how you pry. She has an artist friend here who happens to be male. Don't make so much of it."

"An artist? Do I know him?"

"Possibly. Jenna, why don't you go lie down awhile before dinner so you're refreshed for this evening. You are going to eat first?"

She was more grateful to her mother-in-law than she could show. "I won't leave until around eight, but Aaron's getting hungry…."

"Give me what he needs and go rest. I'll take care of my grandson and call you when dinner is ready."

She nodded, rising to get Aaron's bag. A nap sounded good, and maybe a shower. Travelling always made her feel not-quite-clean.

λλλλ

Spritzing her favorite perfume, Jenna checked the mirror, judging her outfit and her figure. Still following the plain and dark rule, she'd chosen black khakis with a black stretch-knit mock turtleneck covered by a glittery black and gold lace hip-length vest. Appropriate for New Year's Eve, but not too dressy. Her black walking shoes would have to do; pumps made her feet sore too quickly and she wasn't sure how long she would be standing. And maybe it wouldn't matter. Trevor wouldn't necessarily want her to stay.

Jenna knew he was working. He had mentioned it on Christmas, giving her the impression that there was nothing else he would rather do to celebrate the end of the year.

The nerves returned when she kissed Aaron and headed out to the waiting taxi. Jenna was out of place in bars, not used to going to them. And she worried about Trevor's reaction. Would it embarrass him to have some girl check up on him? Though that wasn't her intention. She just wanted to try to keep him as a friend, if he was still willing. Maybe he had a girlfriend. That would explain why he sounded so strange during their phone conversation. She would be with him tonight … his girlfriend, if he had one.

The buildings and street lights moved past, taking her courage away with them. She sensed the driver watching her but didn't dare look at him. He would have told her. Trevor would have mentioned a girlfriend … if he had one.

Unless she was new. Or just a New Year's Eve date. Jenna couldn't see a guy like Trevor without a date for the New Year.

A pressure in the back of her neck began to move into her skull. A bad idea, going to Trevor's bar unannounced. What was she thinking?

The taxi rolled to a stop in front of the gallery. It seemed different at night, with light streaming from the small windows and couples standing around the entranceway. Jenna looked out into the darkness, debating. She could just go back. He would never know….

"This the right address?"

She glanced at the driver. "Yes. I'm just…."

"Sure you wanna go in there alone? It's not the Ritz, ya know."

The Ritz? The black suede trench coat Joan had insisted she borrow must have given the driver the impression that Jenna was more important than she actually was. Her mother-in-law had been right about it being warmer than her short denim coat, and it did match her outfit better. But it was a bit too much for her.

She realized she was stalling and pulled a few bills from her bag, handing them up to the front. "I have a friend here, thank you."

He nodded, eyeing her. "Want me to wait and make sure?"

Jenna considered his offer. What if Trevor had cancelled for some reason? Or if he immediately asked her to leave? She wouldn't want to wait for another taxi.

She took a deep breath, pulling her chin up. "No, thank you. Happy New Year." Pushing the door open, she pulled her coat tighter, not sure whether the shiver was more from the biting cold or her fraying nerves. The couples by the door stared. Was she not dressed right? Doing her best to ignore them, she pushed the metal handle, being sure not to brush her skin across the old, splintered wood.

Music and laughter drummed into her ears and smoke burned her nose. She didn't belong here. Maybe the taxi had waited. Starting to turn, her way was blocked by a group of newcomers. There was nowhere to go but in. Stares caught her eye. What was wrong with her that made her stand out? The women seemed to be dressed as well as she was. But they didn't look nervous. Possibly, her fear showed too much.

"Are you looking for someone?"

She started at the voice. It was slightly familiar. He was tall, broad-shouldered. She didn't recognize him.

"You're in the wrong place, maybe? Someone give you bad directions?"

"Is this a private bar? Should I not be here?"

He laughed, loudly. "Nah, it ain't private. I'm Nate, the owner. Haven't seen you around before, that's all. You're very welcome. Come on in, and if any of these malcontents give you any hassle, just yell for me. I don't put up with no harassment in my bar."

Jenna relaxed slightly. His eyes were friendly and his voice … the guy who answered the phone when she'd called. She wondered if he recognized hers at all.

"Come find a seat and I'll send someone over. What's your name?"

She hesitated, trying to find the right face through the swarm. He wasn't behind the bar.

"You have one, don' cha?"

"Sorry." Did she want to tell him? How could she refuse? "I'm Jenna." She had to yell over the music and surrounding voices. "I was actually looking for someone...."

"Jenna?" His eyebrows furled.

She waited, wondering if he did remember.

"Come on." He took her arm without asking and half-pushed people out of his way, leading her ... somewhere.

The twinge returned to her stomach. He was taking her to the gallery, in the back corner of the bar. Thoughts of escape began to surface, but how would she get through this crowd, away from this huge man who had a firm, though gentle, hold on her arm? She should have just called Trevor, at least let him know to watch for her....

He stopped. She began to panic.

"Hey D-day, ya got company."

Jenna looked up, saw Trevor turn. The man had recognized her name, not her voice. But she hadn't given her name over the phone.

Trevor's mouth dropped open. "Jenna?"

Not sure whether his reaction was good or bad, she waited, trying to figure out what to say. He set the tray of empty glasses down onto the nearest table and moved in close to her, very close. Everyone around them was staring. She didn't care. His thoughts were all that mattered.

"What are you doing here?"

Jenna could easily have touched him, if she had reached out. If her arms weren't frozen at her sides. Just friends? Maybe that wasn't what she wanted.

She had to say something. But what? She began to force words, anything. "It's New Year's Eve ... I ... I know you're working, but...." Gasping for a breath, she stepped back. She sounded like an idiot. "I shouldn't have come. I'm sorry." Trying to turn in to the crowd, her arm was again bound by a firm hand.

"Jen, wait."

Keeping her face toward the floor, she avoided the stares, but allowed him to turn her back toward him, his hands holding both of her arms.

He left barely enough space between them for air to move through. "Why are you here?"

Hell. This was it. She had already stepped across the line and it was too late to back out. Trying to find courage from somewhere in her past, Jenna met his eyes. "I wanted to spend the New Year with you. If you want me to leave, just say so and I'll go back home. But I drove all the way up here … because I had to.… I'm painting again. I've actually finished a few, which is unusual. I seldom finish anything. But it didn't feel like a hobby. I brought one for you … the sketch you saw at Joan's … I painted it. It was the first real thing I've done." She froze. His stare was unwavering. "Trevor? Do you want me to leave?"

Sliding his hands slowly up her arms, he studied her face, pressing closer. "No. I want you to come home with me tonight."

Jenna's heart pounded against her chest. She could barely breath as he lowered his mouth to hers. Finding his shoulders, she held tightly … for support. The space between dissipated and a strong hand cradled the back of her head. The other held her body against his. Surrounded by his presence, Jenna felt grounded.

Twenty-two

She awoke in his bed. Alone.

Taking in her surroundings, Jenna remembered being slightly embarrassed the night before when his aunt heard the door and had come out from her room to wish Trevor a happy New Year. She had seemed surprised that he wasn't alone, which surprised Jenna. Trevor had introduced her to Aunt Nina casually, as if he hadn't taken her home for a particular reason, and had returned his aunt's hug and greeting. Telling her goodnight, he had led Jenna down to his "space," as he called it, in the house he shared only with his aunt.

He had the basement to himself; a very large space considering it was an actual house and not a townhouse like Joan's. Their home wasn't quite as particularly decorated as her mother-in-law's, but it was nice and gave the appearance of comfort. The basement was a separate world, rather messy and dark. She couldn't imagine how he painted with such little light, and looking around, Jenna had to wonder if he had a hamper. Clothes were dumped in small piles here and there, with a couple of shirts hanging over worn chairs. The furniture looked as if it had been salvaged from street curbs or thrift shops. But his artwork was everywhere. It fit in well with the mess.

Even the headboard was a Trevor Dade original; a simple, obviously hand-made, wooden frame painted with a mural. Mostly, the subject matter was undecipherable, but other parts made her cheeks flush when she studied it long enough. She chuckled, thinking about how her parents would react to Trevor and his work, and almost wished he hadn't been such a gentleman the night before.

"Good morning."

She jumped at his voice, pulling the blanket higher around her. Silly, since she was still mostly dressed.

"Cold? It does get chilly down here."

"Oh, no, I'm fine."

"Aunt Nina said I should see if you're ready to eat."

"What time is it?"

He pulled his wrist up to check the too-large black watch. “Nearly eight-thirty.”

“Eight-thirty?” Jenna threw the blankets back and jumped up, faltering a bit. She was still tired. “Joan must be worried to death. I shouldn’t have stayed.”

“I called her.” He waited to make sure he had her attention. “I told her we were talking art too long and you fell asleep. Aaron’s fine; she said not to wake you and that you don’t need to rush back.”

Jenna sat again, the coolness of the basement causing a shiver. Would Joan believe all they had done was talk about art? Most likely not, though it was true. Well, nearly. They had talked about a lot of other things, as well, including Daniel and Alan, and a bit about her parents, and his. Trevor being an orphan and living with his aunt since just after his fifteenth birthday explained the black he always wore. He had been very close to his parents.

His kisses enveloped her even now, along with the memory of her head cradled on his shoulder, her hand resting on his chest. His muscles flexing with his movement…

Trevor wrapped a large sweatshirt around her shoulders, pulling her back to the present and holding her there with a strong arm. “I’m glad you came back.”

Jenna loved the way his eyes constantly reflected a spark of mischief but were always true to their target. And she enjoyed being their target. “You know, when you brought me here last night, I really expected….”

“Yeah, so did I.” He shrugged. “But I was digging just getting you to talk so much. And it got late.”

She noticed how his hair was tousled, apparently uncombed. It was charming. “I would have.”

He grinned, brushing a strand of hair from her face. “You know where to find me.”

λλλλ

Joan greeted her as if it were an everyday occurrence for Jenna to have spent the night with a man. She debated telling her mother-in-law that nothing had happened, though Joan didn’t ask and didn’t seem bothered. And would she believe her anyway, considering that Jenna had agreed to meet Trevor at the bar again that night? Actually, he had insisted on coming to pick them up early enough to have dinner with him and his aunt, both her and Aaron, and Aunt Nina had offered to baby-sit afterwards.

Jenna liked Trevor's aunt. Very down-to-earth and friendly, Nina shared her home with Trevor as an equal. They kept track of each other, but not too closely. They ate and slept and had company on their own schedules. She went away with friends occasionally, and he did the same. Nina had no children of her own and doted on her nephew, who was perfect as far as she could see. He was the exact image of his father, her favorite brother. Jenna hadn't found out whether or not Aunt Nina had ever been married; it hadn't been mentioned and Jenna wasn't sure she should ask. But she expected Aaron would get along with her just fine. If not, she would have to cancel plans to go to the bar with Trevor and either return to Joan's or stay and visit with his aunt until he got home.

Sitting with Aaron on the floor, pretending to be interested in the toys he handed her, then took away again, Jenna hoped her son would cooperate. She very much wanted to go to the bar with Trevor, not only to chat with him during his breaks and whenever possible while he was working, but also to watch him work. He even made serving drinks an art form, over-emphasizing his movements with varying distances between the bottles and glasses as he poured. And he was an exceptional conversationalist.

He had introduced her to most of the regular patrons. A few appeared to recognize her name; all very obviously enjoyed talking with him and did their best to talk with her. Jenna hoped her lack of socializing skills hadn't been misunderstood. She'd had some trouble trying to fit in and add to the conversation since her early marriage and pregnancy had prevented the normal single social life. She was a bit of an outcast in the noisy bar.

Whenever Trevor had heard a song he especially liked, he'd given himself a break and escorted her to the dance floor. He was a good dancer, relaxed and smooth. Jenna felt like a crutch next to him; wanted, but a bit damaging to his image. She wasn't used to dancing as a couple, either. Daniel would never dance publicly and he had been too busy at home.

A sudden slap at her face made her jump and she caught the baby's arm when he lost balance. He had pulled himself up to standing and she had felt the little hands pinching into her skin but apparently wasn't showing the proper respect for his accomplishment.

Jenna took his hand when he raised it again. "Don't hit. I see you."

He smiled and planted a sloppy kiss on her cheek.

"Time for your nap." Wrapping an arm under his legs, she felt his instinctive grasp of her neck. Eight and a half months old. He would be walking before she knew it, before she was ready.

λλλλ

Aaron's comfort with Aunt Nina was nearly as spontaneous as it had been with Trevor. His unwillingness to fuss even slightly about Jenna leaving him was both reassuring and disconcerting. He wasn't old enough to not need her yet.

Trevor closed the door, waiting for Jenna to continue down the stairs, away from the house. "He'll be fine. We'll call now and then."

She perused his face, pulling her coat tighter against the sudden chill. He wasn't pushing and most likely wouldn't have complained if she had suddenly changed her mind. But she still heard no noise on the other side of the door. Aaron had been just fine the previous night with Joan. And she wanted to go with Trevor.

Jenna grasped his arm.

A taxi had taken him to Joan's, and would take him back from Joan's after he dropped Jenna and Aaron off there. But Jenna saw no reason to spend the money on taxis all night when her van was available. She let him drive. Actually, she was glad he agreed to drive.

The wind yanked at the door of the old vehicle, gusting frigid air from Lake Erie. She shivered inside the van, smoothing her hair back down, waiting on Trevor to walk around and claim the driver's seat after closing her door. He quickly revved the engine and switched on the heater.

"Nasty tonight, isn't it?" He rubbed his bare hands together.

They had kept their distance through dinner and visiting with Aunt Nina. Now, alone in the cold darkness and relative privacy, Jenna wanted more. She scooted to her left until their thighs met, completely ignoring her common sense telling her not to get attached, to not start anything.

She didn't have to.

Trevor pivoted in his seat, pressing his mouth against hers, grasping her head to pull her closer. His heat was more intense than the air blowing from the raucous fan. Jenna gave in, let her free hand slip under his coat, rest against his side … move further around his warm body. Cold fingers caressed her lower back, groping until they found bare skin underneath her shirt.

She broke the kiss, trying to find her voice. It came out as a whisper. "Do you have to work?"

His mouth brushed against her neck. "Yes."

"Can you get off early?"

Trevor met her eyes, his fingers still exploring the naked curves of her back. "Are you always so pushy?"

Jenna chuckled. "Not always … sometimes. Am I bothering you?"

"Yes. And I'm enjoying it a hell of a lot." With a slight grin, Trevor pushed back into her lips.

Finally moving away just enough to let him drive, Jenna shivered. She knew it wasn't from the toe-numbing coldness seeping through the floorboard. Or from the van's heater blowing loudly to try to overrule the outside air. She wasn't in love with this man; she barely knew him. But she was glad she had returned to Chicago.

λλλλ

After eight days of vacillating between Joan's and Trevor's and the bar and exploring a couple of art museums Trevor had talked her into, Jenna appreciated the snowfall and light howling of the wind giving her cause to simply sit still. Aaron had fallen asleep in the middle of playing in Joan's living room and Jenna had only moved him enough to lie on top of his blanket, covering him with a second. She had called to let Trevor know they would be staying in tonight, spending time with Joan. She didn't admit also needing time away from … whatever was evolving from their relationship.

They had kept things friendly – so far, not much more than that. Twice, Jenna had expected it to … transform … merge, but she hadn't pushed it and neither had he. She was thinking she should go back to Peoria and hadn't admitted to that, either. There was no real reason to go back, other than the opaque fact that it was home. But it called to her.

One night of hibernation became three. Trevor phoned, once on the second morning, twice on the third day. Something inside wouldn't let her return. He didn't call the next day. Jenna decided to leave in the morning.

Before she could go, she had to drop off the painting she had done for him.

After dinner and helping to clean up, she stole to her room to change out of her house clothes. Winding her hair into a neat bun, Jenna stood back and checked the mirror. She hadn't worn it that way for a long time. Again, it made her look older. It suited her mood.

She grabbed her old coat, pulling it on while stepping into the living room to find Joan. "I need to go out for a little while. Would you mind keeping Aaron for me?"

Her mother-in-law glanced up from the newspaper quizzically. "Is he coming to pick you up?"

"No. I'm taking the van. I've been watching; I can get there fine." And the canvases were still inside.

Joan nodded. "You will be careful. And call me when you're returning so I'll know to watch for you."

"Oh, I won't be long. I just...."

"You're going to tell him good-bye?"

Her stomach fluttered. Good-bye sounded so final. "Well, I have to tell him I'm going back." She picked up her son to give him a kiss.

Joan rattled the paper, setting it neatly on the side table, then stood to take Aaron, who was fussing about wanting to go with his mom. "You're staying with me, Sweetie. And, Jenna, don't be too abrupt. He does care about you."

She studied Joan, who was obviously taking it as a break-up, which it wasn't. At least Jenna didn't think it was. Without answering, she thanked her mother-in-law for watching Aaron and made her way to the van.

The drive made her nervous, though traffic was fairly slow on week nights after rush hour and the snow had melted off the roads. She had figured on arriving a half an hour before he had to leave for work; plenty of time to say she was heading back and to give him the painting.

Sawyer Brown soothed her once more ... until she pulled onto his driveway. After a deep breath, she got out, retrieved the canvas from the back, and made her way to the door. It was strange knocking and waiting for a reply after all the times she had walked right in with him.

Expecting Nina to answer, Jenna was taken aback by Trevor's sudden presence. He was wearing jeans and a T-shirt, like ordinary guys. No loose, hanging shirts. No black covering his real personality.

"Come on in." Not even a trace of annoyance in his voice.

"I can't stay." She avoided his eyes, watching for his aunt while brushing past him into the foyer.

"She's not home. She'll be away a couple more days visiting a friend." He closed the door, staying beside it.

Jenna turned back. "Oh. I'm sorry I missed her. Will you tell her I said thank-you?"

"For what?"

"The hospitality. I should've brought her something, but this is last-minute...."

"You're leaving?"

Another deep breath helped her continue. "Yeah, I need to get back...."

"Why?" He waited for an answer that didn't come. "Have I done something wrong? I'm not pushing, ya know. I know you've been pushed enough."

"No." She stepped toward him, gripping the canvas so tightly it began to make her fingers throb. "It's not.... I'm just going home for a while. I'll be back."

"Back to Chicago? Or back to me?" He leaned against the door, not advancing or retreating. Waiting, for something she couldn't give him.

"I brought this for you and kept forgetting it. The sketch ... I told you...."

"The first real thing you've done. I've been wondering when you would show me." He finally came to her, close enough to begin unwrapping the brown paper.

"No. Wait until ... after work or something. It's not very good and I don't want you to have to try to act like it is in front of me. Don't keep it if you don't want it."

She moved away to prop it against the wall. Straightening, she bumped against him.

"You belong here, Jenna." A hand slid behind her neck. His kiss took her in.

She pulled away. "I'll call you … when I get back … if you want."

Trevor dropped his arm, retreating.

Rushing to open the door, she glanced back, started to speak, and changed her mind. Not worrying about closing it again, Jenna fled half way down the sidewalk then slowed almost to a stop. Then she did stop.

What was she doing? She didn't want to leave.

Standing still, surrounded by the icy blackness of an empty winter night, Jenna allowed the biting wind to whip her unbuttoned coat around her thighs, unable to stop the moisture gathering under her eyes. She didn't love him. She didn't want this. It was too soon to be involved again; too soon for the longing involved with a relationship.

It had to stop now, before it was more than she could handle.

Forcing her feet to continue, she wiped at her face. The cold made her eyes sting. She would have to stop the tears immediately in order to drive through the city at night.

Reaching the van, her fingers shook, fumbling with the keys to unlock the door.

"Stay with me tonight."

She jolted at his voice, turning, then shielding her face. The tears hadn't stopped. She couldn't let him see….

His fingers pulled her chin higher. He hadn't bothered finding a coat. "Stay with me, Jenna. Just for tonight. No promises. No pressure. Just come back inside."

She shook her head. "I can't."

"Why not?" He shivered.

"You need to go in. You'll freeze. You don't even have shoes…."

"Why not?"

Jenna stood, staring at him, no idea how to answer.

"I opened the painting, Jen. You have no reason to play second string to someone else all your life. You can stand on your own just fine. And I'm not looking for … obligations. Hell, I'm twenty-two and just enjoy being a bartender right now. I don't want obligations. But I don't want you to walk out like this."

"Twenty-two?" Jenna studied his face. He couldn't be two years younger than she was.

He shivered again. "I thought you didn't realize that. Does it bother you? Or does it convince you that I'm not…."

"I'm not getting married again. I'm not in love with you. I don't want to do that whole thing again."

He shrugged. "So just sleep with me. I can deal with that."

She pivoted away, toward the van. If she went that far....

"I'm kidding, Jen." He caught her from behind, nuzzling against her hair. "You're not ready for that so let's not even bring it up again. We're friends, right? Come to work with me and just hang, relax. I'm not gonna add to your stress."

Reluctantly, she allowed him to take over, to guide her actions. They returned to the house and he left her to calm down and check her face while he changed into work clothes. She called Joan before they left, trying to keep her voice steady.

The bar was too noisy. No more than usual but irritating in her present state of mind. There was no room to hide in, to get away and pretend she was elsewhere. Instead, she stayed inside herself, avoiding conversation as much as possible, most likely seeming very rude.

They slowly began to leave her alone. Trevor attempted to keep her talking to him as well as he could, but she didn't know what to say to him. She didn't want to talk. She wanted to go home. Which home she meant, Jenna wasn't quite sure.

Strains of a familiar song caught her attention and Trevor looked over from where he was mixing a drink. It was their song – the same as their first slow dance.

He knew she recognized it.

Handing the drink over the counter, he ignored others yelling their orders and walked around the bar, focused on her, stopping when he took her hand. "One dance?"

She nodded, tuning into the singer's voice as she followed Trevor to the small space reserved for the few who used the bar as a club.

"I would want to be there, I could be there where you are
To help you through the late night and be there to lean on.
'Cause every time I'm near you, I feel it deep inside
I feel you as a lover, in you I can confide..."

She kept some distance. He didn't complain or try to move in. She felt, or thought she felt, people staring, wondering why there was so much space between them, why she hadn't been to the bar in nearly a week after being there every night. It made her tense and she scuffed his toes more than once.

"Relax, Jen. It doesn't matter what they're thinking."

She met his eyes. How did he know…? He was right, though. It didn't. "But what are you thinking now? About me? Us?"

He stopped dancing, releasing her hand to brush his fingers against her bare neck. "Me? I'm just enjoying your company while I have it. Trying to frame every detail so I at least won't lose the memory."

Jenna stared. He didn't expect her to stay with him; maybe he never had. He wasn't trying to run her life, or change it. He was simply there.

"So don't hold back, it's not a game we're playing…
Of yours, and mine, and nobody else's
Our love is yours and mine, and nobody else's
Love is yours and mine and nobody else's …
nobody else's…"

She kissed him. As timidly as their first kiss. And he pulled her in.

They blended into the song, refusing to hear the extraneous noise, hearing the music change, become heavier, faster. Couples turned into groups, swarming around them. Still, they remained transfixed.

Trevor didn't bother to ask if he could leave early. He simply informed Nate and took her home. And though there was no music in his basement, Jenna heard it still; the heavy beat, pounding tempo, changing into a slower melody. She was peaceful, lying against his bare skin.

Twenty-three

Jenna rested her hand against Aaron's forehead. It was no warmer than usual. Giving in to his fussy insistence, she pulled him from the playpen. The bags could stay packed for now. Her son rarely demanded so much attention, and even if he wasn't sick, he was bothered. Maybe two weeks away and the long drive home had exhausted him. She didn't remember him being as fussy after their last trip, though.

Settling in her rocker, Jenna cuddled him, soothing them both with the gentle swaying motion. He would be nine months old in just a few days. Nine months. It didn't seem possible. How could she have dealt with so much in the span of less than a year? And her son couldn't be so close to his first birthday. He was still so small. Yes, he was under the average size for his age, but still....

She had spent too much time away from him while running around with Trevor.

Focusing her attention on the changes in the loft, Jenna nearly regretted inviting Carrie to stay with her. She didn't mind the evidence of her friend's presence; it wasn't that she was particular about her decorating. And sleeping on the couch wouldn't bother her. Jenna did that fairly often, anyway. But she had been living alone for eight and a half months and would have to adapt, again.

Through the window, beyond her trees, a translucent red-orange glazed the darkening sky. Despite a bitter wind chill, it had been a good day to travel; no snow and only a few clouds sifting the bright sun rays. The old "red sky at night" proverb told her the following day would also be sunny and calm. Her heart wasn't easily convinced. She had left Trevor ... without further warning. He must have thought she would change her mind about leaving Chicago after their night together. And she nearly had.

While circled in his arms, his bare skin warming hers, Jenna couldn't even think about leaving. His light touch was soothing; his gentleness nurtured her soul. To leave him the following morning had been callous.

Jenna pushed the memory from her consciousness and rose to take Aaron to his crib. He barely stirred as she covered him. Then she shivered and went to turn the heat a bit higher.

Shuffling into the kitchen, she filled a cup with water and set it in the microwave, mesmerized by the slow circular motion until the beeping roused her enough to pull it out again. The mint tea was gone; she'd forgotten to get more. Finding several herb blends, apparently Carrie's addition to the pantry, Jenna pulled out the first one her fingers found and dropped it into the warm water.

She wandered back to the couch, pulling the afghan over her legs, letting her eyes drift toward Daniel's studio ... and his sketches hanging along the wall. Guilt crept into her thoughts. First, the guilt of walking out on Trevor, slowly replaced by how she had broken her promise to Daniel. She had promised to stay true to him.

Sipping the spicy liquid, Jenna's hand shook. Only eight and a half months. It had only been eight and a half months and she had already turned to another. A queasiness overcame her insides and she set the cup on the side table, scrunching her body lower on the couch, pulling the afghan to her chin. The weight of horrendous guilt, mixed with confusion and loneliness, suddenly overwhelmed her brain. Dusk turned into darkness. Her eyes clenched against it ... all of it.

Darkness didn't block it out. The fuzziness of mental and physical fatigue didn't block it out. A throbbing of her temples didn't block it out. It became stronger the more she tried to run from it. Giving in, Jenna focused on it, on her husband. Her promise...

She stroked his hair, trying not to let him see her pain. He had enough of his own.

Daniel's face was drawn, pale, much too thin. It killed her soul to think of how the cancer was devouring the once young and healthy body. It wasn't fair. He had so much left to give. So much....

"Jen." His voice, with only half the strength it used to have, stirred her insides. "It's okay. You're strong. You'll be fine."

Fine? No, not ever again. She attempted a smile. "Don't worry about me. Is there anything you need?"

"Just listen. I'm tired, but I have to tell you..."

"Rest then. Tell me tomorrow. I'll be here." She leaned in to touch his lips. They were cold; it scared her. "Daniel?"

"Jen, I am so sorry ... for everything I didn't do ... for you ... that I should have. For not..."

"No. Don't."

"I have to...." His eyes clenched.

"Daniel? Is the pain bad again? Do you need more..."

His head shook slightly, bringing his eyes back to hers. "Just listen. I wasn't fair to you, by not telling you..."

"It wouldn't have mattered." She fought tears back, again caressing his hair. "It wouldn't have mattered if I had known. I would still be here."

"My angel. You have always been ... my angel; my true inspiration."

Her head dropped. He was trying to say good-bye and she wasn't going to have it. It was too soon.

Daniel's hand raised slowly to her face. Jenna noticed the effort it took and grasped his fingers, letting him borrow her strength.

He gasped for air. "Promise me something."

"Don't do this, Daniel. Don't say good-bye."

"Jenna ... I'm tired of fighting. You have to let go now."

"No. Daniel, no." Her tears fell onto his hand.

"I will be here with you, in our son. Tell him ... how much I wanted him, that I'll be watching ... over him."

She caught her breath. "I don't want you to leave me."

"Promise me, Jen, that ... you will let yourself ... be who you are. More than anything, I want ... you to promise me that."

Jenna stared. He was worried about her. Through all of his pain, and fear, he was worried about her. She rubbed a hand across her eyes, forcing a calm she didn't feel. He didn't need to worry about her now.

"Promise...."

He was getting weaker as she watched. She nodded. For his sake, she would promise him anything. "Okay."

A slight curvature of his lips told her Daniel had accepted her agreement. She laid his arm back down on the bed, keeping hold of his fragile hand. "Rest now. You're too tired."

"So are you. Lie down with me."

She hesitated. It was late, nearly midnight, and she was more than tired. How would she keep herself from falling asleep?

"Jenna...."

She nodded and reclined carefully, aware of how movement caused him pain.

"Stop worrying, Honey. It's beyond that now." His words were softer, barely audible. His face began to relax.

She moved in closer. "Daniel ... you will always be my only true love. I will love you forever. And your son will know you."

His head turned, just slightly. "Raise him ... to be like you. I love you, Jenna. I love who you are."

She met his lips, then cuddled her head on the pillow against his, a hand resting atop his chest, barely feeling the heart beat. It used to be so strong. She had loved resting her head against his chest, listening to the strong melody. She imagined she could hear it now, pounding ... pounding....

Jenna awoke suddenly. She hadn't moved; she was still cradling Daniel's head. Her arm was numb and tingled when she rose enough to see the neon light of the now-unused alarm clock. Just after two a.m. and only the slightest moon glow from the windows. She looked at her husband. His face was purely relaxed, with no trace of pain. She was glad he was getting some sleep ... her hand didn't detect the heartbeat. But she could vaguely see his chest rising and falling, barely. Then it stopped.

"Daniel?" She pushed herself up onto the still-tingling arm, brushed her fingers across his face. "Daniel?" No reply. No movement. She felt for breath she couldn't find. "No."

Realizing he was no longer with her, Jenna surrendered into the mattress, letting her tears flow. What difference did it make now? He was gone. She was alone again.

She should call Joan at Denise's. They would want to know. Not yet. She couldn't pull away from him yet.

"Jenna?"

A voice nagged at her head. Joan? No, not Joan.

"Jenna? Wake up. What's wrong?"

She opened her eyes, slightly aware of dampness on the pillow underneath her face. Carrie. Why was she.... With consciousness alighting, Jenna bolted to sitting. He wasn't there. A dream. No, a memory. She hadn't just lost him – it had been months...

She rubbed a hand across her wet eyes and saw another figure. Alan.

He sat beside her. "What is it, Jen? Did something happen in Chicago? Why didn't you tell me you were coming home?"

She shook her head. "No. A dream ... a ... Daniel ... I...." It was still too vivid. She couldn't relive it enough to tell him.

Alan held her tightly while the tears continued.

He became her best friend again. She sank into him, letting everything out. Blindly accepting tissue from Carrie, her breathing finally calmed, the tears dried. She still held him.

"What happened in Chicago, Jen? And I want the truth this time."

She blew her nose, still sniffling. "I … I spent every day of the week with him … then … I stopped. I was going to leave … and I … went back … to say…."

"To say good-bye, to the painter." Alan's voice wasn't accusatory, just questioning, but he wasn't asking. He knew. "And you couldn't."

Jenna shook her head, wiping again at her nose.

"So don't, Jen. If you want to be there … then maybe you should be."

"But Daniel … I promised…."

Alan pulled away enough to force her release of him. "Promised what? You fulfilled your promise. You were devoted … and faithful." He was being careful with his word choice in front of his sister. "He didn't ask you to be alone forever, did he? I can't imagine he would have wanted that."

"No, he…." She stopped, holding her breath a moment. He hadn't asked her…. Thinking back through the dream, the true memory, Jenna shook her head. She'd had it all mixed up. Her emotions had somehow turned things around. She hadn't promised to never date again; only that he would be her only true love. He hadn't asked her … anything except … to be who she was. He had to know she needed companionship. She needed someone…. Daniel would have known that. He would never have wanted her to be alone.

She stood, walked over to check on her still-sleeping son, and turned back to her friends. She couldn't speak. She just stood there, looking at them, seeing a distance between herself and them that she had never seen before. They belonged here, in Peoria. Jenna didn't. And she no longer had a reason to stay.

Alan went to her, gently setting both hands on the sides of her head. "Call Joan. I'll help you move. And I imagine the Art Institute has a teaching program."

λλλλ

Jenna pulled the van in front of Alan and Cheryl's home, turned off the engine, then checked inside the large box from where constant noises seeped through air holes. The puppy tried to jump out to her. She petted him until he calmed a bit, then grabbed him around the stomach and cuddled him against her chest.

"Okay, you're fine. And you're going to like it here." She stroked the golden hair. He was a beautiful little thing; it would be hard to give him away. But Aaron needed to be older before she took on care of an animal. Fortunately, Denise had offered to keep Aaron while Jenna was running this last errand. She wasn't sure how she would have managed the baby and the puppy both.

Holding him firmly, she made her way to the door. The sun took the bite out of the January cold enough that she didn't mind holding the puppy while waiting for someone to answer.

She was glad it was Alan and smiled at him.

He raised his eyebrows. "Wouldn't it have been easier to get a dog *after* you moved instead of just before?"

"It's not mine. It's for Justin."

"It's what?"

"I told you he needed one and you haven't bothered yet, so…."

"Jen…."

"Alan, this will be good for him. And since I'm taking his playmate away…." She could see her friend starting to give in. "I'll stay out here. Go ask Cheryl."

She waited as he obeyed. The puppy was an active little mutt; they would have their hands full with him. Cheryl opened the door.

"Hi, Jenna! Oh, he's beautiful, Alan. What a sweet little thing!"

Her friend's eyebrows were still half-raised. "Dogs are a lot of work."

"Oh, so are kids, but we have three of those. Justin would love it! The twins are always leaving him out. It would be so good for him! And the yard is plenty big; you can build him a house when it gets warmer and he's older."

Jenna smiled at her friend. With Cheryl on her side, Jenna knew she had won.

Alan shrugged. "Come in; I'll get Justin."

The boy was thrilled. Jenna watched him play with his new best buddy while the twins kept their distance. They weren't sure about the wiggling puppy. But Justin gave Jenna a big hug.

"J.R. – that's his name. Doesn't he look like a J.R.?"

Jenna smiled. "Yes, I would say he does. Is that a friend of yours?"

"It's you. I can't name him Jenna, since he's a boy, but…"

"My initials?"

Justin nodded. She kissed his head. "I want you to teach him to like little kids so when Aaron comes to visit, you can all play together, okay?"

His whole face lit up while hugging his new pal.

She stood, facing Alan. "I have to go, but I have something for you, too. Will you walk out with me?" Giving her farewells to Cheryl and the kids, Jenna led her friend out to the van. She pulled the side door open and carefully grabbed the painting. Holding it in front of her, she watched his face. "I want you to have it."

Alan's eyes were wide. "You're giving me the zoo painting?"

"You said you've always loved it."

"I do, but…"

"I want you to have it. It's … my way of thanking you … for always believing in me … through everything. For pulling me through and helping me move on. This … is what I want you to remember. This is who I am."

"I know. And this is how I have always thought of you, Jen. In a T-shirt and shorts, your hair down and your feet bare. Down-to-earth and content to be there. He captured you at your best." He took it from her hands. "Thank you, and don't throw anything away. Save it for me."

She chuckled. "Okay." Pulling the sliding door until it latched, she opened the front door.

"You know, I'm sure Carrie will have the loft filled in no time, but we do have a guest room."

Jenna turned.

"And Trevor is welcome, too."

She nodded, unable to answer. He was letting her go. She loved him for that.

He held the painting with one hand and touched her arm with the other, planting a kiss on her cheek.

Standing there in his driveway amidst the bustling neighborhood and windows that Cheryl could have been looking out of, Jenna leaned in to touch his lips. Briefly, but warmly. Then she released him. "Bring Cheryl and the kids up to see the art museums and galleries. I'll be your tour guide."

Twenty-four

Jenna knew in which neighborhood she wanted to search for an apartment; on the outskirts of the area the college students had invaded and made their home during their years at the Institute. It was also not far from Aunt Nina's suburb – an easy drive or nice walk, if Trevor still had any interest. She wouldn't blame him if he didn't, but it would have no factor on whether or not she stayed. Chicago fit her well. She could blend in with the other artist-types and non-traditional families. Being a young, single mom wouldn't stand out as much in the city as it would in her hometown. And Peoria was just too close to her hometown, providing less cover from the image people expected her to have because of her parents' careers.

A career; something she would have to work on. While looking through the classifieds for apartments, sitting at Joan's kitchen table, Jenna scanned the employment ads. She wasn't real sure what to look for or exactly how she would deal with working, going to school and taking care of her baby, but she would have to have something. Figuring that her current availability of funds would pay rent in a decent neighborhood for somewhere between two and three years, it didn't give her much time to get a degree and start making a real income. Of course, they had put money aside, in a long-term fund Daniel had insisted on – for their retirement, or for an emergency. She hadn't realized why it had been so important to him until he had become sick.

He had known, somehow. Jenna finally admitted to the pain she felt about not being told he'd had cancer as a child. Until it came back. Daniel felt lucky to have had the years he did, after being told he wouldn't reach puberty. He insisted he hadn't told Jenna because there was no need for her to worry about it. She had truly believed that he meant he could beat it again, since he had once. She couldn't be angry, though. At this point, she wasn't sure she wouldn't have done the same.

She flipped the page. Nothing had pulled her interest, other than a few things that required experience she didn't have. Skimming though the art section, for her own amusement, a small ad jumped out. A part-time gallery assistant; no experience needed, some art knowledge required. She recognized the street name and tried to place where it was. Fairly close to Joan's gallery, if she remembered correctly. She wondered whether she would dare use her mother-in-law as a reference. Joan had offered to get her a job at the gallery she supported, but Jenna refused. That was Daniel's territory; she wanted to leave it that way.

With a deep breath, she picked up the phone and dialed the number in the ad. The line was busy. She tore the piece from the paper and set it aside to try later.

By the time Aaron awoke from his nap, Jenna had a list of apartments. Only three were in the neighborhood she wanted; several others were noted as back-ups. She didn't have time to be too particular. Most of her furniture had been left for Carrie to use, but the books and art supplies and her personal belongings and baby things were either packed into the van or stuffed into the guestroom at Joan's. So far, Daniel's sketches were still hanging in the loft. She planned to take them down to relocate to her new apartment when she went back to trade the van for the Mustang. She saw no reason to keep both vehicles in the city and the van would not be practical in downtown Chicago.

She would need to learn to use public transportation. Trevor generally took the metro – she could do that if he would show her how to keep from getting lost, though she would prefer the El whenever possible. Daniel had taken her on it a couple of times, when she'd asked, but he had preferred the more private taxis. She chuckled. They really did have different ideas about a lot of things.

Handing Aaron his bottle, she glanced at the clock. Trevor would be painting now, she assumed. Late afternoon was his chosen studio time, when he was in the mood. Otherwise, he would be out – doing what, exactly, was hard to guess. Playing basketball down the street or just hanging out with friends. Maybe wandering, looking for someone to chat with whom he had never met. Jenna couldn't imagine Daniel playing basketball or just "hanging." At twenty-one, Daniel had found her and been rushed into marriage. But maybe that was exactly what he had wanted. She hadn't pushed him. She had offered to free him. It had been his choice.

The phone pulled her from her thoughts and she set her baby in his walker before answering. Aaron liked to talk to people, too; in person, on the phone, however.

"Jenna, Honey, I'm going to be rather late tonight. Can you find something there or should I stop? I'll have a sandwich while I'm working, but I do want you to eat."

"I'll find something, Joan. It's fine."

"Are you sure? It's no trouble."

"No, really. I'm fine." After convincing her mother-in-law that she was well able to spend the evening alone, she replaced the receiver and looked over at Aaron. "Well, what should we do tonight?" He smiled, banging his free hand on the small tray, bottle still stuck between his teeth. Lurching for the phone cord, he ran the walker into her legs. "Sorry, Charlie." Jenna pulled it up quickly, draping the cord over the top of the phone. "And just who do you think you're going to call, anyway?"

"Ah dah dah dah."

"I know you want to talk; I just have no clue where you got that from." She rubbed his head and returned to the table. He scooted over next to her, setting the free hand on her leg while working on draining the bottle.

She sat watching him, letting her mind wander. Joan had asked the night before whether she intended to let Trevor know she was in town again. Jenna had been in Chicago four days already and had thought about it nearly every minute but still couldn't answer. How? After walking out the morning after they had.... How did she just go back? Call? Show up at his door? They'd had no contact for just over two weeks. She missed him and thought about him constantly, but would that matter to him?

Glancing at her list of apartments, her eye caught the job advertisement. First things first. She had to get settled. Returning to the phone, she tried the number again.

"Elucidations. Can I help you?"

λλλλ

It was a new, small gallery, but very friendly. As proof that she knew something about art, Jenna had taken the sketchbook she had worked in before leaving Chicago the last time. She had added three new sketches; one of Justin and the new puppy, one of Alan's home, emphasizing the landscaping, the other – kind of her good-bye to Daniel – their loft, as she had first seen it, with him standing at an easel. It didn't resemble him, or anyone. Again, fairly surreal. And she had nearly removed it from the sketchbook.

After a long debate in her mind, she had decided to leave it, realizing no one at the gallery would really understand the sketch, anyway.

The manager in charge of hiring had loved it, all of the work, and apparently had been impressed with Jenna herself. Not only had she hired Jenna immediately, even knowing she was a single mom, but she had pulled Jenna through the gallery to a secluded office to introduce her to the owner. He was young, surprisingly young for an owner, and Jenna hadn't been at all sure that he wasn't flirting. They even agreed to hold the job for the two weeks she needed before she could start.

She flagged a taxi and headed back to Joan's office to pick up her son. Her mother-in-law, of course, was delighted although she would have preferred for Jenna to work in "her" gallery.

"Did they recognize your name?"

Jenna hesitated. "Well, I didn't exactly tell them. I used my maiden name for the interview. I wanted to get this job on my own."

"Oh. So, you're planning on using Givens instead of Rhodes, to stay in hiding?"

In hiding? No, not any longer. "That was just to get the job. I'll tell them when I go back to return the paperwork." Her mother-in-law seemed only party relieved. "I'm not giving up my name, Joan. That is who I am now, and I'm very proud of that. I *am* Jenna Rhodes, for better or for worse."

λλλλ

The sun fell quickly. The further the day progressed, the more Jenna wanted to share her news with Trevor. If he knew she had a job, that she was getting an apartment, maybe.... Suddenly unable to control the restlessness, she used Aaron's nap to change clothes and fix her hair. Dinner was ready for Joan when she arrived home from work, but Jenna couldn't eat. Instead, she thanked her mother-in-law for keeping her son and left to find the catalyst who prompted her return to the city.

It was early; there most likely wouldn't be much of a crowd at the bar yet. He would be getting things in order and chatting with the guys.

The confinement of the taxi did little to warm her, with bitter Lake Erie wind seeping through the windows. The driver was sullen and uncommunicative, which was fine. Jenna hugged her arms around herself for warmth and tried to figure out what she would say to Trevor, and what she would do when he told her to leave. Give up, or try to change his mind? Maybe he would have a girlfriend there with him this time.

The ride ended almost too soon and she forced her half-frozen fingers to open the door. She supposed she would have to invest in a pair of gloves, though she didn't like them. In Peoria, she hadn't been outside for long enough or often enough in the last few years to worry about it. On the city streets, though.... She stopped, just outside the old wooden door, and turned. Through frozen breath, Jenna surveyed the area. Chicago. Her new home. For a moment, she was intimidated by the crowded, narrow buildings reaching into the sky and the bustling locals paying no attention to her as they hurried home to dinner or out for their evening entertainment. Then she smiled, at no one. She had done it. She had broken away from her parents, her past ... her insecurities. Traces of fear still dwelled within, but they no longer ruled her. This was her home, her space.

With a deep, cleansing breath, she turned back again and opened the door, unconcerned about the splintering wood. Entering slowly, the familiar smells surrounded her, the clinking of glasses welcomed her. Trevor was behind the bar, turned away, chatting with one of the regular patrons. Several tables held faces new and faintly recognizable. Nate looked up. She grinned and silently asked him not to give her away.

Jenna was nearly to the bar when Trevor turned, ready to greet the person he had finally noticed walking toward him. She stopped, waiting.

He didn't look as surprised as she had expected. He also didn't seem upset. "Welcome back."

The casualness of his greeting caught her off-guard. But what did she expect in front of his friends? She supposed it wasn't fair not to do this privately so he could say what he was thinking.

"Hi. It's freezing out there tonight." She rubbed her hands together, silently berating herself for sounding so stupid.

He grinned. "Yeah, you know it's January, right? Pretty typical for the Windy City. Have a seat and warm up."

Jenna slipped out of her coat, hung it over the back of the barstool closest to where he was standing, and hoped something intelligent would come to mind soon. Climbing onto the worn, leather-clad seat, she tried her best to look casual, propping an arm on the bar. She felt stiff, again out-of-place in his world.

Trevor maintained his professional stance, treating her as any other customer. “What would you like to drink? It’s on the house.”

“Oh, you don’t have to do that, really….”

“I know I don’t. And you didn’t have to come back.”

Her stomach tightened. He had finally lowered his voice. His eyes were friendly, but … wary. The guilt she felt this time was for him. She had hurt him by walking away so quietly; so viciously. “Yes, I really did … have to come back.” Jenna suddenly had so much she needed to say to him. She caught her breath, a tingling sensation rising from somewhere inside; somewhere she couldn’t quite place. “Trevor, you were right, you know. This is where I belong.”

He leaned in against the bar, arms crossed atop; his face only inches away, his eyes drilling into hers. Jenna could feel the stares surrounding them.

“Do you trust me?”

The tingling moved down through her arms, into her fingertips. The conversation was getting too intense for public view.

“To choose your drink. I know something that will warm you right up.”

She controlled the urge to lean forward to kiss him, grinning instead. “Of course.”

“Right back; don’t go anywhere.” He strolled to the other end of the bar, hiding from her view the concoction he was mixing. He was also talking quietly to Nate, too obviously about her. She began to wonder if she should accept any drink from him. Just as quickly, she scorned herself. Too many movies.

Her heart rate had nearly dropped to normal by the time Trevor returned with a steaming mug, crowned with whipped topping.

“Careful, it may be too hot yet.”

“Thank you.” She gently cupped her hands around the mug. The heat stung her fingers.

Nate interrupted, insisting on covering the bar, and sent Trevor around to sit with her. The silence was awkward until he asked about Aaron and she asked about Aunt Nina and his painting. Everyone left them alone and kept their distance while they chatted about nothing. That was awkward, too. He didn’t ask why she had left, or why she had returned. Jenna could tell he wanted to say more, but kept it in. She wanted to touch him…

"Well, I better get back to work; it's getting crowded. Can you stick around?"

She pulled her eyes away. "Actually, I shouldn't stay long."

"You're not going back again right away?"

"No. I…." He had stood to walk away from her, but waited. Jenna studied him. No black tonight, simply jeans and a T-shirt. He looked incredible. "I was wondering…. I got a job today and I really need to go apartment-hunting tomorrow since I only have two weeks to get a place and move in and…"

"A job? Here?" He sat again.

She longed to move in closer. "A gallery assistant – part-time, nothing big."

"You're staying?"

"Maybe I shouldn't ask, since … it wasn't right of me to just leave that way, but … I was confused … about a lot of things." Jenna took a breath. He was watching her, waiting. "Yes, I'm staying. And I was really hoping … that we could at least…."

"Did you find what you kept going back to Peoria for?"

Her heart pounded. He had leaned closer again so he wouldn't be overheard. His scent was stronger than the cigarettes and alcohol. "Yes. And it had to stay there, where it belonged."

He smiled, gently.

"Anyway, I have a van full of stuff and Joan's guest room is packed and she's being nice about it so far, but…."

"You can stay with me."

The tingling returned. Her breathing was forced. Jenna opened her mouth, trying to speak, then looked away. Move in with him? Briefly, she saw herself in his basement, her clothes hanging over a chair alongside his, their easels adjoined…

"Think about it. I have to get back to work. Stay and we can talk when I take you home." He stood, then leaned in to kiss the side of her head.

Jenna raised her face to see his eyes. He didn't care who was watching or what they thought. When Trevor leaned toward her again, silently asking for more, she met his lips, wrapping a hand behind his head, pulling him in.

λλλλ

She wandered around the spacious three-bedroom apartment. Still mostly empty, except for her art room, it gave out a light echo in reply to sounds. With aching feet, at the end of three days of apartment hunting and three nights of accompanying Trevor to the bar, Jenna had known it was exactly what she needed a moment after stepping inside. Under the process of being remodeled, only the apartment's kitchen and two of the bedrooms had refinished floors, but work had been stalled. Jenna was able to get a good discount for agreeing to take it as it was. And it worked well for her plans. The unfinished bedroom turned into her art room. The tiles had been scratched up and stained, so she wouldn't have to worry about spilling paint. Meant to be the master bedroom, it had two wonderfully large windows on adjoining walls. Jenna didn't need that much space to sleep. The smallest room was large enough for her bed and dresser and would serve as a guest room if needed. A daybed could turn the studio into a sleeping area. The mid-sized room would work well for Aaron's crib and changing table and a play space for when he got older.

The tiny kitchen was no problem since she didn't like to cook, and the living room was open and airy, also with large windows. They had been the selling point. Her paint-splattered rug added life to the apartment. Jenna's first thought had been to put it in her studio, but she changed her mind. She liked the casualness it provided by being the first sight from the front door. So far.

Trevor had done all of the searching with her. They were both tired, but put in the fourth day moving her things out of Joan's guest room and the van and into her own place. Aaron had stayed with Aunt Nina in the evenings and during the move and was perfectly content there. Joan stopped by the apartment briefly, not quite approving, but respecting Jenna's decision. She had been very friendly to Trevor, inviting them both to dinner on his next night off.

Brushing a hand across the sculpture Joan had allowed her to take from Daniel's bedroom to relocate in a corner of her new living room, Jenna sighed and drifted into the studio. She propped herself in front of a window and looked down at the rooftops of neighboring houses, thinking about the extreme difference in the view. She would miss her trees, and the river. But the activity below was energizing. She could let herself daydream about where her "neighbors" were going and what they were thinking....

Strong hands brushed around her waist. She covered his arms with her own.

"Tired?" Trevor's voice was soft against her ear.

"Exhausted. And you should rest before you have to work tonight."

"I'm not going to work tonight."

She turned in his arms, welcoming his kiss. Then she pulled back. She hadn't allowed him to get very close. Although she and Aaron were essentially living with him and his aunt until the apartment was habitable, they weren't actually living *together*. Jenna had insisted on staying upstairs in the guest room with her son. It was just easier to go back to his place after being at the bar so late than to pick up her son and go back to Joan's. Convenience only, or so she told herself. But she had refused his offer to move in with him. She wanted to stay more in control than she had the last time.

"I should go get Aaron. I imagine your aunt is getting tired of babysitting."

His demeanor changed. "No, I'm sure she's not. But, okay." He backed off.

She handed him the keys to the van automatically. He was much better at driving through the city and was more comfortable with the large vehicle.

He was quiet; too quiet. Even at his aunt's house, while they were chatting about the apartment and how Nina had enjoyed taking care of Aaron, Trevor barely joined the discussion. He did watch Jenna, though. She caught him staring several times, until she became slightly uncomfortable.

Aaron yawned, rubbing a fist over his eyes.

She kissed his head. "You're ready to get settled in. Want to go see your new home?"

The baby raised a hand to her face then let his head drop against her shoulder.

"Can I take you home? I'll take the metro back."

Jenna touched Trevor's eyes. "I was hoping you would. And I'll even offer Chinese take-out if you can find the restaurant for me."

λλλλ

He stayed late, talking with her and playing with her son. Jenna wandered a bit in between, pulling a few more things from boxes. After Aaron was asleep for the night, she moved into her art room. Part of her was anxious to initiate the space; the rest of her opposed the thought. What made her think she needed a studio? She could easily turn it into a guest room instead, using it as a den in between guests. If she was going back to school, she could use the desk for homework. Daniel's desk – the only piece of his furniture, other than the easels, that she had relocated to Chicago. Her bed was new; a simple frame purchased quickly the day before, just after signing the apartment lease. Trevor had done that with her, too. It had been slightly uncomfortable, with the salesperson assuming they were living together and Trevor making jokes about trying it out in the store. She chuckled. The look on the woman's face had been priceless.

"What's so funny?"

Jenna turned at his voice. "Oh, I was just thinking about how the woman looked at you yesterday."

"Yesterday?" Trevor handed her a cup full of steaming brown liquid. "Oh, about trying out the bed?"

"Thank you." She could smell the mint. "Yeah."

"I'm used to those looks." He grinned.

Taking a sip of her tea, Jenna went back to digging through the open box next to her, using only the free hand. She was tired of unpacking but it was a useful distraction. Pulling a few miscellaneous objects out to place on the desk, she found her memory albums. Maybe it was a good time to stop unpacking. She had never shared them with anyone.

Trevor moved in closer, hanging onto his glass of iced tea. He didn't drink warm tea, though he did like mint. Watching her pull her hand away, he reached in to grab the book. "Artwork?"

"No. It's just ... well, there is some of that, but mostly...." She set her cup on the desk and took the album from him. "It's a journal, except with more pictures than writing. Some scribbles here and there, but...."

"Can I see it? Or is it personal?"

Jenna held on to the album, keeping her eyes from Trevor. It was the first of five she had done, holding childhood mementos and photos and drawings, a few chorus awards and art show ribbons. Very personal, even Alan hadn't seen it. Neither had her husband.

She looked up at her … boyfriend? Friend? She wasn't even sure what to call him yet. "Only if you won't laugh. There are some old pictures of me and I was a very awkward child, not nearly as graceful as Mom wanted me to be."

Trevor smiled. "You would laugh harder at mine. My parents were very permissive. I had green hair for several months."

"Green?" Jenna chuckled. "Well, you can see mine if I can see yours."

He raised his eyebrows. "I think we've already done that."

His meaning barely started to sink in, making her cheeks grow warm, and he kissed her. Quickly, without asking and without expecting anything in return.

They sat on the floor, against a wall, and she shared not only the first book, but all five.

λλλλ

She felt movement and opened her eyes. He was still there. Somehow, she hadn't expected him to be. It was dark, the glow of the moon streaming through her bedroom window providing the only light. He was completely dressed, other than his shoes. And she had changed to sweats and a clean T-shirt before dropping onto the bed at one o'clock in the morning. The books had taken forever to go through, only because he wanted the stories behind the pictures and drawings. He loved her surrealist touch.

His aunt would expect that more had happened between them, since he had stayed the night. Or maybe she thought he was at work.

Jenna sat up, turned to look at him when he moved again, then left the room. Just after five, if she could see the clock well enough. Not sure what to do with herself so early in the morning, she went to check on Aaron. He was sound asleep, not even flinching when she stroked his head. She should be asleep, too. She was exhausted.

Wandering into the living room, Jenna looked through the so-far-uncovered windows. The street lamps reflected a light snow and highlighted the cold metal of a few passing cars. Apparently, she wasn't the only crazy person up too early.

With a yawn, she moved into her studio. The easels were still propped against the wall. Several paints and a few canvases sat on the desk. Switching on the light, Jenna squinted until adjusting to the sudden brightness. She crossed to the desk, sifting through the partial paintings. Trevor had given her high compliments on all of them, saying he would love to see them finished.

She ran her fingers over her favorite painting, Trevor's bar. It was dark, the age of the building emphasized. And a single bartender taking care of a full counter. With a deep breath, she pulled an easel away from the wall and kicked it to standing with one foot. She placed the painting on it, standing back to get an objective view. It needed … light. There was no light source.

Digging through the rubble on the desk, she found a brush that would work, a palette, and a few paints. The work went quickly, as though something were guiding her hand. Finally, she stood back again. It was done. Satisfaction swelled inside. Yes, she was home here.

"It's wonderful, Jen."

She jumped, nearly dropping the brush.

"I'm sorry. I didn't mean to scare you. Do you always paint so early in the morning?"

His voice was rough, sleepy. His hair was mussed. Jenna studied him, standing in the doorway, his clothes wrinkled from lying in her bed.

"No. I couldn't sleep."

"I was moving too much."

"No." She went to find turpentine to drop her brush into. Where was it? While searching, she watched him approach the easel. He studied it silently. She began to get irritated about everything being in boxes.

Finally, he came to her, took the brush from her hand, and laid it on an unopened box.

"It'll dry out." Her irritation faded with the touch of his fingers lightly pushing through her hair.

"You need to sleep. You're too tired."

Jenna watched his hand move to her shoulder and slide slowly down her arm. His touch overwhelmed her. She did her best to stay in control. "I … guess I felt it calling to me. It had to be done."

"So, now that it is?" He moved closer.

Her body tensed. A palette would have trouble fitting in the space between them. And it was too much. Forcing her breath to slow, Jenna stared into the eyes of the man in her painting, the man who cheerfully waited on others, putting their needs first.

Putting her needs first. She cautiously raised a hand to his face, touching him to ensure he was real. He took her hand, planting a kiss on her palm. Cold shivers consumed her, heightening every sense.

Jenna kissed him, slowly, deeply, letting him inside her world. Allowing him to fill a void she had never noticed. “Trevor….” Her fingers pushed into the warmth of his back. “Move in with me.”

Epilogue

Jenna flexed her calf muscles slowly, causing the old oak rocker to sway back and forth. Trevor had moved it from the loft to their apartment as soon as she realized she would have need for it again.

"Aaron, Honey, sit down."

The eighteen-month-old stared a moment before obeying. Jenna was glad he was still an easy child, especially since the one in her arms most likely wouldn't be. She was fidgety, constantly insisting on being held. Jenna didn't mind just sitting and holding her. Though sometimes Aaron showed his irritation at the attention his sister received. He only climbed up to stand on the couch while Jenna was rocking Anna.

Just over a year ago – four and a half months after losing her husband – she had been rocking Aaron, staring out the window, wondering how she would be able to live alone. Now, she had two babies and a live-in boyfriend. It hadn't taken her long to get pregnant again. Trevor often joked about having a house-full within five years. He didn't seem to mind the thought. He also didn't care that she still had no interest in being married. They were doing fine as they were.

She had finished one semester of school. And Trevor became so interested in her career while helping her study that he had decided to follow her lead. He would be a good teacher. Already, he volunteered at the nearest school, immensely enjoying teaching art to grade school kids. The bar still beckoned to him and he put in a night or two a week there. He was selling quite a few paintings but had taken the more commercial road. His work hung in office buildings around Chicago and other cities in Illinois, Indiana, and Michigan. Joan had connections in those states, as well. She didn't quite believe in the commercialization of artistic talent, but Trevor was pulling in enough money to support Jenna and the kids until she was ready to get back to work. And he painted for himself as he felt the need.

Jenna had worked at Elucidations until she went into labor. They assured her she would have a place whenever she was ready to return. She had enjoyed the gallery so much that she was having second thoughts about returning to school. Either way, at the moment, she was content staying home taking care of her babies.

A rattle in the keyhole caught her attention and sent Aaron running.

Cautiously opening the door, Trevor swept the child into his arms. "Hey, Buddy." He walked across the room, propped Aaron in one arm, and leaned down to give Jenna a kiss. "How are my girls?"

"Girl? I'm older than you are."

"And you are never going to let me forget that, are you?" He grinned, planting another kiss on her head.

"Sure. When we're old enough to want to start hiding our ages."

"You're planning to stay with me that long?"

"Well, the kids are kind of used to you, you know."

"A two-week old can't be too used to anything. Isn't that right, my little Anna?" Trevor stroked his daughter's silky hair. "And I guess we better space them farther apart, so by the time the youngest is over being used to me, you'll be too old to want to run off with some younger guy."

She laughed. "I don't think I could handle anyone even younger."

Trevor took her hand, kissing her palm. "I've missed you today. Come sit with me."

Jenna rose, letting him help her weakened stomach muscles by pulling her arm gently. Anna fussed about being disturbed.

"Okay, Bud, let me take your sister for a few minutes." He set Aaron on his feet and claimed the baby. She continued the soft crying until he sat on the couch, propping her against his chest. Jenna sat next to them, turned enough to hold his free arm. She was tired and glad he was home to take over. Her son grabbed a book and claimed his other side. Listening to Trevor read a story he had to know by heart, Jenna leaned her head against his arm and let her eyes surrender to the peace.

"Love Is Yours And Mine"

Words and Music by Duncan Faure

I would want to be there, I can be there where you are
To help you through the late night and be there to lean on
'Cause every time I'm near you, I feel it deep inside
I feel you as a lover; in you I can confide

So don't hold back it's not a game we're playing…

Of yours and mine and nobody else's
Our love is yours and mine and nobody else's
Love is yours, yours and mine and nobody else's
Yeah nobody else's – yours and mine

So if you get the feeling that I could understand
I'll be there as your lover I'll be there as your friend
So anytime that you need someone all you do is call
I'll be there through whatever, anytime at all

So don't hold back it's not a game we're playing…

Of yours, and mine and nobody else's
Our love is yours and mine and nobody else's
Love is yours, yours and mine and nobody else's
Yeah nobody else's – yours and mine…

www.DuncanFaureMusic.com

To contact the author, visit:
www.elucidations.us